KINGSPORT

The Weird of Hali

Novels by John Michael Greer

The Weird of Hali:

I – *Innsmouth*

II – *Kingsport*

III – *Chorazin*

IV – *Dreamlands*

V – *Providence*

VI – *Red Hook*

VII – *Arkham*

Others:

The Fires of Shalsha

Star's Reach

Twilight's Last Gleaming

Retrotopia

The Shoggoth Concerto

The Nyogtha Variations

A Voyage to Hyperborea

The Seal of Yueh Lao

Journey Star

The Witch of Criswell

KINGSPORT

The Weird of Hali

Book Two

John Michael Greer

Published in 2023 by
Sphinx Books
London

British Library Cataloguing in Publication Data

A C.I.P. for this book is available from the British Library

ISBN-13: 978-1-91257-389-9

Typeset by Medlar Publishing Solutions Pvt Ltd, India

www.aeonbooks.co.uk/sphinx

Vast pyramids of night-hued stone
Rise stark above that nameless strand,
Where on the black and hissing sand
The waves of cloud break endlessly,

Where, in a place of mystery
Beneath the black unhallowed stars,
The pale night-scented nenuphars
Shed perfume for the King alone.

He walks there in the darkling hour
When both the suns have passed from view,
And stops to feel the wind blow through
his tattered robes, from lost Yhtill:

His vow is unforgotten. Still
The Pallid Mask conceals his face:
The shadow of a distant place
And time obscures each floating flower.

Until the blade of Uoht shall rise,
Until the ring of Eibon burns,
Until the one appointed turns
The pages of the *Ghorl Nigral*,

That figure, terrible and tall,
With tattered robes and windblown hair,
Shall keep his nightly vigil there
Beneath those white and wintry skies.

                              —"In Carcosa" by Justin Geoffrey

CONTENTS

Chapter 1: A Letter from Kingsport   1

Chapter 2: The King in Yellow   18

Chapter 3: The Mansion on Green Lane   35

Chapter 4: The Shrine of Saint Toad   50

Chapter 5: The White Ceremonies   70

Chapter 6: The Song of Cassilda   86

Chapter 7: The Terrible Old Man   103

Chapter 8: The Sussex Manuscript   120

Chapter 9: The Ring of Eibon   139

Chapter 10: The Night of the Festival   156

Chapter 11: The Tatters of the King   173

Chapter 12: The Heritage of Carcosa   188

Chapter 13: The Friends of Saint Toad   206

ACKNOWLEDGMENTS   221

CHAPTER 1

A LETTER FROM KINGSPORT

The kitchen phone rang, sending echoes through the house. Jenny Parrish, curled up on the battered couch, heaved the big leatherbound volume out of her lap and started to get up, then settled back again when she heard footsteps crossing the kitchen floor. A moment later, a voice answered: "Hello?" A pause. "Yes, this is Tish Martin." Another, several minutes long. "Oh. Well, I'm sorry to hear that." A third, briefer. "Okay, thanks for letting us know. 'Bye now."

The handset clattered into its place, and a moment later Tish came through the dining room door, gave Jenny an unhappy look. "That was the police," she said. "They found Owen's coat on the riverbank north of Kingsport, just this side of the sea."

Jenny looked up at her from under a mop of mouse-colored hair, said nothing.

"So they've pretty much settled that it's suicide."

"I don't believe that," Jenny said.

Tish sat down on the other end of the couch. "Girl, I hear you. I don't want to think about Owen doing that. Still, he was in Iraq, remember. No way you or I know what that did to him. And then—well, you know his folks got killed in a car crash when he was seven, right?"

"I know."

1

"And the stress he was under the last couple of weeks before he up and disappeared—I mean, who knows what that was all about."

"Tish, I know. I still don't believe he killed himself."

"I hear you," Tish repeated, but the look on her broad brown face told Jenny otherwise. After a moment: "We can bag his stuff and put it in the basement, just in case."

"If the police say it's okay, let's do that."

"Sure thing. I'll call 'em in the next day or two and ask."

She got up and went back into the kitchen. Jenny looked up at the clock on the wall, a blob of green plastic shaped like the silhouette of an octopus, with two waving tentacles for hands— some long-departed grad student's idea of an Arkham joke, no doubt. It showed quarter to one. Half an hour, Jenny reminded herself, and got up, tucking the leatherbound volume under her arm. Then to campus—

And to an appointment that had just gotten even more difficult than it had already been.

She climbed the stairs to the second floor, turned down the dimly lit hallway, unlocked the door to her room. Though the landlord didn't allow anything to be hung from the walls, she'd managed to make the space hers anyway: art prints in upright frames stood all over the top of the dresser and the bookcase; a statue of a unicorn she'd found in a secondhand store brandished its horn from the top of her desk; a bowl of herbal potpourri put a spicy autumn scent into the air; a quilt, another secondhand store find, threw a splash of gaudy colors over the bed. The book she'd been reading went next to half a dozen other nineteenth-century French novels in the bookshelf. That done, she went to the desk, set her smartphone to beep at one-fifteen, perched on the side of the bed, and then let herself fall back into the embrace of the quilt.

It really was strange, she thought. You meet a person in some random way, get to know him a little, go for days at a time barely noticing his existence, maybe having a conversation now and then, going to the occasional music gig with him among others; there's nothing romantic involved, not even a hint in that direction; and then he's gone, and all of a sudden there's a gap in your life where he used to be, a silence where you'd scarcely noticed a voice.

People said Owen had been acting odd the week or so before he disappeared, and then his backpack turned up near the railroad tracks next to the Garrison Street bridge and his coat washed up somewhere on the riverbank downstream. One more student suicide, everyone had assumed right away—Miskatonic had some of those every year, like every other university. Now that the police were saying the same thing, as far as everyone else was concerned, Owen Merrill had stopped being a person and turned into a statistic framed by fading memories.

It would probably be easier, Jenny told herself, if I could just give up and accept that the police were right. She considered the cracked paint on the ceiling, tried to lose herself in the pattern, the way she'd learned to do when she was little. Each thin crack was part of a whole that she could see, maybe, if she took all of it in at once ...

The smartphone on the desk beeped, rousing her from something that didn't feel like sleep. She sat up, blinked, and then remembered where she had to go. She drew in a ragged breath, pocketed the phone, made herself leave the sanctuary of her room and head down the stairs and out the door to keep her appointment with Dr. Miriam Akeley.

* * *

Miskatonic University had two campuses, but these days only the alumni association and the financial aid department used the original campus south of the river, in the old downtown where boarded-up storefronts and vacant lots outnumbered buildings anyone used or lived in. Back in the nineteen-fifties, as veterans with GI Bill benefits flooded into universities across the continent, the Miskatonic administration talked the state government and private donors into funding a big modern campus on land that at that time was just past the northern edge of town, where the Federal Pike ran through abandoned farms and low wooded hills toward Innsmouth out on the bleak Massachusetts coast twenty miles away.

Famous architects converged on the site, summoning contractors and subcontractors who didn't yet have to go through the motions of hiding their connections to Boston's organized crime families. Cyclopean masses of brick, concrete, glass and steel duly sprang up where vacant lots, stone-fenced pastures, and the sprawling premises of Arkham's least reputable used car dealers had once been. Many of the buildings that resulted were stunningly ugly, some were forgettably bland, a few managed to cling to some few misplaced scraps of dignity and taste—and then there was Wilmarth Hall, where Jenny was headed.

Wilmarth Hall rose up on the far side of the Miskatonic quad like a non-Euclidean nightmare that some crazed builder had managed to capture in concrete and steel. The walls bulged and flowed, with windows peering out at random intervals through the wrinkled concrete skin. Up above, a dizzying assortment of spires and cupolas jabbed against the gray winter clouds and the piercing wind. A running joke among Miskatonic students claimed that the Spanish architect who planned the thing, a student of Gaudi's, died screaming in a madhouse, and though that wasn't true—Jenny had looked him up once, a few weeks after she'd first come to Arkham—he hadn't designed another building after Wilmarth Hall.

The main entrance looked a little like a mouth, and rather more like a less polite orifice. Jenny spotted the OUT OF ORDER sign on the sliding doors in the middle, veered over to the smaller door on one side, went through into the curving hallway beyond. There were elevators, but she'd heard enough stories about Wilmarth Hall not to trust them, and found her way to the stair that wandered up the middle of the structure. A glance at her smartphone screen reminded her of the room number. Seven floors up, seven doors down the rambling hallway, and she stood in front of an oddly proportioned door with a wooden sign bolted up above it, bearing improbable words in fancy Old English lettering:

𝔓rogram in 𝔐edieval 𝔐etaphysics

She knocked, tentatively.

"Please come in," said a voice muffled by the door

The room on the other side of the door sprawled half-randomly across an uneven floor to a tall, slightly trapezoidal window. A narrow desk, two big tables, and an assortment of heavily loaded bookshelves huddled against the irregular walls as though expecting some force or other to toss them somewhere else at any moment. The room's one occupant looked no more settled in place than the furniture. Silver-haired and gaunt, dressed in her signature black dress and white sweater, she was twisted half around in her chair at the desk, trying to hold three books open with only two hands and not succeeding very well.

Jenny took this in, hurried over to the desk and caught one of the books, a hefty grammar of medieval Latin, just as it was about to plummet to the floor. "Dr. Akeley? Thanks for being willing to see me."

"You're welcome. If you can hold that up—yes, there would be fine." The professor tried to turn the page of one of the other books, a huge leatherbound volume, and nearly managed to send the third book flying before Jenny got an elbow in its way and stopped it. Finally, after several more near-accidents, all three books were open to the right pages, and Akeley twisted back around and typed two sentences on the keyboard on her desk.

"Thank you," she said. "You must be Jenny Parrish. Pull up a chair—"

Jenny ignored the instruction, as one of the books was making another attempt to fling itself to the floor. It took another few minutes to get all three volumes safely to rest on the cluttered desk. As Jenny went to get the chair, Akeley shook her head disconsolately. "I had no idea I'd lost so much of my Latin. Phil Dyer asked me for a translation to help him make plans for next year's expedition, and I thought it would be easy."

Jenny had heard the name. "Is that for the Miskatonic Greenland Project?"

"Yes, he thinks he has a lead on some runic inscriptions nobody's seen since the sixteenth century. It's all in here—" She tapped the big leatherbound volume. "Arne Saknussemm, *De Mirabilia Septentrionalibus*. Do you read Latin?"

"Just French and English," Jenny admitted. "I hope that won't be a problem."

Akeley looked startled. "No, not at all. This isn't my usual research; it's just that Phil doesn't know a word of Latin and I thought I still remembered more than I did."

"The sign outside the door made me wonder a little."

"Oh, that," said Akeley. "That's a bit of university history—practically the only thing that came with the department from the old campus downtown. The History of Ideas department started out as a program in medieval metaphysics back in the 1920s. I've still got the old syllabus around here somewhere."

"That sounds fascinating," Jenny said. "I'd like to read that sometime."

"I'll see if I can find it for you. It was quite the progressive program in its day." Then, with a shrug: "But I'm wandering. Your background's in nineteenth and twentieth century English lit, as I recall." Jenny nodded, and the professor went on. "That's a good deal closer to my interests—when

I'm not dabbling in sixteenth-century Icelandic alchemists, that is."

Jenny, after a blank moment, realized she must mean the book she'd been translating. "Saknussen was an alchemist?"

"Saknussemm. Yes, his books were burnt by the public hangman in Copenhagen in 1573, and he barely missed joining them." She indicated the book. "That's as rare as anything Orne Library has, but it's not ours. I think Phil borrowed it from the Université de Vyones in France—they're involved in the Greenland project too, you know."

Jenny didn't, and began to wonder how to bring the conversation back around to the questions she needed to ask, but Akeley forestalled her. "But you didn't come here to listen to me babble about alchemists. You'll have to forgive me—I'm still trying to get over everything that's happened over the last month of so."

"I think a lot of people are," Jenny said quietly.

Professor Akeley considered her. "If you don't mind my asking, has there been any further word about Owen?"

Jenny bit her lip, then: "Yes. The police called about an hour ago. I—I don't think there's any easy way to say this." She forced herself to go on. "Somebody found his coat in the river. The police think he killed himself."

Akeley didn't move for a moment, just kept looking at her with the same guarded expression on her face, and then abruptly looked away.

"You don't believe that," Jenny said then. A moment later, before the professor could respond: "Neither do I."

"No," Akeley said after another moment. "No, I don't."

She got up abruptly, crossed the room to the trapezoidal window, looked out it, an angular dark shape against the gray sky. "I was apparently the last person to see him before—whatever happened," she said. "Here in this room. We spent something like four hours sorting through letters and manuscripts by Robert Blake. Owen talked about his thesis, his plans for his doctorate, a paper he was hoping to place in an anthology Jim Willett at Brown is putting together: the kind of thing you talk about when you're planning on having a career and a future. Then he left, and I left about fifteen minutes later, and two days later the police called to ask if I knew where he was." She turned around. "So whatever happened, I don't think it was—that."

The set of the older woman's face, the taut lines around her mouth, meant something. What? Intuition whispered after a moment: she knows something. There's more going on here than she's willing to talk about.

"Neither do I," Jenny repeated. "I don't have any evidence for that, just—" She let the sentence drop.

"Just the fact that you knew him. I understand." She came back to the desk, sat down. "It's good to hear someone else say that." With a little shake of her head: "But we'll see. The upshot, though, is that I'm suddenly short two research assistants."

"Owen said that one of your other grad students quit," Jenny ventured.

"Yes—and nobody's seen her since the night of November twelfth."

Jenny's hand went to her mouth. "Was she in—"

"She was transferring to a program that was based out of Belbury Hall," the professor said. "So, yes, the police think she was inside when it burned."

"I'm so sorry."

Akeley went on as though she hadn't heard. "So your email was—timely, shall we say? Normally you wouldn't be eligible for an assistantship until you start your master's program, but the department has some funds of its own and the administration's agreed to bend the rules a bit this once. If you're willing and your schedule permits, I'd like you to start working for me as soon as the holidays are over."

"I can do that," Jenny said. "You won't need me over break?"

"No, I'll be going up to Vermont for the holidays."

Jenny nodded, and Akeley continued. "Over this coming semester we can talk about what you have in mind for your master's program, and get a jump on that end of things. And this year you're doing postgrad studies in—French literature, was it?"

Jenny nodded a third time. "Yes. Mostly the Decadents this semester."

"*Le Roi en Jaune*?"

"Oh, yes. I read the Oscar Wilde translation my junior year at Oregon State, but the French—Doctor Rice fit it in between Huysmans and Péladan."

"That might be useful," Akeley said. Jenny gave her a questioning look, and she went on. "You know I mostly work on Lovecraft, Smith, Blake, the early *Weird Tales* authors. Recently I've become interested in some of the sources they used for their stories." She was looking past Jenny now, and the sense of words unspoken hung in the air like mist. "Oddly enough, something Owen found earlier this semester pointed me toward that."

"French sources?" Jenny guessed.

"Among other things," said Akeley, "yes."

* * *

Half an hour later, Jenny went down the long stair at the heart of Wilmarth Hall slowly, considering. The next semester would be tough, no question, between working for Professor Akeley and keeping up with her classes in French literature. Still, the assistantship would help keep her student debt from piling up further than it had to, and they'd discussed her plans for her master's and doctorate programs. That was a door she'd hoped she could open, and though it was barely ajar as yet, she thought she could see the first faint glimpses of what might lay beyond it.

A scrap of paper in her hand had a scrawled note on it in Akeley's handwriting. She glanced at it, then tucked it into the inner pocket of her coat before she stepped out through the doors of Wilmarth Hall into the unquiet air outside. It read:

> Abelard,
> At your convenience, I'll need a list of what's still in the collection. Will come by tomorrow after 3 if that's convenient.
>
> Miriam

Professor Akeley had asked her to take the note to the restricted stacks of Orne Library on her way. Doctor Whipple, the restricted-collection librarian, didn't use email or a cell phone, Akeley had said, and the only reliable way to get a message to him was to carry it there; she'd been curiously insistent that Jenny take the paper itself and not put an image of it on her smartphone. Every Miskatonic professor had odd habits like that, though, and Jenny had the spare time that afternoon. For that matter, the thought of getting a glimpse of the legendary restricted-collections room, the one place in Orne Library you didn't go without some very good reason, was another incentive.

She started across the quad toward Orne Library. Off to her left, beyond the stolid brick mass of Morgan Hall, the flame-gutted shell of Belbury Hall stood stark against gray clouds. Odd rumors had murmured their way across campus since the morning after the fire. Students on one side of Chapman Hall, a dorm on the west side of campus right up under the flank of Meadow Hill, claimed that they'd seen running figures in the night, and heard muffled sounds that might have been gunfire: absurd, except that Jenny knew two of the students in question and they weren't the kind of people who would make up stories like that.

She shook her head, walked on. Wind hissed in the leafless branches of the trees lining Federal Street, murmured in the Gothic buttresses of Orne Library, made counterpoint with the background mutter of the traffic. All in all, it was a normal

Arkham day, autumn perched on the edge of an unseasonably warm winter.

Sometimes, in the most ordinary of circumstances, a curious feeling would surge through Jenny's mind, a sense as though the prosaic world around her was on the brink of unfolding into something different, something rich and strange. As she crossed the quad, that feeling broke over her with the force of a wave. Nothing changed, or nothing she could see; the wind hissed and murmured, the clouds slid past overhead, a scattering of students hurried this way or that across the Miskatonic University quad; but all at once, everything around her seemed charged with a presence and a strangeness. Gulls winging overhead called to one another in their keening voices, and for an instant the calls seemed about to communicate some vast secret about the hidden shape of things.

An instant later the feeling vanished, as it always did, leaving the world lessened by its absence. She sighed and trudged the rest of the way across the quad, climbed the stair to Orne Library's main entrance, and passed a bulletin board all but covered with posters yelling about Man's Conquest of Nature— they were announcing a lecture about something called Noology, she noticed in passing, and walked on. Once inside, she turned right and wove her way through the study carrels until she found the door Professor Akeley had told her about.

That let onto a concrete stair leading down to Orne Library's basement. The unmarked door at its foot opened onto a long stark corridor, another door, and a little office with a bare steel desk in it and very little else. On the far side was yet another door; she went to it, found the buzzer beside it, pushed the button.

After a long moment, the speaker next to the button crackled and spat. "Yes?"

"Doctor Whipple," Jenny said, "I have a message for you from—" She pulled out the note and glanced at it. "—Miriam Akeley."

"Ah," said the loudspeaker. The lock clicked, the door opened maybe two inches, and a single bright blue eye gleamed out at her. "And you are …"

"Jenny Parrish. I'm Professor Akeley's new research assistant." Then, remembering some of Owen's stories: "I think you knew Owen Merrill, didn't you? We were housemates."

The door swung suddenly open. "Come in, come in," said the old man on the other side. "Yes, I know Owen quite well. Pity about that business."

Jenny nodded uncomfortably, let the old man wave her through the door, heard the lock click shut. She found herself in a windowless room with bare concrete walls, where long rows of steel bookshelves held the rarest items in Orne Library's collection, and harsh fluorescent lamps glared down from above.

She handed Whipple the note, watched him as he read it and nodded slowly. "Well, well," he said. "If you'll wait a moment." He turned and ducked into the gap between two of the shelves, muttering something to himself that Jenny couldn't make out at all.

Having nothing better to do, she glanced around the room. Next to the door stood an old steel desk. The sheets of paper strewn across the top were covered in penciled notes and what looked like complicated geometrical diagrams. On top of one stack sat a slender hardback in a dust jacket printed in fine Art Deco style. *The People of the Monolith and Other Poems* was its title, and the author, whom she'd never heard of, was Justin Geoffrey. It seemed incongruous enough, sitting there atop a flurry of paper covered in incomprehensible scrawls. She wondered what it was, but had heard too many stories about the restricted collection and its elderly guardian to risk picking it up and turning the pages.

The old man came back after a few minutes. "Thank you," he said. "I'll send something to Miriam tomorrow morning;. You can tell her that if you see her before then." Then, before she could respond, he indicated the book on the desk.

"Couldn't help notice that you were looking at that," he said then. "Do you know Geoffrey's poetry?"

"I haven't read it," Jenny admitted.

"Ah, indeed," said Dr. Whipple, as though the answer disappointed him. "Well, good afternoon, then."

She said the polite thing and let herself be ushered out the door. Her footsteps whispered down the concrete corridor and up the harsh angles of the stairwell. A few minutes later she was out in the blustery air, rounding the northeastern corner of Orne Library on her way home. The clouds still rolled past overhead, the gulls circled and cried, but every trace of the magic that seemed to haunt the afternoon ever so briefly had vanished.

South of Orne Library was the old gray Arkham Sanitarium building, now the Lovecraft Museum, and in front of the parking lot stood a big bronze statue of Cthulhu, the tentacle-faced, dragon-winged Great Old One that H.P. Lovecraft dredged up out of obscurity back in the 1920s and turned into one of the icons of modern fantasy fiction. Hardly a day passed without at least one absurd decoration showing up on the statue, courtesy of some campus wag or other; that afternoon, in honor of the approaching holiday, the bulbous head had a Santa Claus hat perched atop it, and a garish plastic candy cane was clutched in the mighty devil-god's upraised claw.

Cthulhu Claus, Jenny thought, amused. I wonder what kind of gifts he'd bring. She passed the statue, waited at the crosswalk beyond it, waited again on the far side to cross the other way. Tall houses well over a century old loomed over her as she made her way to Halsey Street and the old gambrel-roofed house that was the nearest thing to a home she had in Arkham.

The door slammed shut behind her as she ducked into the entry, shed her coat, went into the living room. Barry Holzer, one of her housemates, and his friend and perennial study partner Kenji Nakamura were arguing about something in the dining room, their voices a random tangle of software-engineering jargon as incomprehensible to her as any incantation in Love-craft's stories. Closer by, Tish Martin sprawled on her end of the living room couch, and looked up from one of her med-school textbooks.

"Hey," Tish said. "How'd it go?"

"I got the assistantship."

Tish whooped, causing a sudden silence in the dining room. "Really? You *go*, girl." She motioned to the shelf next to the door. "You got a letter, too. Know anybody in Kingsport?"

The smile abruptly vanished from Jenny's face. After a moment, she turned and went to the shelf. In among the bills and junk mail was a squarish envelope of cream-colored paper, addressed to her in the elegant handwriting of an earlier day. She stared at the return address for what seemed like a long while:

Sylvia Chaudronnier
730 Green Lane
Kingsport, MA 01947

"Girl," said Tish, "you okay?"

"Yeah," Jenny said. "Yeah, I'm fine."

"Somebody you know?"

"Family." Then, before Tish could ask any more questions, she bolted up the stairs toward the privacy of her room.

* * *

She shut the door, sat on her bed, stared at the envelope in her hands. It took her a long moment to work up the courage to open it, and when she finally managed to nerve herself up, she was shaking so hard that she couldn't slide a nail under the flap and tear it open. Stop it, she told herself. Stop it. It's only a letter. Her hands paid no attention to the lie, but she managed to get the thing open anyway, and pulled out the letter inside.

It was on the same cream-colored stationery as the envelope, and a faint scent of lavender came from it, stirring recollections she didn't want to face just yet. Still, she made herself unfold the letter, and read:

My dear Jenny,

Your letter came as a very welcome surprise, and the news that you're living in Arkham now, so close to us, even more so. It's a bit of a reach for me to imagine you grown now, and attending college—it seems like only a little while back that you came to visit in Newport, though I know it was more than fourteen years ago. Do you remember at all how I looked then? My hair is all white now.

Of course the family would love to see you, and sooner rather than later. Are you possibly free to come down to Kingsport over the winter break? It's a bit of a special time for us— an old festival that's held here in Kingsport now and again will be happening, and you'd be very welcome to take part. Don't worry about presents—the family has its own traditions, like most of the old Kingsport families, and we don't keep Christmas in the usual way.

If you can come—and even if you can't—please call me at 839-135-0193 so we can make arrangements. It will be so good to hear your voice again! Your uncle Martin, aunt Lisette, and cousin Charlotte send their very best wishes, as of course do I.

Your great-aunt,
Sylvia

Great-aunt Sylvia. The name brought up a torrent of memories—the old houses of Rhode Island, so startling to the eyes of a child used to the raw newness of the architecture out west; the blue-green-gray of the Atlantic reaching out to the southern horizon, dotted here and there with sails or the dark purposeful shapes of fishing boats, like and yet unlike the vast emptiness of the Pacific she'd seen from Oregon beaches so many times; her mother in jeans and a T-shirt, her face not yet hollowed out by illness; and a woman with short graying hair and big round glasses who took them to lunch at a seaside restaurant, and then sat with Jenny's mother on a bench, where they talked in low intent voices while Jenny, standing by the railing at the edge of the pier, tossed fries to the gulls and watched them catch every single one in the air.

They'd spent, what? Four days in Newport, if she remembered right. Then it was back to Providence and the Greyhound stop there, to board a bus that looked just like the one that brought them. Days and nights crossing the continent to the rhythms of the engine's roar and the swaying of the coach framed Jenny's Newport memories on both ends, all but identical to one another, except that her mother laughed and smiled more than usual on the way out, and told stories about her family Jenny had never heard before, while on the way back she was silent and withdrawn. Jenny had taken refuge in the books Great-aunt Sylvia bought her at a bookstore close to the harbor: *Misty of Chincoteague, Justin Morgan Had a Horse, Brighty of the Grand Canyon, King of the Wind*. She could see the covers in her mind's eye, recalled vividly the daydreams they'd set in motion, even though the books themselves got misplaced during one of the many moves they'd had to make, looking for work, looking for a place to live, and finally looking for a hospital where the staff would do something besides shake their heads and turn Jenny's mother away.

Great-aunt Sylvia. Other threads of memory wove themselves into a hopeless tangle around the name: pictures she'd been shown in Newport, faces of the family she'd never met—Uncle Martin, her mother's brother; Aunt Elizabeth, his wife; Charlotte, their only child—and a single faded photograph of a place Jenny had never been.

She set the letter aside, went to the battered dresser on the other side of the room, knelt down and got something out of the lowest drawer: a little photo album covered in cheap brown plastic, sized to fit a single picture on each page. Inside were photographs—antiques, really, taken before digital cameras and the internet swept the humble film camera into history's trash can. There were snapshots her mother took when she had the money, half a dozen of them from that trip to Rhode Island, and one other photo, older, in the very back.

She knew every detail before she looked at it: the wrought-iron fence along the sidewalk, the lawn and the closely pruned evergreens behind it, the red brick and white trim of the old Georgian mansion behind those. Two great bays pierced with windows faced the street, and between them was a white porch with Doric pillars and a double door. Above the heavy white cornice were tall chimneys and little attic windows, each in a gable of its own. Long rambling wings stretched away behind, though the photo showed little of them, and there was a rose garden, too, for her mother had told her stories about it more than once.

That was the Chaudronnier mansion in Kingsport, the place where Jenny's mother spent her childhood, then left at the age of eighteen and never visited again.

And now—

The sentence would not complete itself. Jenny put the little album away, tucked the letter and envelope under the unicorn statue on her desk, drew in a long ragged breath, and went downstairs to cook something for dinner before Tish came up to ask her what was wrong.

CHAPTER 2

THE KING IN YELLOW

When she got to the foot of the stairs, Tish glanced up from a medical textbook and gave Jenny a worried look, but said nothing. Jenny forced a smile and went past. Barry and Kenji were still arguing in the dining room, but the topic seemed to have wandered away from software engineering. When Jenny stepped through the open door on the way to the kitchen, Barry turned toward her and asked in a portentous voice, "Have you seen the Yellow Sign?"

Jenny stared at him, then started laughing. Barry's face, framed with blond hair above and an improbable brown goatee below, wasn't spooky no matter how absurdly he twisted it, and he was trying his best. "You've been reading *The King in Yellow*," she said.

"No," Kenji said. "He's been trying to talk me into taking a class where I'll have to read the damn thing."

"You gotta take care of your humanities requirements somehow," Barry reminded him.

"Dostoevskii," Kenji said. "Proust. Doctor Seuss, if I have to. I just don't want to have to put time into the tentacle stuff."

"Why on earth did you come to Miskatonic, then?" Jenny asked him.

"It's got a great software engineering program." Kenji threw his hands up in an eloquent gesture. "That's all I wanted—a BS in software design. Nobody told me before I signed the paper-work that H.P. Lovecraft is this town's patron saint."

"It's just one play," Barry said, "and it's not even by Lovecraft."

"What's the class?" asked Jenny.

"Kate Ashley's survey course on modern English drama—you know that one?" Jenny shook her head, and he went on. "Starts with *The School for Scandal* and ends with *Equus*, and yeah, Oscar Wilde's translation of *The King in Yellow* is in the middle there."

"What, not *The Importance of Being Earnest*?"

"Nah, Ashley can't stand Wilde's comedies. But that's the only play she covers that even comes close to the spooky stuff, and she skims over that part of it pretty quickly." He turned back to face Kenji. "Thing is, that's about the only thing in the catalog that'll fill the requirement and fit your schedule next semester—you know that."

Kenji hung his head. "Yeah, I know. I just feel a need to utter one final wail of protest before the tentacles slide out of the abyss and drag me under."

"There aren't any tentacles in *The King in Yellow*," Jenny told him.

He looked up with a wry grin, his spray of black hair reminding her even more than usual of a cockatoo's feathers. "That's reassuring," he said, not sounding particularly reassured. "What's the play about?"

"The last days of the kingdom of Alar," Barry said. "Scene, the royal palace. Cast, Aldones, the king. Camilla and Cassilda, his daughters. Two ambitious young dukes, Thale and Uoht, who want to marry the daughters. A scheming high priest, Naotalba, and his mute acolyte Jasht. Two servants, three guards in full armor who might be machines made of brass instead of people, and a madwoman. Then comes a masked stranger—"

"'Hi-yo, Silver! Away!'" Kenji interjected, and Jenny burst out laughing again.

"*As* I was saying," Barry went on, with a fine though unconvincing display of wounded dignity. "The stranger, who might just be the mysterious Phantom of Truth, comes from the city of Carcosa, where the King in Yellow rules. Both princesses fall in love with him, but he's only got time for Cassilda. And away we go; there's romance, jealousy, plotting, dancing, wine, madness, murder; the Phantom gets stabbed with a poisoned dagger and dies, so does Cassilda; she calls on the King in Yellow with her dying breath, and then he shows up and things really come unhinged—and bit by bit, as everybody else in the palace dies too, you figure out that the characters onstage were the only people left on earth, going through the motions of ruling a kingdom that's been dead for hundreds of years. It's really good."

"Positively heartwarming," Kenji said, rolling his eyes.

"No, seriously," said Barry. "It's really *really* good."

"Well, I'll consider it." Kenji tilted his head at an angle. "Why'd they ban it, anyway?"

"People were easy to shock back then," Barry said. "This was when piano legs had little skirts on them to keep them from being indecent, remember. The play drops some coy hints about Camilla and Cassilda sharing a bed, and the madwoman tears open her clothes at one point—that was more than enough to get it on the banned list."

"Well, but it was more than that," Jenny said. "The first act is basically bland romantic melodrama, and then you get to the second act and Castaigne takes apart the plot he's built, bit by bit, showing just how empty it is. It starts to sink in that the people of Alar, the last people on earth, are still going through the same motions of love, jealousy, ambition, and so on that we go through today. Castaigne never says this in so many words, but he makes you feel that nothing you or I can do will ever mean anything to anybody but us. Progress, civilization, morality—the play isn't exactly against those, but you can't read it without seeing those as just notions in our minds, nothing that means anything to the rest of the universe."

"A case could be made," Kenji said.

"But that sort of thinking was even more shocking then than it is today," she went on, "shocking enough that some people ended up in institutions because they couldn't stop brooding about it. It didn't help that Castaigne got the King in Yellow and most of the other characters out of old books about magic—"

"Not the same ones Lovecraft used," said Kenji with a shudder.

"Well, some of them—Castaigne's one of the writers that gave Lovecraft the idea of borrowing things from those, you know. But the Archbishop of Paris got bent out of shape because the play had a connection to the occult, and between that and everything else, the government shut it down after just one performance." She shrugged. "It's been performed since then, of course."

"Without tentacles."

"I promise," Jenny said, laughing again.

She extricated herself from the conversation, went into the kitchen, fixed herself mac and cheese and a bagged-lettuce salad. When that was ready, she ducked back through the dining room—Barry and Kenji were arguing about software again—and settled on her side of the old couch, propping her dinner unsteadily on her knees.

Tish, on the other end of the couch, looked up from her textbook again. "That play you all were talking about," she said. "It sounds pretty good."

"Oh, it is," said Jenny. "You ought to read it sometime."

Tish snorted. "Not 'til I'm through med school. I swear I hardly remember the last time I read something that wasn't required for a class."

Jenny had a mouthful of mac and cheese by then, and had to be content with a nod. Tish turned back to her textbook.

* * *

That night, after retreating to her room with a cup of coffee and giving the laptop on her desk a bleak look, she pulled out *Le Roi en Jaune* from the shelf of French books, settled onto her bed, and started reading. It wasn't quite an escape from study, since she'd have to discuss the play in one of her finals that semester, but it was a refuge nonetheless. It gave her something to occupy her thoughts besides the letter under the unicorn statue on her desk, and the unanswered questions that surrounded it.

By the time she finished reading the play it was nearly two in the morning. The terrible final image, as the King in Yellow gazed in silence over the open tomb of Aldones and the ruins of the empty city beyond it, seemed to hover in the air as she turned out the lights. Plenty of people found *The King in Yellow* troubling, she knew that in an abstract sense, and she also knew people who wouldn't read it after dark, but she didn't share that reaction at all. The desolate mood of the last scene was familiar enough to be comfortable, its harsh edges rounded off like a stone carried long in a pocket, and she drifted off to sleep easily enough.

The alarm went off too early, jolting her out of unremembered dreams, and since she had no classes that day, she made up for the previous night's reading with a marathon study session in her room, emerging only for two simple meals and the occasional bathroom break. Once toward evening, when her brain felt so thoroughly stuffed with details of French literature that she half expected a subjunctive phrase or two to drip out of her ears, she sat back for a while, got the little photo album out of the dresser and looked at the last picture again, then put it away and stared out at the darkening sky.

After so many years—

She stifled the thought, plunged back into her studies.

The next day she had two classes to distract her, and by the time she walked to the first of them, workmen had showed

up on campus to demolish what was left of the insides of Belbury Hall. That was a distraction of a different kind, and it set
the campus rumor mill buzzing. Jenny half-listened to class-
mates talking in low voices about some of the wreckage they'd
glimpsed as the demolition crews carried it out bit by bit, or
tossed it from upper floors into a couple of big steel dumpsters:
broken chunks of electronic gear that looked as though someone had set off bombs nearby, doors twisted off their hinges
by some unnamed force. It didn't help that the dumpsters and
trucks had no identifying markings, and the license plates on
the trucks were so caked with mud that they couldn't be read
at all.

She came back from campus and buried herself in her studies. Finally, though, as evening darkened over Arkham's roofs
and the last daylight trickled in through her window and
pooled on the bare linoleum floor, she made herself leave her
books and notes and call the phone number that had come
with the letter. The phone on the far end rang once, twice, and
then clicked as someone picked it up. A man's voice, precise
and formal, answered: "Good evening."

"Hi," Jenny said, trying without much success to keep
her nervousness out of her voice. "Can I speak to Sylvia
Chaudronnier?"

"May I ask who is calling?"

"Jenny Parrish."

A long moment of dead silence followed. Then, in a different tone, the voice said: "Of course. It may be a few minutes."

"Sure," Jenny said.

She sat there waiting for what felt like half of forever, staring out the window at the great dark masses of the university
buildings and the whaleback curve of Meadow Hill beyond
them as the first stars came out through jagged tears in the
clouds. Finally the phone clicked and clattered, and a voice
that stirred half-forgotten memories said, "Jenny?"

"Yes," she said. "Great-aunt Sylvia?"

Bubbling laughter came over the line. "Oh, for heaven's sake, just call me Sylvia. It's such a delight to hear you—I'm so glad you got my letter."

"So am I," Jenny said.

"And will you be able to join us over the holidays?"

She hadn't been sure what she would say, when the moment arrived, but the words came without hesitation: "Yes. Yes, I will."

"Oh, that's wonderful! Do you have a way of getting down here?"

"I can catch the bus."

"Is there still a county bus line out here? That's good to know. Now you'll be busy with finals right now, won't you? When can we expect to see you?"

They got that settled, and then Jenny worked up the courage to ask the question that had been troubling her since the letter arrived. "You mentioned a—festival. What's that about?"

"Oh, nothing to worry about, child. It's an old tradition that happens every so often—I imagine you'll find it quaint. Did your mother tell you anything about the family traditions?"

"No," Jenny admitted.

"We can certainly talk about that once you're down here. Ours is a very old family—it's been in Kingsport since colonial times, you know."

"I didn't."

A pause, and then: "We're going to have so much to say to each other once you're here."

They talked a little longer about things that didn't matter, and then said their goodbyes. Jenny set the phone down when the call was over, and stared at nothing in particular for a while.

After that one visit to Newport, more often than she liked to remember, she'd daydreamed about packing a suitcase, walking out the door of whatever temporary home she and her mother were living in that year, heading for the nearest

Greyhound station, and catching the next bus across the country to Kingsport and the mansion she knew only from that one fading photo. Something would happen there, she would make believe, something that would be full of the wonder her own life so obviously lacked. There would be—

Magic. She cherished the word, though she'd been taught over and over again that magic couldn't be real. For that matter, the trip could never be more than a daydream, with money too scarce for a ticket, and leaving home was never really an option: her mother needed her help more and more as the years went by and the cancer spread through the crawlspaces of her body.

Years passed, dreams faded, and then Jenny was out of high school. The graduation ceremony was six days before her mother's funeral, and she'd worn the same dress to both. The next stop was Oregon State University on a National Merit scholarship, plunging into an unfamiliar life that seemed worlds away from the dim memories of Newport and the few stories her mother had ever told her about her Kingsport girlhood. Only when one of her professors at OSU suggested Miskatonic University as an option for graduate school did the old daydream come to mind again. Even after she'd made the decision to go there, taken Greyhound across the country and settled into the house on Halsey Street and the familiar rhythms of classes and study, more than a month went by before she finally nerved herself up to open the Essex County phone book and run a finger down the columns to the entry she hoped and feared to find:

CHAUDRONNIER Martin & Lisette 730 Green Lane Kingsport 839-135-0193

She'd written a letter weeks later and pushed it through the slot at the little post office branch downstairs in the Armitage Union, half terrified that it might get lost somehow on its way to Kingsport and half hoping that it would never arrive.

The response had come, and so, in due time, a choice that had just gone too far to be evaded any longer.

"I'm going." She said the words aloud, as though daring the night to disagree.

* * *

Three more class sessions, a weekend obsessively reviewing her class notes and looking up one last set of details from the books she'd studied, and then finals: the end of the semester was a familiar drill for Jenny, if a stressful one. When she came back to the house on Halsey Street after her last exam, on a blustery morning under heavy gray clouds, the sense of empty space that blew down the streets with the wind was familiar, too. Students made up much more than half of Arkham's population when Miskatonic University was in session, and most of them would be going somewhere else over the holiday break. She'd planned to spend the holiday alone in town, as she'd done four years in a row at Oregon State University. It seemed unreal that she would be doing something else instead.

That evening she and Tish went up to Owen's room and packed everything he'd owned into plastic garbage bags, then tied them shut and hauled them down to the basement. Neither of them spoke much until that was finished and the basement door clicked shut behind them.

"Well, that's over with," Tish said, shaking her head. "I'll pray for him."

Jenny nodded, didn't say anything. Tish was quiet about her faith most times, but everyone in the house knew that she spent every Sunday morning at the Asbury Methodist Episcopal Church a few blocks away. Now and then Jenny wondered what it would be like to make room for something like that in her life, but her experiences with Tish's religion hadn't inspired her with any great desire to find out.

They came out of the back hall into the living room. "After that," said Tish, "I'm going to want a little brandy. You?"

Jenny rarely drank more than the occasional beer, but decided to make an exception. "Please. I think I could use that."

"I bet." Tish vanished into the kitchen as Jenny sank down onto her side of the battered old couch. One of Barry's running jokes had it that the same bottle of brandy had been in the same upper cupboard since it was put there by old Keziah Mason, the famous witch of Arkham's colonial days, but Jenny knew better; it was the one extravagance Tish allowed herself, a single bottle purchased at the start of each semester, and poured out a little at a time until the last days of finals week emptied it.

"Here you go." Tish came back with two mismatched glasses, handed Jenny one, slumped onto her end of the couch. "To this semester—I'm glad it's done."

"Me too," Jenny said. The glasses clinked discordantly. Jenny sipped the brandy a little at a time, felt the heat of it spread shimmering through her body.

They talked about their finals and the semester just past, and shared the latest rumors about Belbury Hall. Then Tish asked, "You staying here over break, like you planned?"

"No," Jenny admitted. "I'm going down to Kingsport for the holidays."

Tish gave her a startled look, then: "That letter you got."

"Yeah. I've got family there."

"You say that like it's a bad thing."

Under other circumstances Jenny might have shrugged and changed the subject, but the brandy made it hard not to speak of her thoughts. "I don't know them, Tish," she said. "I met my great-aunt once when I was nine. I've never even seen any of the others. They live in a big Kingsport mansion, and—I have no idea what they'll think of me." There was more to it than that, much more, but the brandy only went so far.

"Girl, they're *family*," Tish told her.

Jenny looked across the brandy at her housemate. "I'm not sure I know what that means."

Tish took that in, nodded slowly after a moment. She had family down in New Jersey, Jenny remembered, grandparents, aunts and uncles and cousins and a baby nephew whose framed picture was on Tish's desk upstairs, so many that when everybody came home for Christmas the children had to bed down on half a dozen spare mattresses in the family room.

"Good time to find out," Tish said then.

"I know. I'm probably just being silly." Then: "You're leaving tomorrow?"

"Yeah, bussing down to Boston to meet Will." Jenny raised an eyebrow, and Tish laughed and mimed a swat at her. "Just for lunch. Then I'll be meeting a couple of my cousins and riding with them the rest of the way home. You?"

"Friday," Jenny said, and shivered a little, as though saying it out loud somehow made it more real. "Friday morning."

"Well, there you go," Tish said, and took another sip of her brandy. "I bet you have the time of your life down there."

The next evening, Jenny stood at her window and watched the stars come out. On the sidewalk below, a trio of young men stumbled past, yowling an off-key rendition of the old Miskatonic drinking song "Shagged by the Shoggoth from Shaggai." They vanished from sight, and their voices faded to silence some minutes later. The house was empty; Tish had gone home, Barry was out partying with friends to celebrate the semester's end, and Owen—

She forced the thought aside.

She'd checked the county bus website three times, made sure at least as many times that she could find her way from the bus to Green Lane, set and then doublechecked the alarm: all the little rituals that brought her some sense of security when that was in short supply.

"I'm going," she said aloud once again, and this time it wasn't a challenge. This time it was as though an astonishing fact had finally sunk in. Then, just as in the old daydream, she pulled her one battered suitcase out of the closet, and began to pack.

* * *

She left the house before noon the next day, suitcase in hand. The bus wasn't due to pull out of the station on Dyer Street for almost another hour, and it was only four blocks to the station; Jenny laughed at her own nerves but couldn't make herself wait longer. A sharp wind out of the east set raindrops fleeing down Arkham's dark streets, keened in the bare trees and the gaps between sagging gambrel roofs as she walked. The station was busy, and the little lobby with its racks of schedules was already crowded with passengers sheltering from the weather. Outside, in the big open shelter where the buses pulled up, she looked for a place to sit.

The front page story on that day's *Arkham Advertiser* was about the unseasonably warm weather—two Miskatonic professors were quoted arguing about whether global warming was responsible—but the morning felt cold enough that Jenny was glad to find a bench where a nearby pillar gave a little shelter against the wind. She huddled there in her thin coat, tried not to think about Kingsport and the Chaudronniers. She'd slept little during the night, and only the raw weather kept her from dozing.

One by one, more passengers came to the station and hunched on the bare metal benches. One by one, county buses rolled up with grumbling engines, let off passengers and took others on board, and rolled away toward the far corners of Essex County; now and again a big white MBTA bus showed up to take commuters to the light rail station in Salem. Finally, a county bus came around the corner with 13 SALEM VIA KINGSPORT on the sign above the front window.

Jenny hauled herself to her feet, collected her suitcase, and was waiting on the curb when the bus groaned to a halt. Hiss of the doors and rattle of the farebox ushered her to her seat just behind the driver. A few other passengers boarded after her, and then the doors hissed again and the bus pulled out onto Arkham's streets, rolling past the Lovecraft museum and the Santa-hatted Cthulhu statue on the way to Peabody Avenue.

A few minutes later the bus rumbled across the Miskatonic River on the Peabody Avenue bridge, into Arkham's old downtown. Jenny had been on that side of the river only on the few occasions she'd been to the financial aid office in Miskatonic University's original campus, and each of those trips was an experience in urban blight. Peabody Avenue was well to the east of the old campus, but things were no better there. From the window Jenny saw scores of abandoned houses and boarded-over businesses, with here and there a vacant lot where the city council had found the money to level a building before it tumbled down without outside help.

Finally Peabody Avenue turned into Old Kingsport Road and began to climb up out of the Miskatonic valley. The buildings thinned out, and then the bus passed a cluster of big blocky buildings with a sign out front that read FAIR ISLES MALL, in letters that tried to look tropical and exotic and only managed to look fake. The parking lot was empty, with dead grass sticking up through cracks in the pavement, and the doors had long since been boarded up with plywood sheets. The big tacky palm-tree logo on the side of one of the anchor stores had fallen down into the rank shrubbery around its base, leaving behind a pale shape that looked weirdly like some tentacled creature. Jenny thought she recalled an article on the *Arkham Advertiser* website, mentioning that it had been five years since the mall's last store shut its doors, and rumors among Miskatonic students had it that homeless people had moved into the abandoned buildings. Jenny considered the blank windowless walls, and nodded; there had been times when an abandoned mall would have been a tempting option for her and her mother.

Beyond the mall, the road wound through hills thick with gaunt bare willows that clawed at the passing clouds. That country had once been full of farms, or so Jenny guessed; certainly the landscape was dotted with old barns, most of them fallen into ruin. Miles passed and signs of human presence grew fewer, until Jenny, amusing herself with stray thoughts, imagined that the bus had somehow taken a wrong turn in time and was traveling through a Massachusetts of the distant past or the far future, when human beings had not yet arrived or had long since passed away. It reminded her of the dead land of Alar in *The King in Yellow*.

Then the bus crested a rise, the scenery changed in that indefinable way that tells the attentive traveler that the sea is near, and Kingsport came into sight.

At first glance, the town did little to dispell Jenny's daydream. Off ahead, a crazy-quilt patchwork of rain-darkened roofs spilled up the slopes of a central hill crowned with a great brown brick building with dark windows, and then down the other side to the harbor and the sea. For all she could tell at first glance, it could have been a forgotten ruin unpeopled for centuries. The cliffs beyond it added to the air of fantasy, great rugged crags climbing one after another into the distance, the nearest rising above the building on the central hill, the furthest and highest a dim gray bulk that soared up to blend in with the winter clouds. Below that last pinnacle and out to the left, the old North Point lighthouse thrust up out of the gray turbulent expanse of the sea, blinking at intervals. The mouth of the Miskatonic River lay just past the light, Jenny thought she recalled, and shivered, remembering what had been found on the riverbank not far upstream from that distant shape.

A mile or so down the road was an outer belt of condominiums, some finished, others half-completed shells, interspersed with bare lots where once-gaudy placards announced yet another luxury development with completion dates already a year or two in the past. Faded FOR SALE signs sprouted everywhere. Jenny thought she recalled something about Kingsport from an online article about the latest housing market bust, but none of the details would surface.

Only when the bus rattled further down the slope and reached the edges of town did Jenny see lights in windows and cars picking their way through the streets. First came a narrow belt of tract housing from the 1950s and 1960s. Further on, older houses began to appear, a scattering of them at first, then more and more of them, elbowing the tract housing aside. A few more blocks, and the bus plunged into the dark heart of old Kingsport, weaving through crooked wet streets lined with ancient trees, fieldstone walls, and tall clapboard-covered houses, their windows divided into small panes, their roofs a jumbled forest of gables and peaks silhouetted against the gray wet sky.

She pulled out her smartphone, watched the thing struggle to find a signal and fail. Fortunately she'd downloaded a map of Kingsport the night before. Her phone didn't have GPS, she hadn't had the cash to spare for one that did, but a well-timed street sign told her the bus was on High Street, and the left turn onto Orient Street gave her her bearings. That also marked the beginning of the old waterfront, full of shops and warehouses so weathered by the years that they looked as though a tall ship's masts and rigging ought to be visible past the sagging rooflines—and suddenly, blinking in surprise, she caught sight of stark lines that could be nothing else.

The bus turned right onto Franklin Street, and the stout black hull and three soaring masts of a tall ship stood clear against the gray unquiet waters of the harbor and the paler shapes of the sky. A big wooden sign beside the ship gave it a name she recognized, the barque *Miskatonic*, and Jenny tried to recall what she'd read about it: it had been, she thought she remembered, the flagship of Miskatonic University's polar exploration and research program back in the day, a whaler before that, and some kind of naval vessel back in the Civil

War, before setting into its latest career as one of Kingsport's tourist attractions.

That day, though, the tourists had drier places to be. The only person Jenny saw near the ship was an old man with a long white beard. His heavy pea coat and wool hat kept the wind and rain at bay as he stood, back turned to the road, looking up into the rigging. He glanced over his shoulder at the bus as it passed him, and his gaze met Jenny's. She blinked again, for his eyes were the oddest color she'd ever seen, the rich yellow of polished gold.

The bus rolled on, and within moments the outbuildings of the public marina hid the lone figure from sight. A few more blocks and a left turn brought the bus back onto High Street, and Jenny pocketed her phone and pulled the bell. The bus wheezed to a halt at the next corner; she caught hold of her suitcase, went to the front, thanked the driver and went down the steps onto the wet sidewalk.

The bus started up again with a grumbling diesel-scented roar and headed on its way, and a few cars followed it. Jenny waited until they were past, and then crossed the street. Her courage had already begun to fail her, but there was nowhere she could go but forward, to whatever waited for her on Green Lane. She checked the map on her smartphone again, and began picking her way through the narrow twisting streets of old Kingsport, climbing always upwards, with the hill at the center of town rising higher still to her right. The big brick building atop the hill, she could see now, had plywood covering most of its windows and a general air of decay; Jenny wondered idly what it had been, kept walking.

She passed, unexpectedly, another brick building of nineteenth-century date, with the words KINGSPORT PUBLIC LIBRARY emblazoned above the doors in great bronze letters, and tall windows letting light out onto the wet sidewalk. Beyond it were houses ancient even by Kingsport standards, tall narrow buildings with sagging ridgelines and jutting second stories half sheltering the street below, and what light came out of the small-paned windows to either side was so dim that Jenny wondered if the residents still used candles or oil lamps. She saw no one on the streets, and tried to tell herself that the raw weather explained that.

A faded street sign touched with rust gave her the last guidance she needed: *Green Lane*. She turned right, walked uphill through the shadows of ancient houses and great spreading trees for a block or so. Then the houses drew back on one side; a black wrought iron fence ran along the verge, with a lawn and closely pruned evergreen shrubs behind it. Rising above them, all red brick and elegant white trim, stood a mansion in the Georgian style with two great bays facing the street and sprawling wings reaching out behind.

Jenny's breath caught as she recognized the house from her mother's old photograph. She made herself keep going, to the place where the walk from the pillared white porch passed through a gate in the fence, and stopped. A little numbered plaque to one side of the gate had the house number, 730, on it. She paused, then opened the gate and went up the walk to the great white door under the shadow of the porch. Above it was a shield carved from white stone, with the image of a cauldron and three serpents on it.

By the time she got to the door she was shaking, and not from the cold. Frantic thoughts passed one after another through her mind. Still, she reached for the doorbell, pushed it, and heard the faint chime sound inside, as though from some great distance.

CHAPTER 3

THE MANSION ON GREEN LANE

Minutes passed, and then suddenly, without any warning sound, the great white door swung open. Behind it stood a short stocky man in a black suit of old-fashioned cut. Hair the color of steel was combed straight back from a pale, oddly expressionless face. "Yes?"

She recognized the voice at once from her phone call. "I'm— I'm Jenny Parrish," she stammered. "I—"

In a single precise motion he stepped out of her way, motioned her inside and deftly took the suitcase from her hand. "Of course. Please come with me, Miss."

Jenny followed. The entry hall was on the grand scale, with pilasters rising up the walls on either side to a vaulted ceiling where shadows hung like cobwebs. Ahead, pale light filtered down a wide staircase carpeted in red. "Mr. Martin and Miss Sylvia planned to be here for your arrival," the man went on as they walked. "I am sorry to say they were both unavoidably delayed. Perhaps you'd like to be shown to your rooms to freshen up."

"Please," Jenny said. Portraits from the better part of three centuries gazed down at her from the walls; she thought she recognized some of the artists.

"Of course." At the far end, corridors ran left and right, and the great staircase rose up ahead. The man who'd greeted

Jenny—a butler, she guessed—went to the wall, pressed a button twice, then turned back to her. "I believe this is your first visit to Kingsport," he said.

"Yes." She tried to think of something else to say, and failed. The butler's impassive face and the grand scale of the mansion left her feeling hopelessly out of place.

A door opened somewhere along one of the corridors, and Jenny turned, expecting another servant. Instead, a middle-aged man appeared, gave her a startled look, and then came down the corridor toward them. He wore a dove-colored suit and a loud tie, and his face had the flat florid look Jenny associated with those whose minds count as blunt instruments.

He stared at Jenny for a moment, then turned to the butler. "Who's she?"

In an austere voice: "A guest of Mr. Martin's."

The man made a irritable noise in his throat and walked on past them, as though her presence offended him. Jenny bit back her irritation, glanced after him, then turned back to the butler. He had evidently been watching her the whole time out of the corner of one eye. He said nothing, and she couldn't trust herself to speak civilly, so they stood there in silence for an uncomfortable minute or two.

Finally soft steps whispered down the corridor, and a dark-haired and dark-eyed woman Jenny's age in the black dress and white apron of a maid came toward them. "Yes?"

"Miss Jenny Parrish," the butler said. "You'll please show her to her rooms."

"Of course. If you'll come with me, Miss."

The suitcase changed hands, and the maid led Jenny up the stair. The carpet on the steps hushed their footfalls. They went up two floors and then down another long corridor to the left, to a six-paneled wooden door at the far end.

"These will be your rooms," the maid said, opening the door. "If you'd like me to see to your clothes?"

"No," Jenny said. "No, thank you." At that moment she wanted nothing more than solitude. She took her suitcase from the maid, went inside, and closed the door. After a long moment, she set the suitcase down and turned to see where she'd be staying for the holidays.

She was standing in an old-fashioned sitting room, the kind that would have done justice to a scene from a Victorian novel, with rose-patterned wallpaper and a lush Persian carpet on the floor. A settee and two mismatched chairs upholstered in velvet sat near the door. Further in, a little round table stood next to the room's one window, with a lace tablecloth on it and two ladderbacked wooden chairs next to it; the window itself was curtained in billows of crimson damask, tied back with ornate cords striped in crimson and gold. A bookcase on one wall held an assortment of books in dark bindings, their titles illegible to a casual glance, and an ornate clock hung on the wall above. The facing wall had an alcove—it had probably been a fireplace when the house was built—and whatever was in the alcove was hidden in shadow.

Two doors opened off the wall with the bookcase on it. One turned out to lead into a bathroom with an immense clawfooted bathtub in it; the other went through a short hall to a bedroom nearly as large as the sitting room, with a great four-poster bed heaped with pillows and quilts filling one side of it, a dresser nearly as tall as Jenny standing guard on the other, and a closet on the wall between them. That cheered her; the thought of having so much space to herself, even just for two weeks, was hard to believe. She hauled her suitcase into the bedroom and got her things put away, then went back to the sitting room and noticed the shadowy alcove again. A floor lamp with an ornate brass shade stood next to the settee. She turned the switch, went over to the alcove.

It was maybe two feet deep and three feet wide, with a shelf a little above waist height, a single deep drawer beneath that, and intricate woodwork styled like a Gothic arch to frame the whole. At the center of the shelf, resting on a thin cushion of black silk, was an odd little statue of black stone some eight inches high. It looked rather like a toad on a first glance, something like a bat on the second, and a little like a sloth on the third. Its pointed ears stood up straight, the tip of its tongue showed absurdly between its wide and oddly angled lips, its surface was carved to look like thick short fur, and it regarded her and the world with half-lidded eyes and a drowsy expression. Looking at it, the French phrase *joli laid* came instantly to her mind; the statue had exactly that quality, an ugliness that was somehow endearing.

Two new beeswax candles in ornate holders stood to either side of the statue, and a bowl full of what looked like a potpourri blend sat in front of each candlestick. The whole arrangement looked like a little shrine, the sort of thing that might house a devotional painting of Jesus or a statue of the Buddha in some less eccentric household. Laughing partly at the thought and partly at herself, Jenny curtseyed to the little statue, turned to go.

All at once the idea of lighting the candles entered her mind. Where it came from, she had no idea, but she had turned back to the alcove before the thought had finished crossing her mind. She started to wonder where matches might be found, and knew instantly that they would be in the drawer under the shrine, if that was what it was, along with something else that was needed.

The matches were there, a little box of them, just in front of a long row of candles and a fancy silver candle snuffer. Next to the matches was an ornate bottle with an eyedropper in the stopper. She lit one of the matches and got the candles burning, sending the warm scent of hot beeswax into the room. Then she picked up the bottle. It was for the potpourri, she knew at once; she unscrewed the top, raised the bottle to her nose, and sniffed.

The scent was so extraordinary that Jenny let out a little wordless cry. It smelled of sleepy summer afternoons in rose gardens she'd known or imagined in childhood, where the hum of the bees as they went from flower to flower drowned all other sounds, and furtive things crept beneath the tangled canes. It smelled of resins from gnarled trees that grew in secluded valleys between gaunt gray mountains, brought by caravans along winding desert tracks that were old beyond memory when Babylon was young. It smelled, in a way she couldn't begin to define, of time itself, of long ages cascading one after another back beyond thought to the uttermost beginning of things. One drop, she knew at once, went into each bowl of potpourri. She let the drops fall—they were the color of red amber, and each one caught the light from the candle flames and sparkled as it fell—and watched as the petals and herbs in the bowls shifted and curled in response to the moisture.

Then, all at once, something released her. That was certainly what it félt like; whatever wanted the candles lit and the porpourri refreshed with scent was satisfied, and she was free to put out the candles and go. Half-dazed, she closed up the bottle, returned it to its place, took out the snuffer and used it. The snuffer went back where it had been; she shut the drawer, and then for good measure curtseyed to the statue before going to the settee and collapsing onto it. She sat there for a long while, trying to make sense of what had just happened.

* * *

Maybe ten minutes later, she'd gotten far enough past the confusion to get up and go to the bookshelf with an eye toward looking at some of the old books there. Just then a knock sounded at the door. Startled, she went to the door and opened it, to find an old woman outside whose face almost seemed familiar to her. She had white hair cut short and wore a blue shirtwaist dress with a cardigan over it, and her dark eyes were magnified by thick rimless glasses. "Jenny," she said, with a broad smile. "I'm sure you don't remember me at all."

"Sylvia?" Jenny guessed.

"The one and only. I'm sorry to say Martin is still busy. Still, I've brought tea and a few things to eat, in case that's of interest." She turned and started to bend down, then winced and put a hand on her lower back.

"Please come in," Jenny said. "I'll get that."

"Thank you," Sylvia said, and came into the sitting room. Jenny stepped past her and out the door. "That" turned out to be a lacquered tray sitting on the floor. On it was a teapot and cups, a plate of little triangular sandwiches with no crusts, and a plate of ginger snaps. She picked up the tray, carried it into the sitting room, set it on the table by the window and turned.

Sylvia had closed the door and was looking at the shrine, if that was what it was, with an astonished expression. She turned to Jenny. "My dear," she said, "is it possible that you're already a friend of Saint Toad?"

"I don't know what that means," Jenny admitted after a moment of confusion.

"No?" She gestured at the burned tips of the candles, the scented potpourri.

"I'm—not sure what happened," said Jenny. "I'm really not. It felt as though something wanted the candles and the scent, and—and showed me."

Sylvia nodded, as though she understood. "That's often the way of it." Jenny wondered what that meant. "Tea first," the old woman went on. "And catching up—I've heard next to nothing about you since you were nine, you know. Then we can talk about *him*."

The tea was Earl Gray, scented with lavender. The sandwiches were some gourmet variation on chicken salad with something green that didn't look or taste like lettuce, and the ginger snaps were fresh and crisp. Jenny had dreaded having to describe her mother's last illness to her relatives, and was relieved to find out that Sylvia already knew the gist of it. "Sophie wrote to Martin just before she died," the old woman said, gesturing with a sandwich as though she had the letters in her hand. "It was literally the first time we'd heard from her since I met the two of you in Newport, and only about the third letter she sent here since she left home. And then there were some things that came back to the family after she passed away."

Jenny nodded glumly.

"That must have been so very difficult for you." Then, with another motion of the dwindling sandwich: "But you're—twenty-three now, isn't it? What have you been doing?"

Jenny sipped more tea, closed her eyes for a moment, and then tried to sum up the last fourteen years of her life in some sort of order. It wasn't easy, and Sylvia's gently probing questions didn't help, but finally she brought the story up to her move to Arkham, the house on Halsey Street, and her just-finished first semester there.

She took refuge in a second sandwich as Sylvia nodded her approval. "French literature was a passion of mine when I was your age," the old woman said. "Did your class on the Decadents cover *The King in Yellow*?"

Jenny choked on a bite of sandwich, swallowed, and then started laughing. "That's funny," she said. "You're the third person who's mentioned that in the last two weeks."

Sylvia's eyebrows went up. "Oh?"

"The professor I mentioned, the one I'll be working for next semester, asked me if I knew the play; then it came up talking with one of my housemates; and now you. But the answer's yes—we studied Castaigne between de l'Isle Adam and Péladan, and I read Wilde's translation in an English drama class back at OSU." She sipped more tea, remembered Barry's mock-serious question, and added: "But I haven't seen the Yellow Sign, in case you were wondering."

"All in good time," said Sylvia.

Jenny glanced up from her tea, startled. The old woman's gaze met hers squarely. "How much did your mother tell you about the family traditions?"

"Almost nothing." Jenny finished the cup, accepted a refill. "She wouldn't talk about the family or her childhood most of the time. When we were on the bus on the way to Newport, that time I met you, she told me some stories about growing up here, and there were times she'd mention something in passing—but if I asked her about anything, she'd say that it was all in the past now, and then she wouldn't say another word."

"That's too bad," said Sylvia. After a moment, she went on. "It's simple enough, really. Our family belongs to a very old religion—so old that it doesn't even have a name."

Jenny indicated the shrine with the statue. "And that—" She tried to find words, failed.

"The shrine of Saint Toad? Yes." Seeing her perplexity: "Saint Toad's a nickname of sorts from the Middle Ages—it was *Sainct Crapaud* back then. His proper name is Tsathoggua." The name seemed to echo faintly, in a way that none of Sylvia's other words had. "Some people call him the least of the Great Old Ones, though I'd dispute that."

"And he's the god the family worships?" Jenny asked, confused.

"One of them. There's a way of figuring out which of the Great Old Ones will guide and protect a newborn child. Back when we first learned that Sophie had a daughter, we cast the omens and found that you're of Saint Toad's folk." She smiled. "So am I. So when we knew you were coming, I set up a shrine in the rooms where you'd be staying, just like the ones the rest of us have. I'd planned on talking to you about it once we'd had a chance to get to know each other a little better—but I gather that Saint Toad decided to talk to you first."

"Well—" said Jenny, stopped, and tried again. "It wasn't—talk."

"Of course not. The Great Old Ones don't speak human languages—well, most of them, most of the time, at any rate."

Jenny took that in. "But—" Then, after another awkward silence: "But the family religion—do you have to believe in something, or, like, not eat some kind of food, or—" Her voice trickled to a halt.

"No, it's nothing like that," said Sylvia in a tone of voice Jenny couldn't interpret at all. "There are ceremonies, and some other things, but that's—well, for later. The heart of it, and the thing I'd like to encourage you to try if you're minded to, is talking to the Great Old One who's your guide and protector— or more precisely, listening for him."

Jenny considered that for a long moment. Finally: "How do you do that?"

"It's very simple. Just after getting up in the morning and just before going to bed at night, you light the candles and refresh the scent, just as you've done, and sit down in front of the shrine. There are words—" She searched the pockets of her cardigan, found a slip of paper and a pen, wrote something and handed the paper to Jenny. It read:

Iâ, Iâ, G'noth-ykagga-ha,
Iâ, Iâ, Tsathoggua.

Jenny tried to parse the words, failed. "It's in a very old language," said Sylvia, "the Aklo language. You say it like this." She repeated the words several times, and got Jenny to attempt them until she could pronounce them without stumbling. "Say those aloud, once, and then simply set your thoughts aside and listen— with your mind, not your ears. Do that for a few minutes, see what happens, and then put out the candles and there you are."

"That sounds easy enough," Jenny said.

"Oh, it is. If you feel like it, you might give it a try."

"I think—" Jenny started to say, and stopped again. The words on the paper seemed to exert an odd fascination on her, just as the little shrine had done. "I think I'll do that."

"Good." The old woman smiled broadly. "I'm very glad."

They talked about other things for a long while, and then Sylvia finally sighed and said, "Well, we'll have plenty of time to talk, and there are things I still have to do today. Dinner's at seven; we dress for dinner—I don't imagine you're used to that."

"Not at all," Jenny admitted. "Thanks for letting me know."

"You're very welcome." Then, with another smile: "It's so good to have the chance to meet you, after all these years. I'm sorry I never got to know the little girl I met in Newport that one time, but the accomplished young woman from Arkham—well, here you are."

Jenny blushed. "Did you know Mom when she was growing up?"

"No, I'm sorry to say—I didn't live in Kingsport during those years. We can talk about that some other time, if you like."

A minute later she was gone, and Jenny considered the door for a long moment before returning to the settee. Sylvia's talk about the family religion stirred feelings that combined equal parts of curiosity and unease. She'd known since before she'd come to Miskatonic that there were people who believed in the traditions that Castaigne borrowed to provide plot engines for his drama, and H.P. Lovecraft and plenty of others had taken up in their turn. The professor who'd introduced her to *The King In Yellow* had mentioned as much, with an uncomfortable look on his face, and the comment had stirred an idle curiosity in her, which she'd never followed up. It had never occurred to her that he might have been talking about her mother's family.

That intrigued her, and the unspoken things that seemed to hover all around during her conversation with Sylvia intrigued her even more, but they troubled her as well. Lacking anything else to do, she went back to the shrine, considered the strange little statue in it. The scent she'd put on the potpourri still hovered around it. She shook her head, wondering what she'd gotten herself into, and picked up her smartphone. It couldn't get a signal, though, so she put it down and went to see if there was anything interesting in the bookshelf.

* * *

The ornate clock up on the wall chimed half past six, and Jenny glanced up from a book she'd taken from the shelf—a light romance by Amadeus Carson, a Massachusetts author from the 1930s she hadn't encountered before. Remembering what Sylvia had said about dressing for dinner, she set the book aside, got out the best dress she had, gave it a critical look, and put it on. A ribbon to tie her hair back, the one pair of earrings she had that were real pearls and not something cheaper, a little understated makeup, a touch of perfume: she considered herself in the mirror, nodded in satisfaction, and left the room.

Her steps made no noise on the carpeted stairs as she descended. Voices came up from below: she followed them down to the first floor and along the main hall to what she guessed was the dining room.

It took only a glance to tell her that she'd guessed correctly. A great wooden table covered with antique lace filled the middle of the room, with ladderback chairs around it; the walls were dark wainscoting to elbow height and a faded off-white that had probably once been peach color above that, and paintings at intervals showed still-life scenes, mostly baskets of fruit. An ornate chandelier mostly of lead crystal hung overhead; below on the table, white candles in silver candlesticks burned. Around the table, talking among themselves, were the Chaudronniers.

Jenny stopped in the open doorway, uncertain. The man with the florid face she'd seen briefly by the stair was there; he was leaning on one side of the table and talking to another man in his forties, who was tanned, dark-haired and fashionably thin, while an older man with gray-brown hair and a mustache the same color stood near the head of the table and frowned at nothing in particular. They were all in black evening dress, and the ladies were in silk gowns. Sylvia and another woman, who had skin as pale as porcelain and the pink hair that redheads get in old age, stood on the far side of the table, discussing something in low animated voices. On the near side, closest to Jenny, stood a middle-aged woman with bottle-blonde hair and a hard discontented face, talking to a brown-haired woman a little younger than Jenny who looked like her daughter and didn't seem to be enjoying the conversation much. After a moment she looked past her mother, saw Jenny, and said something in a low voice.

The middle-aged woman turned, saw Jenny, and let out a little shriek that stopped conversations across the room. "Charlotte," she said in a piercing voice, "you will have to get that poor thing something fit to wear."

Jenny, mortified, tried to think of something to say. Sylvia started toward her, but the middle-aged woman got there first. "You must be Jenny—Parrish, isn't it."

"Yes, ma'am. You must be Aunt Lisette?"

The older woman allowed a faint smile. "Yes. You'll be staying with us for the holidays, I understand." Her tone of voice made it clear how little she relished the prospect. "Well. I suppose introductions are in order." She took Jenny's arm firmly and turned, neatly cutting off Sylvia. "My daughter Charlotte." The young woman gave Jenny a frightened look, took her hand briefly. Aunt Lisette propelled Jenny past her. "Your uncle Martin." The man with the mustache nodded a distracted greeting. "My brother Roger." The man in the dove-colored suit looked away with a disgusted look.

"We've met," Jenny said.

Aunt Lisette ignored her. "And our friend Willis Connor."

"Pleased to meet you," said Jenny.

Willis Connor took her hand, considered her for a moment with cold gray eyes, released it. "Likewise."

"And your great-aunt Sylvia and her friend Claire," said Aunt Lisette, indicating them with evident disapproval and a perfunctory nod across the table. Sylvia closed her eyes briefly, obviously upset. The other woman managed an encouraging smile. Jenny wondered what exactly Lisette meant by "friend."

"Well," said Aunt Lisette. "I believe dinner's ready. You may as well sit here, Jenny." She indicated a seat next to hers. Jenny, already miserable, braced herself for a wretched evening.

She was not disappointed. As the butler poured wine and the maids brought in the soup, Aunt Lisette asked her a series of perfunctory questions and responded to each of her answers with a pained sigh or a moment of icy silence. Uncle Martin said very few words to anyone, and though the one thing he said to Jenny was encouraging in its way—"I'm glad you could come, Jenny. We'll make time to talk sometime"—that was all. Roger and his friend talked about investments or chatted formally and pointlessly with Aunt Lisette; Sylvia and Claire, across the table, murmured to each other. Charlotte, on the other side of Jenny, said nothing at all.

The dinner dragged on. Jenny ate little and drank only a few sips of the wine. The main course, baked halibut with hollandaise sauce, came and went. Aunt Lisette, having apparently finished with Jenny, kept up a desultory conversation with Roger and his friend, whose name Jenny had already forgotten. Finally the servants came out with coffee and dessert. "No, thank you," Jenny said when the maid with the plate of little ornate tarts came around to her.

"Oh, but you must try one," Aunt Lisette said. Her tone suggested that turning the tarts down amounted to a personal insult.

Jenny didn't let herself answer, and the maid made a fractional curtsey and went on. She sent the coffee on its way with a shake of her head, not trusting herself to speak, and sat there not looking at anything until the meal was finally over.

Finally the chair at the head of the table slid back with a groan, and Uncle Martin got to his feet. "Well, then," he said. "Jenny, would you like to join the rest of us in the rose parlor?"

"I'm sure she's much too tired for that," Aunt Lisette said at once, in in a dismissive tone.

For Jenny, that was the last straw. "Yes, as it happens," she said, getting up from the table and directing a hard level gaze at Aunt Lisette, "I'm very tired." Facing the others: "Uncle Martin, everyone, good night." Then, biting down on her lip to keep from saying anything else, she turned and left the dining room as quickly as she could without running.

By the time she got to the stair, she could hear voices echoing down the hall, but she paid them no attention. One thought circled over and over through her mind: she could pack her suitcase, slip out the door, make her way through the streets to the nearest bus stop, and catch the late bus home to Arkham. She was at the first landing before she recognized the thought as her old daydream turned inside out. That was almost more than her self-control could take, and she fought back tears of anger as she trudged up the stair.

Just at that moment, a voice came up from below. "Miss?"

Jenny stopped, turned. One of the maids was at the foot of the stair.

"Would you like breakfast in your room tomorrow?"

Great, she thought. Even the servants don't want to be seen with me. The thought of a solitary breakfast sounded infinitely better than a repeat of dinner, though. "Please," she said.

"Anything in particular, miss?"

"Surprise me," she said, and fled up the stair.

The room at the end of the third floor hall was blessedly silent, and the lamp by the settee was the only illumination. She slumped on the settee and sat there for what seemed like a long time, trying not to think of what the rest of the holiday break would be like. Finally, she got up, went into the bathroom, and washed her face in cold water straight from the tap. It was icy, and the shock did her some good. She untied the ribbon and shook her hair out, glanced at herself in the mirror—red-eyed, pale, her hair an unruly mop—and left the bathroom with her chin up.

Across the sitting room, the shrine of Saint Toad waited. She stopped, considered it. She didn't feel particularly reverential, if that was how you were supposed to feel when you invoked the Great Old Ones, but there was the not-quite-promise she'd made, and whatever had happened when she'd first encountered the shrine that afternoon was the one thing that even hinted at the magic she'd daydreamed about all through her childhood. After a moment, she pulled a chair over in front of the shrine, lit the candles and put a drop of the scent in each bowl of potpourri.

Only then did she remember the scrap of paper with the words on it. She tried to remember where it had ended up, finally tracked it down atop the bookshelf, sat on the chair facing the shrine and read the words aloud, as she'd been instructed.

"Iâ, Iâ, G'noth-ykagga-ha." She tried to say them the way Great-aunt Sylvia had, but they came out sounding like nonsense syllables. "Iâ, Iâ, Tsathoggua." Make something happen, she said silently to the strange little statue in the alcove. Please.

Nothing happened.

She sat there for something like a quarter hour, trying to keep her mind quiet and failing miserably, waiting for the smallest shimmer of magic to show itself and feeling nothing. The mingled scents from the potpourri and the burning candles smelled heavy and cloying. Finally she got up, extinguished the candles, and crept off to bed, feeling utterly defeated.

CHAPTER 4

THE SHRINE OF SAINT TOAD

Pale sunlight woke her, splashing in through the lace curtains of the bedroom window. She let herself enjoy the warmth and the softness of the bed for a long while, then finally got up, threw a worn plaid robe over her nightgown and padded out of the bedroom on bare feet. The same pale light was streaming into the sitting room as well, and one of the chairs was where she'd left it, in front of the shrine.

She stood in the doorway for a while, then with a sigh and a shake of her head, went over to the shrine. Pointless as the whole ritual seemed, she'd agreed to try it morning and evening, and it gave her something to do other than think about how she was going to get through the rest of her stay in Kingsport. After a moment's hesitation, she lit the candles, put a drop of oil in each bowl of potpourri, and sat down with the slip of paper in her lap.

"Iâ, Iâ, G'noth-ykagga-ha." The words still sounded clumsy when she said them. "Iâ, Iâ, Tsathoggua." The little statue sat there on its cushion. I guess we have something in common, Jenny thought at it. You're supposed to be the least of the Great Old Ones, and I'm apparently the least of the Chaudronniers. She let out a long uneven breath and tried to relax and quiet her mind, the way Sylvia had told her to do.

50

Only after several minutes did she realize that something was happening—or, rather, that she'd finally managed to notice something that had been happening all along. She was, in some sense she struggled to define, not quite alone in the room. The little statue in the shrine wasn't alive or conscious, but there was a life and a consciousness that seemed to flicker ever so faintly through it, like moonlight through a window thick with dust. She understood, without knowing quite how, why the sculptor had made the statue look sleepy. Some faint hint of calm seemed to gather around her as she faced the shrine, and a small part of the misery of the previous evening wandered off into the stillness and didn't come back again.

Then it was time to extinguish the candles. She felt that, though it was nothing like the definite shift she'd sensed the day before. She got up, used the snuffer, and curtseyed to the statue, feeling confused, a little embarrassed, and a little—what? She wasn't sure. It was as though there was a thread of connection linking her to whatever she'd sensed through the statue of Saint Toad. It was subtle and tenuous as spider's silk, and could be snapped just as easily, but she didn't want to snap it. She wanted to follow it and find out where it led.

She compromised with her confusion and the feelings she couldn't define by running a bath. The pipes clanked, gurgled, and spat out water a good deal hotter than the decrepit water heater in her temporary home in Arkham could manage, and the tub was gargantuan, big enough to provide ample room for someone much taller and wider than she was. A shortage of housemates ready to pound on the bathroom door at inconvenient moments was an additional guilty pleasure. She slipped into the water, got everything but her face underneath it, and let the rest of the universe go somewhere else for a while.

After she'd finally made herself leave the hot water and towelled off, she came out of the bathroom and stopped in surprise. One of the maids had come into the sitting room while she'd been bathing, and put breakfast on the round table by the window. There was a silver coffee pot with a bowl for sugar and a pitcher for cream; there were poached eggs; there were croissants fresh from the oven that looked practically light enough to levitate, and butter for them; there were clementines in one bowl, strawberries in another, and a flower arrangement of hothouse roses in back of it all. She stood there staring at it all in disbelief for a moment, then sat down in one of the ladderback chairs.

She paused, though, fork in hand, wondering: did one say grace to the Great Old Ones? Thanking Saint Toad for breakfast seemed somehow inappropriate; probably, she guessed, one of the other Great Old Ones was supposed to make the crops grow and keep the hens doing whatever it was that kept them laying. "Whoever you are, thank you," she said aloud, and then tucked into the poached eggs.

The sun had drowned itself in gray winter clouds before she was done with breakfast. She poured herself one more cup of coffee, fixed it up the way she liked with cream and sugar, then went into the bedroom and dressed for the day. When that was finished and her hair was brushed into submission, she picked up the cup again and sipped meditatively, considering her options. The thought of leaving the house and taking the next bus back to Arkham occurred to her again, but a night's sleep left her rather less willing to give in to Aunt Lisette's bullying. If everyone else but Sylvia found her an embarrassment, she decided, maybe they wouldn't mind if she kept to her rooms until the break and the festival, whatever that was, were over and done with. The idea of being left alone, she decided, definitely had its appeal.

Just as she reached that conclusion, a tentative knock came at the door.

She turned, hoping it was the maid. A moment later, though, a half-muffled voice came through the door: "Jenny? It's Charlotte."

Jenny let out a weary sigh, went to the door and opened it. "Please come in," she said unenthusiastically, and only then noticed that Charlotte looked very much as though she expected to have her head bitten off for breakfast.

"I'm so sorry you had to put up with Mother at dinner," Charlotte said as soon as the door was shut. "She can be such a battle-ax sometimes."

Jenny choked. "Thank you," she managed to say after a moment. "It was—" She stopped, tried to find a sufficiently diplomatic word.

"Oh, I know," said Charlotte. "I practically wanted to crawl under the table, I was so embarrassed at the way she was behaving. And then after she practically drove you out of the dining room, Sylvia lit into her, the men fled to the billiards room, and the two of them screamed at each other for I don't know how long. Of course Sylvia finished by reminding her that she wasn't Lisette until she married Father but just plain Betsy Applegate, which is true, but you can't mention that to her. So Mother stormed off to her room and probably won't be to dinner for days, and Sylvia and Claire drank half a bottle of brandy to celebrate and won't be up much before dinner, and Father's out planning for the Festival, and Roger and Willis are out doing I don't know or care what, and everything's going to be perfectly quiet and pleasant today."

Jenny, feeling more than a little overwhelmed by all this, motioned toward the settee. "Would you like—" she began, thinking to offer Charlotte coffee, then stopped in confusion, remembering that she only had the one cup.

"No, no, I'm fine." Charlotte plopped onto the settee, looking a little less apprehensive. "But it was so unfair of Mother. I don't imagine you grew up with any of this sort of thing." She gestured around at the sitting room.

"No," Jenny said, settling on a nearby chair. "Not a bit. Mom couldn't always find work, so we lived in homeless shelters a lot—and then for a couple of years we lived in a trailer in an abandoned campground outside of a little town in Oregon."

That stopped Charlotte cold. "I can't even imagine doing that," she said after a moment, her eyes round.

"I thought it was pretty neat at the time," Jenny admitted. "I was young enough that it was an adventure." Then: "But the dress that upset your mother—that's the nicest one I have."

"I thought so," said Charlotte, who still seemed to be trying to process the trailer in the abandoned campground. "It really didn't deserve the scream." She pursed her lips, then, as if trying to decide whether to say something. Jenny waited.

"But the fact is," Charlotte said slowly, looking frightened again, "Mother wasn't just putting on airs when she told me to get you something nicer to wear. If you want to wear your own clothing, there's nothing wrong with that, but the family has ..." Her voice trailed off.

Jenny waited again, then prompted her: "The family has?"

"Dresses," Charlotte said. "More than a hundred of them, from the very best designers—now of course they're all from last century, when the family had more money than it does now, but a dress by Christian Dior or Pierre Balmain never goes out of style, you know. I'm sure I can find you seven or eight dinner gowns and at least as many day dresses that will suit you and make Mother horribly jealous, because she can't wear them any more and you can."

Jenny wasn't sure that sounded like a good strategy, but said, "I'm willing to try."

"Oh, good," Charlotte said. "Shall we go look at them now?"

"Please."

Moments later they were heading down the third floor hall, Charlotte talking excitedly and Jenny listening with a certain amusement. The thought of wearing antique designer dresses seemed as improbable to her as sprouting wings, but it had a certain appeal as well, and after the previous evening, it helped that Charlotte was so obviously disposed to be friendly.

"This will be so fun," Charlotte was saying. "It'll be like the time three summers ago when we were visiting our cousins in France, and Mother kept on trying to tell me what to say, and her French—*c'est barbare!*"

Jenny glanced at her. "*Voulez-vous parler en Français?*"

Charlotte lit up. "*Certainement!*" As they started down the stairs, she launched into a lively if disjointed account, in better-than-average schoolroom French, of how Aunt Lisette had been gently assisted by Charlotte and her cousins to make a fool of herself in front of half a dozen elderly French relatives, an event that still couldn't be mentioned in her presence without a fine quarrel and a sulk at least three days long. "There really is a dear person in there," said Charlotte sadly, lapsing back into English. "But these days, you have to work so hard to find it. I think she spends too much time these days brooding about the Festival. The Applegates aren't one of the families that keep it—they're from Danvers, you know."

"I didn't," Jenny said. "I don't know anything about the Festival at all, really."

"I don't know much," Charlotte confessed, as they left the stairs and headed down the second floor hall. "All the old families here in Kingsport have kept it every hundred years since I don't know when. It's got to do with our religion." She gave Jenny a nervous glance, went on. "And Father says there are people who will stop us from keeping it if they can."

* * *

The hall ended in a six-paneled door nearly black with aged varnish. Charlotte pulled it open, reached through it to turn on the lights. Inside was a long narrow room. Down each side ran a gleaming brass rod at shoulder height, with dress bags hanging below and a dark wooden shelf above burdened with hatboxes, shoeboxes, and other containers Jenny didn't recognize.

The window at the far end had heavy curtains over it and a vast dark bureau beneath it.

"Here we go," Charlotte said cheerfully. "There should be a measuring tape here—oh, there it is." She went to the bureau, picked the tape off the cloth runner on top, came back to where Jenny was standing. "Now let's get you measured."

The next half hour was a surreal experience for Jenny, who'd dressed all her life in clothes off the rack from low-end stores when she didn't have to settle for whatever thrift stores or charity clothing banks had on offer, and thought of measurements as three numbers and a shoe size. Charlotte clearly had a more expansive understanding of the concept, and used the measuring tape more than a dozen times before she was satisfied. Thereafter she scurried up and down the room, unzipping this dress bag and that one, holding a sleeve or skirt against Jenny's face or hair, all the while keeping up a steady stream of talk about dresses and designers and members of the Chaudronnier family, none of which stirred the least echo in Jenny's memory.

Jenny, feeling herself wholly out of her element, followed Charlotte back and forth in the room, offered her cheek or her hair for comparison with the dresses when asked, watched the whole process with a bemused look on her face. There was, she gathered, more than a little art in what Charlotte was doing, for the younger woman's face showed an abstracted concentration that reminded Jenny at once of friends of hers in Miskatonic University's art department, and even more of the two times she'd sat on a platform in Pickman Hall with her clothes off, modeling for a life drawing class to bring in a little extra money.

The choosing of dresses took only about as long as a plein-air sketch, though, and finally Charlotte went to the door and rang the bell. "This'll be fun," she said with a bright smile with just a hint of slyness around the edges. "You have nearly the same coloring as Sylvia did when she was our age, and most of the dresses she wore then will fit you perfectly. You'll look splendid, Mother will be terribly jealous, and that brother of hers—" She said these last words with a flip of her head and a disgusted look. "—won't know what to say at all."

Charlotte pulled the door open, then, and a moment later one of the maids came down the hall. "Henrietta," Charlotte called out to her, "some dresses need to be taken to Jenny's room."

"Of course, Miss Charlotte," said the maid. "But your mother's asking for you."

"Is she in the lilac parlor?"Charlotte asked, in a less than hopeful tone.

"No, in her rooms."

Charlotte let out an exasperated sigh and turned to Jenny. "Well, that's annoying. I'll have to go, or there'll be no putting up with her for days." She turned back to the maid and rattled off a long and disjointed list of numbers and descriptions which the maid apparently had no trouble following. Then, to Jenny: "I'll get free as soon as I can. Until then—" She stopped, as an idea evidently struck her. "You might like the library. You're family, so you shouldn't have the least trouble finding it. It's on the first floor. Go past the dining room, turn right, and it's on your right just before you get to the conservatory. I'll see you there soon, I hope!"

She hurried away. Jenny watched her go.

"Miss," said the maid, "I hope breakfast was a pleasant surprise."

Jenny gave her a startled look, and only then realized that she was the same maid who'd called up the stair to her the night before. "Yes, very much so," she said. "Thank you, Henrietta."

"You're very welcome, Miss." The maid curtseyed, paused briefly, and then went to get the first of the dresses. Jenny turned away after a moment and went to the stairs.

Go past the dining room, she repeated to herself, turn right. She managed to follow that part of Charlotte's instructions without any difficulty, but the hall that went to the right had no doors on either side, just a door at the far end with a large window in it. Through the window she could see greenery and, above it, the glass and iron of a nineteenth-century conservatory. She retraced her steps, looking for anything that might lead to a library, and found nothing. Puzzled, she decided there must be another corridor to the right further along, but couldn't find one. Had Charlotte meant to turn left? That didn't help either, for there was no hall leading to the left at all.

She went back to the dining room door, thoroughly confused. Just then the butler came out from one of the parlors and spotted her. "You look lost, Miss," he said as he approached her.

"I am," she admitted. "Charlotte told me how to find the library, but I think I've gotten turned around or something."

The butler considered her for a moment. "There's a trick to it, Miss," he said then, "one that's for the family alone. If you'd like to come with me."

He went down the same hallway Jenny had already explored, and after a moment of bafflement, she followed. "Keep your eyes on the left hand wall, Miss," he said. "Don't look to your right until you see a face."

A dozen steps later her breath caught, because she had seen the face in the pattern of the wallpaper. It was not a human face. It looked rather like a toad's face, something like a bat's, and a little like a sloth's. She nodded, recognizing it, and then looked to her right.

A short corridor, where she was sure no corridor had been, led to a heavy wooden door.

Jenny stood there for a long moment, astonished. "This way, Miss," the butler finally said, and she shook herself and followed his lead. When they got to the end of the corridor, he opened the door, ushered her into the room beyond, and then reached into his pocket and handed Jenny an old-fashioned key on a ring.

"As a member of the family, Miss," said the butler then, "you have a right to this. It opens the bookcase at the far end of the library."

She took the key. "Thank you."

"You're welcome, Miss." Then: "I trust it will not be out of place to say that there are some who regret your mother's departure, and take a certain consolation from her daughter's presence."

A lump in Jenny's throat kept her from answering at once. "Thank you," she managed to say after a moment. "That— means a lot."

"You're most welcome, Miss," the butler said. With a precise bow, he left the room and closed the door behind him with the faintest of noises.

* * *

Jenny stood where she was for a while, and then blinked the wetness out of her eyes and looked around. The room was everything she would have pictured in her mind if she'd tried to imagine the library of a Kingsport mansion. Oaken bookshelves black with old varnish lined the walls, straining under the burden of massed volumes bound in leather and cloth. Thick carpet covered most of the floor, and a massive oaken table stood at the center of the room with chairs around it. Above, a stained glass skylight that had to be from Louis Tiffany's own workshop let in diffuse illumination from the winter clouds, while globes of white frosted glass hung at intervals from the ceiling spilled a brighter light. The rich dry scent of old books, the scholar's aphrodisiac, hung heavy in the still air.

Jenny gazed around herself for a moment, then went to the nearest bookshelf and started reading the titles on the spines of the books. That shelf had reference books: an *Encyclopedia Brittanica* from the 1920s, copies of *Burke's Peerage* and the

Almanach de Gotha, dictionaries of a dozen languages, and more of the same sort, along with a few oddities—a French translation of the *Steganographia* of Abbot Trithemius, a very old book on codes and ciphers she'd read about in her undergraduate days, was among these. The next two shelves had Latin classics, mostly nineteenth-century editions, and the two after that were Greek classics of the same vintage. After that came a shelf full of philosophy in which the Cambridge Neoplatonists and Thomas Taylor were very well represented, along with Morryster's *Marvells of Science* and a stray volume or two of Borellus, and another shelf of theology and religion in which Jacob Boehme and the early Theosophists took up more space than anybody else.

That brought her to the far end of the room, and a locked bookcase with old volumes dimly visible through the glass panes on the doors. She considered that, decided to leave it for last, and went to the other side of the room. That turned out to be literature, a fine jumble from the late eighteenth to the mid-twentieth century. There were books by authors Jenny had never heard of alongside collected editions of Goethe and William Morris. All twenty-two volumes of Joséphin Péladan's *La Décadence Latine* filled a shelf, and just below was a pristine first edition of Wilde's translation of *The King in Yellow*, complete with the Aubrey Beardsley illustrations that scandalized half of Britain when they first saw print. Jenny noted another familiar title, and pulled out a copy of Justin Geoffrey's *The People of the Monolith and Other Poems*; it was the same edition as the one she'd seen in the restricted collection room at Orne Library, with the ornate Art Deco design on the dustjacket. She considered it, slid it back into its place.

By the time she finished the circuit of the library, Jenny already had a mental list of more than a dozen books she wanted to read before she caught the bus back to Arkham, and the thought of burying herself right away in one of Péladan's lurid tales of Parisian decadence and sorcery had a decided appeal. Still, the locked bookcase at the far end of the room waited. After a moment's indecision, she went to the case and unlocked it.

A glance at the bindings showed that the books inside dated from the Renaissance or before, and there was something about them that reminded her of the statue of Saint Toad in her sitting room upstairs. One of the volumes in particular had a Saint Toad-ish air, and the same curious compulsion that led her to light the candles and refresh the scent at the shrine the first time she'd entered her room seized her again, directed her hand as she reached for that great leatherbound book.

Something hovered around the book beyond the odd compulsion, though. After a moment she recognized it: the familiar, magical sense of a presence and a strangeness, of the prosaic world opening out into something new and unknowable. She clutched the book, and waited for the moment to pass. When it was gone, she went the table with the book in both hands, set it down, slipped into one of the heavy oaken chairs, and opened the cover.

Inside were three blank pages spotted with the brown dots of foxing, and then the ornate title page, all elaborate copperplate engravings and text in antique fonts. *Livre d'Ivon*, it read, and below that a cascade of sixteenth-century French prose, from which she gathered that Ivon was a sorcerer of great repute from an age long before Atlantis, and Gaspard du Nord, who translated the book out of Greek in the thirteenth century, had quite a reputation for sorcery as well.

She turned the page, flipped past the florid and fawning dedication to Antoine de Perigon, Sieur des Flèches, evidently the nobleman who paid for the publication. After that came a brace of erudite and formal Latin poems, brandishing the hackneyed metaphors of the time to praise Gaspard du Nord for his erudition and the Sieur des Flèches for his generosity; then, finally, the first page of the translation. She leaned forward, began to read.

Afterwards, Jenny could never recall more than the vaguest memories of her first reading of the *Livre d'Ivon*. Like every other literate person, she knew the experience of getting lost in a book, but this was something deeper and stranger, something that drew her into bright broken images that might almost have been memories, except that they were not hers. Sometimes a single word was enough to set pictures cascading through her mind—*Voormithadreth* called up images of a soaring dark mountain looming above a plain covered in green jungle, *Uzuldaroum* evoked views of a city of marble and alabaster in an elaborate architectural style Jenny had never encountered before—while other passages took a sentence or a paragraph to accomplish a similar magic. Before long, she was wholly wrapped up in a world not her own, a world of strange gods and goddesses and stranger sorceries.

Then someone touched her arm, and Charlotte's voice broke in on her thoughts. "Jenny? Are you all right?"

Jenny blinked, looked up from the book. "I—" Then: "I must have dozed off." She hadn't, she knew that at once, but it seemed easier to say that than to try to explain something she herself didn't understand.

"I bet," said Charlotte. "That's from the locked cabinet, isn't it?"

"The butler gave me a key," Jenny said.

"Michaelmas? Oh, good. If he hadn't given you one yet, I'd have gone looking for him and made sure you got one."

"Have you read the books in there?"

"Me? No." Charlotte dimpled. "Well, I've looked at some of them, but I don't understand them at all." She gestured at the book open in front of Jenny. "Like that. Do you have any idea what that's about?"

Jenny looked. The *Livre d'Ivon* was open to its last printed page. On it was a circle with the words *Iâ Iâ G'noth-ykagga-ha Iâ Iâ Tsathoggua* written around it, and an elaborate geometrical design within it. Below were the words: *Cette figure est la symbole hiéroglyphique dernière et interdite de Sadogui.*

"'The final and forbidden hieroglyphic symbol of Tsathoggua,'" Jenny translated. "Don't ask me what that means, though."

Charlotte laughed. "I won't, I promise."

Jenny closed the book, then considered her cousin. "Do you know about Saint Toad?"

The laughter went away in a hurry. "Sylvia knows about him," Charlotte said in a low voice. "She's told me a little, and prays to him for me, but he scares me. I pray to Shub-Ne'hurrath instead."

The thought of being scared of the sleepy, almost shy presence she'd sensed that morning left Jenny blinking in surprise. "I don't know much about the family religion," she said. "Mom never told me anything about it."

"You should ask Sylvia," Charlotte said. "Or Father. They can tell you whatever you want to know. I don't know much—of course I've learned the White and Green Ceremonies, and I know about the Scarlet." For some reason, she blushed. "And the Mao Games, and the songs and the Circles—well, everybody in the old families here in Kingsport learns those by the time they're seven or eight." She looked at Jenny, then, and in a different tone: "But you probably didn't get to learn any of that, did you?"

"No," Jenny admitted. "No, Mom didn't tell me about any of that."

Charlotte considered her for a moment, then: "If you want, I can show you the Games and the Ceremonies, at least."

"I'd like that." Jenny got up, returned the *Livre d'Ivon* to its place among the other old books, locked the case and turned back to Charlotte.

"Oh, good," said Charlotte. "I'd show you the first voola of the first Game now, but dinner's only about an hour away—Mother was tiresome, and I only just got away from her.

I thought—" She looked away. "Since you haven't worn that sort of dress before, and there are some tricks involved, you might want some help."

"Yes, I would," Jenny said at once. "And thank you."

Charlotte brightened up, and the two of them left the library. When Jenny saw the face of Saint Toad in the wallpaper, she laughed. "That was quite a little prank you played on me," she said. "I had to ask the butler how to find the library."

Charlotte gave her a horrified look. "Oh, I'm so sorry! I didn't even think—" She looked as though she was about to burst into tears.

"It's all right," Jenny said, perplexed. "I'm not upset at all."

"You're not?"

"Not a bit," Jenny reassured her, and they started walking again.

Charlotte took that in. "I wasn't thinking," she said contritely as they reached the stairs. "I'm very sorry. It's just second nature to look at the wall until her face appears, and then turn."

Her face? Jenny wondered. "Charlotte, whose face do you see there?"

"Why, Shub-Ne'hurrath's, of course. Oh, of course—you see Saint Toad's, don't you? So does Sylvia, of course."

"I wonder who your father sees," Jenny said.

"Oh, he told me once. He doesn't see a face there. He sees a white mask with a pointed chin, with a line for the nose and two dark eyeholes. It's the Pallid Mask." Her voice dropped low, so that Jenny had to strain to listen. "The mask of the King in Yellow."

* * *

There were indeed tricks to wearing antique designer dresses, but Charlotte knew them well, and presently Jenny was arrayed in a gorgeous evening gown of dark red silk. A jewelry box made its appearance—"This one just has to have gold to bring out the color," Charlotte said, "and that'll go very well with your hair"—and before long Jenny found herself wearing a necklace and earrings worth a good deal more than she wanted to think about. Still, the image in the mirror was improbably elegant. Charlotte, in a pale blue gown that could have graced John F. Kennedy's inaugural ball, nodded her approval, for all the world like a portraitist who had just put the last spot of paint in the right place. "Shall we?"

The voices coming up the stairs echoed much as they had the previous evening, and Jenny felt a moment of panic at the thought of a repetition of that unwelcome experience. When they got to the dining room, though, Aunt Lisette was nowhere to be seen, and her brother's friend—Willis Connor, Jenny recalled after a moment—had apparently found somewhere else to be that night as well. Roger, standing near Uncle Martin and talking to him in a loud voice, caught sight of the two young women first, stumbled over a word, turned redder than usual, and then looked away. Sylvia noticed them a moment later, murmured something to Claire, and then came over to greet them.

"You look splendid," she said to Jenny, pressing her hand. Then, in a low voice: "I'm so sorry Lisette was such a—well, I won't say it. But I had no idea she'd behave so badly, and I honestly don't know why she did."

"It's okay," Jenny said quietly, and then in an ordinary tone: "I'm sorry I didn't have the chance to see you earlier today. I was in the li—"

Sylvia's hand closed on hers, hard, warning; her head shook back and forth fractionally.

"—lac parlor this morning," Jenny managed to say, remembering something Charlotte had said. Fumbling for a way to end the sentence: "Looking at the pictures."

"You're interested in art?" said Uncle Martin, unexpectedly. He had come around the table and was standing just past Sylvia. "That's good to hear. We have quite a few old masters in the house, as I imagine you've noticed already."

"Martin's the family art connoisseur," Sylvia said.

"A moderately well-read amateur," Martin said. "Nothing more. Still, Jenny, if paintings are of interest to you, we should certainly talk."

"Please," Jenny said. "I think we have quite a bit to talk about."

He gave her an odd sidelong look, nodded.

With Lisette absent, Charlotte took the seat at the foot of the table and motioned for Jenny to sit next to her. The others took their places and the butler came in with wine, followed by the maids with the soup course. The conversation around the table wandered aimlessly from the mansion's art collection to Jenny's classes the previous semester to the latest scandal among Kingsport's old families, the disappearance of a rare and valuable book from the Amberville mansion on Derby Street—the Ambervilles were cousins of the Chaudronniers, Jenny gathered, by some tangle of marriages and common ancestry she couldn't follow. She did much more listening and observing than talking, and so couldn't help noticing Roger, a mostly silent figure up near Martin's end of the table, watching her with narrowed eyes.

She limited herself to a few sips of each of the wines that Michaelmas the butler brought around, and very modest portions of each course, but even so she was comfortably full and more than usually cheerful by the time the meal ended. Roger added considerably to her good mood by rising from the table, wishing everyone a good night, and heading out into the hallway. His heavy tread on the stairs faded slowly into silence thereafter.

As everyone else stood, Sylvia glanced at Claire, who nodded fractionally and said aloud to the others, "Well, it's been a bit of a long day for me as well. Jenny, it was so good to meet you; everyone, good night." She left the dining room as well. Sylvia glanced at Martin, who said, "Since it's just family tonight—" He turned to the butler. "Michaelmas, we'll have coffee in the blue room."

"Of course, sir." The butler turned and left without the least whisper of sound.

Jenny followed the others through a door at the far end of the dining room. The smallish chamber beyond had the blue wallpaper Jenny expected, but also blue velvet upholstery on an assortment of chairs and divans, and blue-figured porcelain fittings on the chandelier overhead. The lavish Persian rug on the floor had scores of colors in it, but a dozen shades of blue were the most prominent, and the low table in the middle of the room, a Victorian piece by the look of it, had a top of translucent blue glass framed by wood.

Martin settled into an overstuffed armchair, waved the rest of them to seats. Jenny sat on one side of a nearby divan, and was cheered when Charlotte plopped herself down on the other side and Sylvia settled into a chair close by. A moment later Michaelmas came in with a burdened tray, poured coffee for each of them, put down a bowl of mints, set cream and sugar within easy reach, and left as noiselessly as he'd entered.

"I understand you've been to the library," Sylvia said to her then.

Jenny gave her a startled look, and the old woman smiled. "The library and the things in it—those are for the family, and it's best not to talk about them around others, but we can certainly discuss them among ourselves."

"Family by marriage doesn't count?" Jenny ventured.

"Unfortunately not," said Martin.

Jenny nodded. "I'll do my best to keep mum about it."

"Thank you," said Martin. "Sophie told you nothing at all about the family traditions?" When she shook her head: "I can scarcely imagine what all this must be like for you, then. I hope it doesn't seem too outlandish."

"Well—" Jenny said. Then—perhaps it was the wine— words she hadn't intended to say came spilling out: "I made Saint Toad's acquaintance this morning."

The room went very silent for a moment. Martin and Sylvia glanced at each other, and then Martin said, "That's very good to hear. I hope you pursue the acquaintaince."

There were any number of questions Jenny wanted to ask, but uncertainty stopped her. Charlotte, after a few moments, mentioned something about the dresses she'd found for Jenny, and the conversation veered off in other directions from there, losing itself in the ordinary doings of Jenny and the Chaudron-nier family over the years they'd led their separate lives.

It was close to two hours later that Jenny said her goodnights and headed up the stairs to her rooms. She was tired, and the burst of energy she'd gotten from the coffee had long since gut-tered out, but as soon as she'd washed up and changed into her nightgown, she lit the candles and refreshed the scent at the shrine, pulled the chair over and sat on it, facing the statue. The words seemed less awkward to her tongue this time: "*Iâ, Iâ, G'noth-ykagga-ha, Iâ, Iâ, Tsathoggua.*" She cleared her mind as best she could, and all at once the presence was there, aware of her as she was aware of it.

Once again, the sleepy hush that seemed to surround the statue surrounded her as well, and another part of her worries and fears lost itself in the stillness. She sensed somehow that she had passed a test of some sort by repeating the little ritual she'd been taught; sensed also that others had failed it, fleeing in panic from the presence of the other, profoundly unhuman mind on the far side of the strange little statue. Now that she had passed that test, portals awaited her, and she could open them if she chose.

When the ceremony was finished, she snuffed the candles, curtseyed, and went to bed. She lay there in the darkness for what seemed like a long time before sleep finally came, caught up in a tangle of emotions she could scarcely name.

Delight was part of it, delight that the magic she'd dreamed about had come to her, however improbably, in the place she'd always expected it, but another part was fear. She knew with perfect clarity that she could turn back at any moment, break the subtle link that she'd formed with the Great Old One Tsathoggua. She knew just as clearly, though, that no matter what waited beyond the portals before her, she would do no such thing, and that knowledge sent cold shudders of dread deep into the silent places of her mind. Caught between the delight and the dread, she finally drifted off to sleep.

CHAPTER 5

THE WHITE CEREMONIES

The days that followed left Jenny feeling as though she'd somehow slipped across the boundary into a different world, a world with its own rules and laws that she could learn only a little at a time. Part of it was the gaping social chasm that separated the Chaudronnier mansion and its residents from the impoverished settings where she'd spent most of her life: the presence of servants, the changes of clothing from day dress to evening dress, habits of a way of life she'd only read about in books. She wondered from time to time what it must have been like for her mother to make the transition the other way, and tried to imagine a child of a moneyed family trying to find her feet in a world of soup kitchens, temporary housing, and part-time jobs.

Still, there was more to the strangeness than that. Presences she could not name brooded over the mansion, moved silently along the carpeted halls at night, gazed down from time to time from the age-darkened portraits of Chaudronnier ancestors on the walls. Jenny guessed that the presence had something to do with the upcoming Festival, for on the rare occasions when Martin spoke of that event a tension seemed to build in the air.

She noticed also that he never mentioned the Festival in front of Lisette, her brother, or Willis Connor. Claire politely absented herself whenever the subject came up, and among the servants only Michaelmas was present during those conversations. Sylvia was as deeply involved in preparations for the festival as Martin, and the two of them would meet with members of the other old Kingsport families in the afternoons or at night, closing themselves in one of the downstairs parlors with Michaelmas standing near the door to ward off any risk of intrusion.

Jenny herself, like Charlotte, was politely excluded from those discussions, and merely informed from time to time of something she needed to know. One chilly afternoon Martin had the two of them meet him in the library, taught them words in a language Jenny thought sounded like her prayer to Saint Toad—

Iâ, Hastur, khai'wan shrai-ghnagh'gwa,
Iâ, Hastur, khai'wan khlw'mna.

—and coached them in the way it was to be chanted until they had every word and note of it by heart. Jenny gathered that they, and probably others, would be chanting it at some point during the Festival, but that was little more than a guess. Information on the Festival was given out on a need-to-know basis, and she and Charlotte obviously didn't.

Other than such details of the Festival as she was given, there was little that demanded Jenny's attention. Sometimes Charlotte was free, and the two of them would sit in the library and talk. That was where Charlotte taught her the Mao Games.

A box of dark chip-carved wood sat in a drawer underneath the locked bookcase, all by itself except for an oddly angled crystal the size of both of Jenny's fists put together. In it were polished marble disks the size of pennies that generations of Chaudronnier children had used to play the Games. Charlotte taught her each of the Games, one voola at a time, and coached her in the rhymes that the children of the old families in Kingsport had chanted in singsong tones since time out of mind to recall the details. Each voola and each Game, Charlotte explained, had some purpose; some blessed and some banished and some, done in the right manner, would give glimpses of the future. Jenny nodded and tried to make sense of it all.

There were also the White Ceremonies to learn. Between All Hallows Day and May Eve, Charlotte told her in a low voice, the White Ceremonies welcomed the voor, the secret force of life, as it cascaded down from the heavens and sank beneath the soil. Between May Day and All Hallows Eve it was the turn of the Green Ceremonies, to welcome the voor as it woke with the sap and streamed up toward the skies. The Ceremonies were simple enough, a matter of a few steps and gestures and words, but they had to be done each morning just so, and Jenny repeated the White Ceremonies in the library beneath Charlotte's practiced gaze until she'd absorbed every detail. The Green Ceremonies, she learned, would have to wait for another visit, for during each half of the year, the Ceremonies of the other half were not to be practiced or even described.

"And the Scarlet Ceremonies?" Jenny asked. "You mentioned those, too, I think."

Charlotte blushed. "Well, yes," she said in an embarrassed voice. "But those are for—well, marriage, and, you know—"

"Okay," said Jenny, laughing. "Never mind, then."

At other times the two of them would go burrowing into one of the odd corners of the mansion where, Charlotte assured her, something fascinating was to be found. She was invariably right. One morning it was an improbable device in a dusty back room off the south wing with a triple keyboard like a church organ, which once, Charlotte told her, dispensed blended scents through a forest of glass tubes on top. Their attempts to play it mostly generated sighing noises and little puffs of dust, but one key released a piercing bittersweet scent that smelled like the distilled essence of autumn and had both of them silent for a long while.

On another afternoon, it was a huge clockwork orrery that filled an attic room, with painted planets suspended from tracks in the ceiling around a gilt sun. The two of them strained to turn the handle that wound the great spring under the floor, finally managed to budge the thing into motion, and were rewarded by a deep steady tick-*tock* as the painted planets moved in their orbits with little tarnished moons dancing around them.

When Charlotte was busy—placating her mother, Jenny guessed, and guessed also that this was something close to a full-time job—she'd found early on that her smartphone wouldn't get a signal from anywhere in the house, so much more often than not she went down to the library and buried herself in books. Novels and poetry received a share of her time, and she also spent some time with several of the other books from the locked bookcase—*Mysteries of the Worm*, *Le Sept Livres Cryptiques de Hsan*, *The Book of Nameless Cults*, and others. Day after day, though she found herself returning to the *Livre d'Ivon*, turning the stiff brown pages and trying to make sense of the tales and teachings it contained.

As much as anything else, the sheer strangeness of the contents brought her back to that tome. She read of the formless demiurge Ubbo-Sathla, whose mindless bulk flowed among star-quarried tablets carved with the wisdom of gods who died before the Earth was born; she read of the terrible worm-wizard Rlim Shaikorth; she read of seven temples older than the human race, spread across the deserts of an ancient land, and stopped short at one of the many marginal notes Gaspard du Nord had added to the text: *These are the holy places that were laid waste in the time of Alexander, and shall not be made whole again until the stars are right.*

One passage stirred her imagination so deeply that she returned to it again and again. The world, that passage explained, was greater than the part of it known to humans. Alongside north and south, east and west, and at the same right angle to up and down as these, were another pair of directions the book called anth and ulth, and the world curved away anthward and ulthward just as it did in the directions that humanity knew. Along the curvature of that greater world, it said, were many little worlds, side by side though unseen to human eyes; and it noted in passing—casually, as though it was the most ordinary thing in the greater world—that the sky, blue in our world, had different colors in the anthern and ulthern reaches of the greater Earth.

From time to time, at breakfast or late at night, she would look out the window of her sitting room and wonder what was happening in the world outside. The lawn between the mansion and the nearest houses on her side looked rank and drear in the rain, but directly below the windows of her rooms lay a set of brown beds that had to be a rose garden in summer. Now and then she wondered if she would have the chance to see it in flower, and those thoughts led through fragmentary daydreams about spending summers at the mansion to questions about the Chaudronnier family and her place in it that she had no way to answer.

She considered taking a walk in the garden on those few times when the rain stopped and the sun peered down through gaps in the clouds, partly for the sake of the walk and partly in the hope of getting a signal on her smartphone, but somehow she never got around to it. She had too many other things to occupy her thoughts—and the most important of those was the little dark statue in the shrine in her sitting room, the image of Saint Toad.

* * *

She'd imagined any number of things happening at the mansion of the Chaudronniers, back when that ancient house was no more to her than a comforting daydream in the shabby temporary dwellings of her childhood. To the best of her memory, finding a religion had never been one of them, but then what she'd seen of religion in those years was not suited to a child's daydreams, nor any conceivable source of comfort in that harsh time. Street preachers roaring threats of eternal damnation, prayers blaring from loudspeakers in church-run soup kitchens, sermons that always seemed to circle around to how to vote in the next election, people with feverish eyes insisting that the end of the world was about to happen this time for certain—it was all very loud and public, a thing of raised voices, harsh lights, and milling crowds.

This was different. When she lit the candles, renewed the scent, and sat facing the image of Saint Toad, she could be utterly alone if she wished to be. The Great Old One invited her company but didn't require it, and demanded no obedience from her. He simply showed her possibilities, and left her to make whatever choices she would. She quickly learned the way of sitting and breathing that made stilling her mind easier. Once those were thoroughly mastered, she sensed, there would be other things. She would be—trained, perhaps?—in certain things, if she wished, and only if she wished. She shivered now and then, sometimes with fear, sometimes with excitement, knowing that she would follow the path before her no matter where it led.

She could ask questions. Saint Toad showed her that, one gray morning when rain drummed on the windows of the sitting room, and showed her how to frame them without words, as they had to be framed to pass from her mind to the very different mind on the far side of the strange little image. It took several tries for her to learn the trick. Once she'd managed it, questions she'd been too nervous to ask Martin and Sylvia came spilling out all at once in a tangle of wordless perplexity: who was the King in Yellow? Who was Shub-Ne'hurrath? How did they relate to Saint Toad, and—were there others?

She managed to still her mind, then, and the answers took shape there, one after another.

A.vast hall of night-colored stone, hung with great embroidered banners, rose in her mind like a distant memory. At the far end stood a mighty throne, and on it sat a gaunt figure, titanic and unhuman, clad in heavy robes of yellow brocade scalloped at the hems. Pallid hair cascaded down past his shoulders from beneath a crown that might have been unnaturally red gold and might have been motionless flame. His face was covered with a mask the color of bone, broad at the top and tapering to a point at the chin, the features reduced to pure abstraction: a vertical line for the nose, dark gaps for the eyes. An air of brooding silence filled the hall. Something that was not a voice coalesced into patterns of meaning in Jenny's mind: *He is king among the Great Old Ones, and his name is not to be spoken lightly.*

The image faded, and another rose in its place. The moon stood high amid winter stars, seen through bare branches that twisted and bent like the claws of some archaic beast. Against these, a vast dark form rose up from the ground below. She had a woman's face and breasts and rounded hips, though great curving horns swept back to either side of her brow in majestic arcs and what lay below the hips bristled with coarse shaggy fur. Moonlight gleamed on dark skin as her strong arms spread out and up to either side, and in answer the wild things of the forest came to gambol about her. *The black goat of the woods with a thousand young*, the not-voice told her. *The mother of all that lives. Few of us have dwelt on this world as long as she has, and only one has dwelt here longer.*

That image shrank, the image of the King in Yellow appeared alongside it, and then all at once others too numerous to count appeared in her mind. *There are some hundreds of us on this world*, the not-voice told her. *Think of us as members of one great family—parents and children, siblings and cousins, grandparents, great-grandchildren. Some wandering the world, some dwelling in secret, some—otherwise.*

As the not-voice finished, two more images took shape in her mind: fleeting and tinged with sorrow, as though the presence on the other side of the image had thought of them only briefly, and grieved to recall them. The first was a silent form lying in a dimly lit vault of stone, human in shape except for the great branching antlers that rose from her head. A cloak that seemed to be made of many different kinds of fur wrapped her body from shoulders to ankles, leaving face and feet bare. The figure looked young, though her long tumbling mane of hair was white, and her flesh was the terrible bloodless color of the dead. A sense of bitter loss framed the image, and there seemed to be, Jenny thought, something tautly focused, almost personal to it.

It was gone in an instant, and replaced for another instant by something so dark and vast that Jenny could barely begin to process the image before it vanished. She sensed salt water, heavy and cold, eddying through vast cyclopean vaults that didn't seem to fit together in any way that made sense to her mind's eye. In the midst of the waters lay a colossal shape she couldn't see clearly at all. She caught fragmentary glimpses only: the mighty muscles of an immense arm, the tip of a folded wing, a long sinuous shape that reminded her of the limb of an octopus, the arc of a closed eyelid greater than the room in which she sat. An instant later the image was gone, leaving behind only a whisper of tremendous grief in which there was nothing personal at all. It felt to her the way a frozen world might mourn for its dead sun.

Then Jenny was blinking awake from something that wasn't quite a doze, knowing that it was time to extinguish the candles, knowing also that she'd brushed against something far deeper and more terrible than she had any way of understanding. She curtseyed to the little image of Saint Toad when she put out the candles, and framed a wordless thought. If it had been in words, they would have been something like *I'm sorry my question grieved you.*

The response came at once, a flicker of reassurance, as though a great furred paw had stroked her cheek. She broke into a sudden smile. It made, just then, perfect sense to her that

Sylvia always spoke of Saint Toad as having not worshippers but friends.

* * *

Another day brought different discoveries, as blue and yellow flames rose from the alcohol burner beneath a silver-plated pan, browning butter within. "You've never seen a chafing dish?" Claire asked with every evidence of surprise, and when Jenny shook her head, went on: "I suppose they're not as common now as they once were. Still, I can't imagine doing without one. We—I've lived fairly often in places without any kitchen to speak of, but there's always a spot to set a chafing dish."

"Do you still do a lot of your own cooking?" Jenny asked.

"Just to keep my hand in." Claire smiled. "And for friends."

The evening before had been enlivened—if that was the right word—by Aunt Lisette's reappearance. Jenny, hearing her voice as she came down the stair to dinner, braced herself for a scene, but all that happened was that Lisette glanced up, saw her, stiffened, and turned sharply away to talk to her brother. The dinner proceeded without discord; afterwards, the men went off to the billiard room, Lisette complained of a headache and left with Charlotte in tow, and Jenny, Sylvia, and Claire had coffee in the blue room. That was when Claire had tentatively invited Jenny to lunch the next day.

Now she, Claire, and Sylvia sat in a room that could have been the twin of Jenny's sitting room, though the doors and the shrine had switched sides, and the view through the window showed the roof of the carriage port instead of the rose garden. Beyond that, fitful gleams of sunlight splashed across the wet roofs of Kingsport as they spilled up the side of the hill toward the abandoned building that crowned it—the old Congregational Hospital, Sylvia had mentioned. Inside was a comfortable clutter in which the main features were brightly painted furniture, books, an assortment of curios, a wooden easel with a half-completed watercolor landscape on it, and a shrine to the Great Old Ones all but identical to the one in Jenny's room.

Two statues sat in the shrine, each on its own cushion. One was a statue of Saint Toad; the other was a statue in moon-colored stone of a cat with woman's breasts—an image of the goddess Phauz, Sylvia had said. There was something about Phauz in the *Livre d'Ivon*, Jenny thought she remembered, but just then she couldn't recall what it was. She watched the flames under the pan, smelled the browning butter, and considered the two old women on the couch across the cluttered table from her.

Claire stirred flour into the melted butter and then added milk a splash at a time. "Some years back," she said, "Syl and I visited Cornwall, and met the most fascinating old woman there, a Miss Morgan. She made a fine art out of cooking in chafing dishes—I'd never realized just how many things you can do with one. But she was kind enough to give me some of her recipes, and taught me a few tricks as well. There we are." The mixture in the chafing dish had turned into a white sauce; Claire added salt and herbs, and then began slicing hard-boiled eggs.

"The two of them used to go down to the seashore and paint for hours," Sylvia said to Jenny, "and they'd come back and Miss Morgan would cook up the most astonishing things with nothing but a big copper chafing dish and—what did she call the warming thing?"

"A Sluggard's Friend," said Claire, still slicing eggs.

Jenny laughed at the absurdity of the name. Sylvia leaned back in the couch and then said, "That was quite a time. I wish we'd been able to stay there longer."

A brief companionable silence filled the room, and Jenny glanced from Sylvia to Claire. The Chaudronnier mansion had no shortage of puzzles, but she thought she could guess the answer to one of them. "If you don't mind my asking," she said then, "how long have the two of you been together?"

The silence stiffened around her momentarily, and then Claire gave Sylvia a rueful glance, and Sylvia returned a look that said "I told you so" more clearly than words.

"Since the summer of '78," Claire said after another moment. "Sylvia was staying with friends down in Provincetown— I don't imagine you've been there?" Jenny shook her head, and Claire went on. "And I drove out from Boston for the weekend. We both got invited to the same party, and—well, I ended up staying in Provincetown a good deal longer than I'd planned."

"It was a lovely summer," Sylvia said then. "Bright and clear but never too warm."

"I honestly don't remember the weather at all," said Claire, looking at Sylvia. They both laughed, and Claire turned back to the chafing dish.

"I certainly don't mean to pry," Sylvia said to Jenny, "but is there anyone special in your life?" When Jenny shook her head: "Ah. Well, someday, maybe."

"Maybe," Jenny said, looking away. Sylvia nodded, and let the subject drop.

"Now for the lobster," Claire said then. A jar in a bowl of ice gave up shredded lobster meat. "And we'll need to get the toast points started soon. Syl, do you feel like risking it?"

Sylvia's face took on a slightly glazed look, and Jenny, who recognized that look from college housemates with no cooking skills, said, "I can make some toast, if that'll help."

"Please," Sylvia said. "I can't boil water without burning it."

Claire laughed but didn't argue, and got up from the couch long enough to take a well-used toaster oven out from a cupboard, find a place for it atop a desk, and hand a loaf of bread to Jenny. Before long the aroma of toast joined the scents of lobster and white sauce in the room.

A final flurry of preparations, and then Jenny handed Claire plates of toast points, Claire ladled creamed egg and lobster over them, and Sylvia served up fresh pineapple rings and poured a tart white wine—"Just a little for me, thanks,"

Jenny said. Then Claire and Sylvia bowed their heads and folded their hands in what looked very much like prayer. Jenny copied them. Sylvia said, "Ever the praises of Great Cthulhu, of Tsathoggua, and of Him Who is not to be Named. Ever their praises, and abundance to the Black Goat of the Woods. *Iâ Shub-Ne'hurrath!*"

"*Iâ Shub-Ne'hurrath,*" Claire repeated, and Jenny managed to join in. Grace having been said, they started eating. Jenny cut off the lightly sauced tip of one toast point with the edge of her fork—she had never eaten lobster before, and tended to caution when it came to new foods—and took a tentative bite. Her eyebrows went up, and she cut a much larger piece and tucked in.

"Good?" Claire asked.

"Amazing," Jenny said, when she'd swallowed and could speak. Claire beamed, and the three of them busied themselves with lunch for a while.

When the last of it was gone, Sylvia took the dishes into the bathroom for later washing while Claire poured coffee. Jenny asked her, "Did you grow up praying to the Great Old Ones?"

"Me?" Claire looked startled. "No, not at all. My family was Catholic, but I dropped out of that in my teens. When Syl told me about her religion, I was a little uncertain at first, but only a little—old religions were rather in vogue in those days, you know. But we cast the omens to find out which Great Old One I should pray to, and I met Phauz, and—well, that's been part of my life ever since. I think you understand."

"I think I'm starting to understand," said Jenny.

"I imagine so," Claire said. "Saint Toad's a strange one. Of course they're all strange to us, being what they are, but Saint Toad—there you've got depths within depths."

Sylvia, who had just come back out of the bathroom, laughed quietly but said nothing.

Jenny nodded. "Does Aunt Lisette pray to any of the Great Old Ones?"

"No," said Sylvia. "Martin and I cast the omens for her, but at first she wasn't interested, and since then it's become rather more than that. You'll hear the story sometime, I'm sure, but I don't want to spoil a very pleasant lunch by telling it now."

Jenny nodded again and sipped her coffee.

* * *

That afternoon Jenny was at loose ends, as Charlotte had been called away to deal with her mother, who had another headache. She decided to leave the library for another time, and wandered down the main hall on the first floor, looking at the paintings on the walls. She'd considered starting at the lilac parlor, but the door was open and Willis Connor was sitting on a sofa that faced the door, reading a newspaper; he glanced up at her as she passed by. She made what she hoped was a civil nod and went further down the hall. Something about Connor's presence there bothered her, though she wasn't sure what it was.

The paintings were well worth her attention, though. She'd picked up a smattering of art history at Oregon State, and her friends in Miskatonic's art department talked constantly about this or that long-dead painter: the neoclassical revival had arrived in Arkham two years back by way of a new art professor, and half the students in the art department were veering away from the waning star of the Suppressionist movement to embrace what was clearly the coming trend.

Staring up at the canvases, then, Jenny had some idea what she was seeing. This quiet eighteenth-century domestic scene had to be by Chardin; that crouching nightmare was certainly a Pickman; the sprawling, sphinx-filled allegorical piece that took up most of the space between two doors didn't need Moreau's name on it to announce its maker. A little further along the hall, a full-length portrait by Lawrence caught her attention—a brown-haired, dark-eyed boy of maybe ten, wearing the ornate coat and knee breeches of late eighteenth-century nobility, gazing down at her with a somber expression on his thin pale face. Behind him was a tapestry with a coat of arms repeated on it, a cauldron surrounded by three serpents. She studied the painting for a long moment, wondering why the boy seemed so familiar.

"Do you know who that is?" said a half-recognized voice behind her.

She glanced over her shoulder to see Martin standing there, arms folded, looking past her at the painting. The thick carpet on the floor had erased all sound of his footsteps.

"Oh, hi," Jenny said. "No, I don't. An ancestor of ours?"

"Very much so. That's Marc d'Ursuras, who built this house. Have you looked at the paintings in the brown parlor?"

"Not yet, no."

He gestured down the hall, and she followed.

"Jeanne-Marie d'Ursuras," he said as they walked, indicating a painting of a delicate-looking woman in the ornate finery of the middle eighteenth century. "When she was in her teens, she dressed as a man and fought in the French army during the War of the Spanish Succession. Up there—" He pointed to another painting. "Michel le Chaudronnier, who was a pirate captain for a while, and then settled down and became a banker in Vyones. He used to insist that of the two, piracy was the more honest trade."

Jenny laughed. Martin gave her an owlish glance, as though he hadn't expected the words to amuse. "The man in black next to him is Raoul de Malinbous, who nearly got burnt at the stake for witchcraft at Ximes in 1672, and fled to Québec afterwards. Over here is Patience Magbane—her father Stephen was another of the family pirates; she inherited half his estate, never married, and was the talk of Providence for something like half a century before she finally moved here. Her niece Abigail married Paul de Malinbous, Raoul's son, and their daughter was one of your six times great-grandmothers. And here's the brown parlor."

Inside, the walls were paneled in brown oak, the furniture covered in leather and brown velvet, and the chandelier overhead spilled golden light over all. Above a fireplace that looked as though it hadn't been used in decades, another full-length portrait gazed down with the same expression that had been on the boy's face: a middle-aged man with graying hair, dressed in the plainer clothes of the eighteen-thirties.

"Marc again," Martin said. "Your seven times great-grandfather, and the first of our family to settle here in Kingsport. His daughter Marie married his secretary, Jean-Luc Chaudronnier—they're over on that wall." He gestured, and Jenny turned to look.

The painting was the opposite of memorable, a run of the mill portrait of a prosperous American couple by some academic painter of the eighteen-fifties. The only thing that made it stand out to Jenny was that the woman's face was very nearly identical to the one she saw in the mirror each morning.

"The resemblance has been noted," Martin said after a moment.

"I bet," said Jenny.

Unexpectedly, he laughed. Then, serious again: "There were—questions, when you first wrote to us. I'm pleased to say they haven't been raised again since your arrival."

She watched him, unsure what to say, or whether to say anything at all.

Martin pursed his lips, then said, "Which brings up a question that's delicate enough I'm by no means sure I know how to ask it."

"You want to know if I know who my father is," Jenny said at once.

He drew in a sudden sharp breath, paused before going on. "Essentially."

"No," said Jenny. "No, I don't."

"I see," he said after a frozen moment. "And—the Parrish name?"

"Oh, that. Mom married a man named Rick Parrish when I was six. It didn't work out, and they got divorced when I was nine, but by then I'd already started school as Jenny Parrish, and she kept the name herself because it was easier for other people to spell."

Martin took that in, and finally nodded. "I suppose it would be. Well."

"Under the circumstances," Jenny said then, "I'm grateful to have been invited here. I really am."

Abruptly Martin faced the window and the blurred shapes of the shrubs and the lawn beyond it. "I would have welcomed Sophie back at any time," he said, "no matter what it involved or what it cost. When Sylvia came back from Newport without her—" His voice broke, and it took him a moment to master himself. "I certainly won't turn away her daughter."

"Thank you," said Jenny.

He turned back to face her. "It really is the least I can do." He considered her for a moment longer, then forced a smile. "I'm sorry to say there's work waiting for me. I won't distract you any longer." He nodded a farewell, left the room.

CHAPTER 6

THE SONG OF CASSILDA

Then there was Aunt Lisette.

Each evening, when Jenny came down the stairs just before seven and went to the dining room, she listened for Lisette's sharp voice. If she heard it, she looked for her aunt the moment she got to the door and went at once to whatever side of the dining room was furthest from where she stood. Inevitably, Sylvia and Claire had gotten there before her. Quiet greetings and conversation followed, and it often wasn't until dinner started that Lisette noted her presence and looked pointedly away. Now and then, when the room fell silent, Jenny noticed Lisette watching her with a curious intensity, but the moment Lisette noticed that Jenny had seen her she turned to someone else and started talking.

Then, one cold afternoon when Charlotte had other things to do, Jenny left the library around six to get dressed for dinner. She'd spent most of the day leafing through books from the locked bookcase at the far end of the library, sorting out the handful in French or English, which she could read, from the ones in German, Latin, Greek, or languages she didn't recognize at all. The simple process of turning the pages and glancing at the text left her feeling oddly unsteady, and it didn't help that Roger Applegate was sitting in one of the parlors close to the hall that led to the library, all too obviously watching through the open door. She was distracted enough that she didn't notice who was coming down the stairway until she got to the foot of it.

"Jenny," said Aunt Lisette, "where were you earlier? I tried to find you before lunch."

Jenny was sufficiently startled by the question as much as by her aunt's sudden appearance that she said without thinking, "I was in the library."

Lisette drew back suddenly as though she'd been stung. In a brittle voice very different from the one she'd used a moment earlier: "This house has no library."

"I meant the public library," Jenny said, trying to cover her slip of the tongue. "I went out for a walk."

It was apparently the wrong thing to say. Lisette drew back even further. "You went to a *public* library?"

The contempt in her voice was more than Jenny's temper could take, and she was just sure enough of her standing with the other members of the family by that point that she let herself speak. "Why, yes," she snapped. "Since you've made it painfully clear that I'm not welcome here, I thought I'd spare the household the embarrassment of putting up with me all day, and took a walk—and yes, I stopped at the public library. Now if you'll excuse me!"

Furious, she crossed to the other side of the broad stair and started to climb.

"Jenny," Lisette said, in an odd strained voice. Jenny almost ignored her but decided against it, and stopped and glanced back over her shoulder.

"I'm sorry the two of us have started off our acquaintance so awkwardly," Lisette said then. "You're hardly responsible for the circumstances of your upbringing, after all."

Startled, Jenny turned to face her. "Thank you."

"In fact," her aunt went on, in the same strained voice, "that was why I hoped to find you earlier. I wanted to invite you to have lunch in my rooms—just the two of us, to have a little talk and sort things out between us. Tomorrow I have a luncheon with the garden club, I'm sorry to say—the day after tomorrow, maybe?"

"Please," Jenny said. "And thank you."

"Very good." Lisette pasted on a smile she obviously didn't feel. "Noon, perhaps? I'll expect you."

"I'll be there," Jenny said. Her aunt nodded, turned away, and went down the hall to the right, toward the lilac parlor.

Jenny watched her go, then turned and climbed the stair. If she could work things out with Lisette, she reflected, future visits to the Chaudronnier mansion might be much easier to arrange; somewhere off in the distance, there hovered the possibility that words like *home* and *family* might stop being labels that applied only to other people's lives. Still, there was too much she needed to know, too many secrets in the sprawling old house to be sure, and the forced smile on her aunt's face left her wary.

When she got to her room, before she dressed for dinner, she got out a set of stones for the Mao Games that Charlotte had found for her, and played the fourth voola of the First Game, which was supposed to offer glimpses of the future. The stones clicked down on the table one after another, and Jenny chanted the old rhyme under her breath until the pattern was complete. She still had much to learn about the Game and its interpretation, but the meaning of the pattern she got was clear enough: danger.

* * *

That evening, Martin and Sylvia had an evening meeting at another house about the Festival, and Roger Applegate and Willis Connor headed off to some party in Arkham. Lisette retired right after dinner, taking Charlotte with her—there was a television program she liked to watch, Charlotte had explained to Jenny, but she didn't like to watch it alone—and that left Jenny and Claire by themselves in the blue room, with steaming cups of coffee and a plate of crisp spiced cookies to fill in whatever crevices dinner hadn't reached.

They talked about nothing in particular for a while, and then Jenny gathered up her courage and said, "I've been wondering about what Sylvia said about my aunt Lisette—the story that would have spoiled a good lunch. I don't know if it would spoil the dinner we just had, but nobody else seems to be willing to talk about it."

"That's true enough," said Claire. She sat back, sipped coffee. "I can tell you the story, if you like. It's probably easier for me, since I was on the outside of most of it."

"Please," Jenny said.

"I should probably start with your grandfather Charles, Syl's older brother. He's the reason I know how to cook with a chafing dish, in a certain sense. He had control of the family money, and when he found out about me and Syl, he threw her out of this house and cut her off without a cent. We managed—it was easier to get by in those days, and people in the gay and lesbian scene helped each other out a lot. So she waited tables in a lesbian bar in Boston, I already had a job in a bookstore in Somerville, and we lived in one cramped little place after another in one rundown neighborhood after another, as often as not without a kitchen. Partly that was so we could scrape together enough money every few years for a vacation—we went to Cornwall, Mexico, Thailand." She laughed, shook her head. "We could have gone to France and her family over there would have taken us in, but she wouldn't do that—there's the Chaudronnier pride for you. But we didn't have too bad of a life, all things considered."

"And your family?"

Claire's expression tightened. "When I came out to my parents they told me to my face that they wished I was dead."

Jenny winced. "I'm sorry."

"Don't worry about it. It's common enough in my generation." Jenny nodded, and Claire went on. "Syl and Martin worked out some way of staying in touch—he was at Miskatonic by then, and I think they used one of his friends as a mail drop. We heard all about his romance with Betsy Applegate, he let us know when your grandmother Audrey died, and he kept us posted about how your mother was doing—she was in the Kingsport high school orchestra, playing clarinet, I think, and we got the programs from every single concert they had."

"I didn't know about that," Jenny said.

"No? Ask Syl sometime; I think she still has all those letters. But everything seemed perfectly normal, or as normal as you get in Kingsport, and then something happened. I don't know what it was. I don't know if anybody knows what it was. But all of a sudden Charles was dead and your mother was gone—we found out afterwards that she'd taken the county bus to Boston and ridden Greyhound to the other side of the country—and right around nine months later, you were born."

Jenny looked up from her coffee then. Claire met her gaze, and said, "I don't know what happened. I really don't." Jenny nodded after a long moment, and she went on. "So when he graduated from Miskatonic, Martin married Betsy and moved into the mansion. Syl and I came to the wedding, and right there in front of everyone he told us that we were welcome in his house and he didn't give a damn what anyone else thought. So we came to visit, after he and Betsy had a couple of months to settle in together, and then we visited again about eight months later, and finally moved in about two years after the wedding.

"And the thing is, Betsy was delighted to have us. She'd just had Charlotte and had a very hard time with the birth, and having a couple of middle-aged women around who were more than willing to sit up with a colicky baby wasn't exactly unwelcome. So we settled in, and everything was fine. Martin and Betsy had friends and relatives staying here as often as not, and neither of them minded at all when Sylvia and I had some of our friends visit for a week or two.

"And then, maybe ten years ago, things started to go sour. It didn't happen all at once—it was a bit at a time, and Syl and I told each other at first that it was just a phase, something that would blow on past. Betsy never really was interested in the family religion, but she got really brittle about it, so you couldn't even mention it around her. She started complaining when Syl and I had friends to visit, and there started being trouble whenever anyone stayed, except for her family—and lately, only her brother and maybe a friend or two of his. She insisted after one visit to France that everyone call her Lisette, and started to put on the most embarrassing airs—I hate to say it, but the sort of thing you'd expect from someone who didn't grow up with old money but wants to pretend she did."

"I know," Jenny said. "I mentioned the public library to her earlier today and she acted like I'd dropped a dead rat in her salad."

"Now there's an idea," said Claire. Jenny nearly choked on her coffee.

"The thing is," Claire went on, "she wasn't anything like that when I first met her. Syl and I both tried to get her to talk—we thought she was upset about something—but she insisted there was nothing wrong and got really nasty with us when we didn't drop the matter. And it just went downhill from there. To this day I don't know why."

Jenny considered that. "How did Uncle Martin take all that?"

"Not well," Claire admitted. "He won't confront Lisette most of the time. He used to get into terrible fights with your grandfather, but when Lisette behaves—well, for example, the atrocious way she did that first night you were here—he just withdraws. I don't know why."

After a moment, Jenny nodded. "Mom never told me anything about her family, so all of this is new to me. She wouldn't talk about her parents at all, or—" She shrugged.

"I never met your grandmother," Claire said. "Charles— I met him once. He was older than Syl, fifteen years older, I think, and he already looked like an old man when he was younger than Martin is now. He was quite a serious scholar, and he studied a lot of very strange things." She shuddered visibly. "I've never met anyone who scared me more. But there was just that one time, when he showed up at my place one night when Syl was there." She leaned forward. "And to this day nobody in the family has been willing to tell me how he died."

* * *

Not long after, Jenny climbed the stair to the third floor, her head full of unanswered questions. Once she'd washed and changed into her nightgown, she went to the shrine, lit the candles, refreshed the scent, and settled on the chair. It took her longer than usual to still her mind, but presently her thoughts stopped chasing each other in circles and she became aware of the other mind on the far side of the strange little statue.

You are troubled, the not-voice said.

Jenny let out a ragged sigh. *Is it that obvious?*

In answer, a brief fragmentary glimpse of an awareness that was not hers broke over her with the force of a wave. It was not a human awareness; it contemplated the world through senses she didn't recognize and arranged its thoughts in patterns her mind couldn't grasp; but in that awareness, simultaneously present to it, were countless human and near-human faces, minds, thoughts, each of them expressing some slight variation on the mood she felt just then.

The glimpse vanished before she could quite make sense of it, but it left her dazzled and trembling. It took her some time to bring her mind back to stillness and return her attention to the presence of Saint Toad. One of the things the glimpse had shown her, though it had nothing to do with her or the perplexities she faced, stayed at the center of her thoughts, and once she had cleared her mind sufficiently, she framed the question: *Is that true? Do you remember the first human beings that ever lived?*

The answer came with a hint of amusement. *Why, yes.* Through the not-words came a sense of time even more forceful than the one that had overwhelmed her the first time she'd smelled the scent-offering at the shrine. She could sense memories reaching back incalculably far beyond earliest humanity and its ancestors, all the way to the original stirrings of life on Earth. Faint broken glimpses of that primordial scene whispered through Jenny's mind, and a sudden wild desire seized her, to know what that first beginning had been like.

In answer, the room dissolved around her.

She stood on a beach of rough gray sand. Before her, a sea as clear as distilled water reached into the distance, where a conical mountain topped with fire broke the surface. The smoke that belched from its summit rose in lightning-edged billows to unguessable heights. Elsewhere, the sky was dark blue dotted here and there with bright stars.

Something turned her, and she gasped. A moon twice the size of the one she knew hung vast and pale in the sky before her. Only a few of the great dark blotches she remembered had yet appeared on it, but little smoldering points of red light here and there on its face spoke of the volcanic fires that would put those markings in their places in due time. She stared at it for a long moment, and then, again without intending the movement, started walking toward it.

Sand forced its way between her toes, and she looked down in surprise. Absurdly, she was on that primordial shore barefoot and dressed in her nightgown, just as she'd been when she sat before the shrine. *Am I actually here?* she asked, astonished.

Physically? No. Something that would have been a smile, if the Great Old One's face had been capable of such expressions, came through the not-voice. *The air would choke you, and there are—other issues. But this is what you would have seen, if by some chance you happened to exist rather more than two billion years before your species was born.*

She nodded vaguely, dazzled by the thought, as she walked on toward the vast pale disk of the moon. As she followed the line of the beach, she could feel a vast presence moving behind her. A compulsion she couldn't name kept her from glancing back at it, but it didn't seem to be the familiar shape, rather like a toad, something like a bat, a little like a sloth, that she associated with Tsathoggua. Something deep in her mind hinted at many wings and many eyes, coiling shapes and vast prismatic surfaces. Whatever it was, it made no sound and cast no shadow, though she could hear the waves hiss on the beach and the distant roar of the eruption across the water, and her own shadow stretched out before her across the sand as she walked.

The presence guided her to a shallow pool edged with rock maybe twenty yards back from the sea's edge, just within the line the last high tide had traced on the sand. On the shores she knew, a tidepool so neatly placed would have barnacles clinging to the rocks, starfish and sea anemones on the sandy bottom, seaweed here and hermit crabs there, but she knew that none of those familiar creatures had yet come into being, nor would exist yet for countless ages. Even so, the pool lacked the sterile purity of the sea. In its deepest corner, something faint and shapeless clouded the water and blurred the sand and rock underneath.

The first of all living things on Earth, the not-voice said. *The loremasters of Hyperborea will one day call it Ubbo-Sathla. When it has grown strong I will give it certain treasures to guard. Then it will swell and slough parts of itself into the sea; over the cycles of time, those fragments will grow and mate and multiply, and from them will come—you.*

Then all at once she was back in her sitting room in the Chaudronnier mansion, in the chair before the shrine of Saint

Toad, without so much as a single grain of gray sand on her bare feet. She laughed, shaking her head in amazement, then considered the vast span of time she'd been shown, the infinitesimal length of her own life, and the greater but still tiny span allotted to her species, and asked in wonder: *why do you even bother with us?*

The answer this time came in the form of one of her own memories. That autumn, looking out the window of her bedroom in the house on Halsey Street, she'd seen a bright-eyed little wren hopping here and there on the outside sill, and watched it for most of fifteen minutes until it finally darted off in a flurry of tiny wings. The image came back to her in perfect clarity, vanished as suddenly as it had come.

The image delighted her, and she laughed again. A sudden stray thought tried to convince her that she should take offense at the comparison, brought up all those claims she'd heard that human beings had some grander role in the scheme of things than wrens or hermit crabs or faint shapeless blurs at the bottom of Archaean tidepools; a slogan from a poster on a Miskatonic University bulletin board tried to force its way into her mind. At that moment, it might as well have tried to convince her that squares have five sides and rocks fall straight up into the sky. *I hope we entertain you*, she said, still laughing.

Now and again, the not-voice responded, amused. Then, serious again: *But there is another matter. Some things can be done by a wren that a human cannot do as easily, or at all.*

She had wondered, since her first contact with Saint Toad, if one of the doors that would open before her would lead her to do things at the Great Old One's direction. She could refuse, she knew that at once, and there might be good reason to do so, but the thought was a distant abstraction. *If there's anything you want me to do ...*

All in good time, the Great Old One replied.

* * *

The next morning she woke early, when the sky was still dark. The weather had turned stormy, and the mansion whispered and sighed to itself as mixed rain and snow blew past the windows, driven before the wind's whips. Her morning devotion to Saint Toad was a simple comfortable silence. Afterwards, she rang the bell to call for breakfast, then suddenly felt ashamed that she'd called one of the maids at so early an hour.

"Good heavens, don't worry about it," said Henrietta, when Jenny stammered an apology. "It's no trouble at all. Mr. Martin has breakfast every morning at six sharp, and then everyone else starts ringing for theirs at nine or thereabouts. If you want yours in between, that makes things easier for me and Fern both—not that we mind either way, you understand."

They settled on the details of Jenny's breakfast, and Henrietta left. Jenny watched her go. Since their first brief interactions, she and Henrietta had become—what? Not friends, not with the inescapable fact of their different places in the household, but linked by some formal but companionable relationship for which Jenny had no name.

"It's really quite a decent job," Henrietta had explained the previous morning, in response to Jenny's tentative questions. "The pay's good, and I don't have to worry about renting an apartment—you can't imagine how much that helped a couple of years ago when rents went way up." She'd shaken her head. "My sister Lettie works at the Kingsport Grand out Harbor Street, and she'd give anything to get a place at one of the big houses. She has to work a lot harder at the hotel, her schedule's just plain crazy, and—" Her face twisted in disgust. "Some of the men who stay there get real creepy sometimes, if you know what I mean."

Jenny had nodded. "I hope you don't have to deal with anything like that here."

She'd already gotten used to the quick assessing glance that told her Henrietta was trying to decide how much to say. "Well," said the maid, "I'm sorry to say it, but Mr. Applegate gets handsy sometimes. If he ever gives you any trouble, you talk to Michaelmas right away and he'll put a stop to it. Me and Alison, we watch out for each other, and of course we make sure that Fern stays out of his way." Fern, the assistant cook, had Downs syndrome; Jenny had seen only a few glimpses of her so far, a plump little red-haired woman with a round face who scurried out of sight if she thought anyone was watching her. The thought of Roger Applegate pawing her made Jenny's fists clench.

Breakfast showed up promptly—shirred eggs, toast, half a baked apple, and plenty of coffee—and Henrietta headed off to other chores. The first uncertain light had just begun to show in the sky when Jenny finished the meal. She'd brought one of Péladan's novels from the library to read before bed, and common sense suggested another chapter or two before venturing out of her rooms, but a restless mood was on her, and the White Ceremonies, which she did most days right after breakfast, did nothing to dispell it. She pulled a cardigan over her morning dress and went out into the hallway outside.

A whisper of sound came up from below, barely audible at first, though she moved as silent as a cat down the carpeted stair. She was on the second floor before she was sure it was music, and halfway to the first before the sound unfolded into a voice and the notes of a piano weaving odd harmonies around it. The voice, Jenny thought, sounded like Charlotte's. As she reached the bottom of the stair, she could make out the words:

> "Je songe à cette terre ancienne
> Où des couchants longtemps déchus
> Dorent des grandes cygnes perdus
> Pagayant dans une eau païenne …"*

---

* "I dream of that ancient land
Where sunsets long departed
Gild the great vanished swans
Swimming in a pagan water …"

The music came from a door to the right of the stair, not far from the brown parlor. The door gapped open just enough to show pale light and a glimpse of green wallpaper. Quietly, hoping not to interrupt, Jenny slipped down the silent hall and looked inside.

It was Charlotte, as she'd thought, sitting at a grand piano that looked well over a century old. Her eyes were shut as she sang, and her fingers darted across the keyboard with a fluid grace that bespoke years of practice. Jenny stood there listening for a long moment, and then turned to go, feeling uncomfortable. There was something intensely private about the younger woman's concentration, the carefully muffled playing and the low voice.

As she stepped back, a floorboard beneath the carpet moaned audibly. All at once Charlotte stopped playing and turned toward the door, eyes wide and frightened.

"Please don't stop," Jenny said. "That was lovely."

Charlotte stared at her for a moment, and then sagged in evident relief. "I thought that Mother had come downstairs early," she said.

"Doesn't she like you to play?"

"It's—complicated."

"As far as I know everybody else is still sound asleep," Jenny said, wondering what the complications might be, and half afraid she could guess. "If you'd rather, I can go away—I was headed for the library when I heard you."

"You don't have to," Charlotte said after a moment.

Jenny considered that, then went into the room. "That really was lovely."

"Do you know the song?" When Jenny shook her head: "It's by Erich Zann—well, the words are by Honoré-Leclerc Fréneville-Forgeron, of course, one of his most famous poems, but Zann put most of those to music, you know. Old Jean-Laurent d'Ursuras, who's our third cousin twice removed, knew Zann personally."

"I don't think I've heard of Erich Zann," said Jenny. "Or—" She stopped, trying to recall the name of the poet.

"No? I suppose they're mostly famous in the *département Haute-Isoile*. Everybody there reads Fréneville-Forgeron, he's the most famous poet of that part of France. As for Zann, there's a bronze statue of him in Vyones—the old mute fiddler of the Rue d'Auseil, they call him, but he was quite a prolific composer as well, and there's a concert of his music there every year at midsummer." Charlotte sighed, shook her head, and for a moment the frightened look left her face. "Father and I went three years ago, when we were in Vyones for the summer, visiting the cousins. It was wonderful. Have you been to Vyones?"

"No," said Jenny, trying to keep track of poets, fiddlers, and the rest. "I've been to France; I had a six week summer program there, but that was in Paris."

"Vyones is two hours south of Paris by train," Charlotte said. "That's where our family is from, you know—the old province of Averoigne."

"I didn't," Jenny admitted.

"Oh, you'll have to come with us next time we go there! We usually stay with the Greniers, who are cousins on Grandmother Jeanne's side—their house is a great sprawling thing just a few blocks from the cathedral, and Emmeline Grenier is a professor at the Université, so you ought to get along wonderfully. Do you get time off from classes in the summer?"

"Sometimes," Jenny said, taken aback but far from displeased at the thought of a summer in France. "I could probably arrange it."

"I'll talk to Father about it," Charlotte said, as though the matter was settled.

After a moment, Jenny asked, "But you were playing— I don't know the song."

"*Un Paysage Paîen*," said Charlotte, a hint of tension slipping back into her voice.

Jenny guessed at the cause of it. "Would you like me to sing with you?"

Charlotte brightened at once. "Could you? I didn't know that you sang."

"Well enough to get into high school choir."

Apparently that was higher than Charlotte's ambitions had ever reached. She gave Jenny a wide-eyed look, then shook her hands to loosen them, set her fingertips on the keys, began to play. Jenny considered the sheet music on the rack above the keyboard, found one of the vocal parts that fit her range, and joined in as Charlotte began singing. The younger woman gave her a delighted look, sang a little more loudly.

They sang two more Zann pieces together, and then Charlotte got up from the piano bench and went to a cabinet near the piano. "Here's something I think you'll like," she said, "and it really does need two voices to sound right. Do you know *Le Roi en Jaune*?"

"Yes," said Jenny, startled at the recurrence of the question. "Yes, in fact, I read it for a class last semester."

"Oh, good. Then you probably know all about the 1895 Paris production."

"The one that got shut down by the government after one night? Yes."

Charlotte beamed. "We have some of the music."

It was Jenny's turn to stare wide-eyed. "Seriously?" When Charlotte nodded: "Erik Satie is supposed to have written that."

"Oh, yes," Charlotte said, leafing through sheet music in the cabinet. "One of our d'Amberville cousins was a friend of Satie's—they used to play four-handed in I forget which Paris nightclub. Here they are: the *Prelude*, the *Sonnerie d'Aldones* and the *Sonnerie du Fantôme de Vérité*, the *Valse Masqué*—and here's the one I had in mind, *Le Chant de Cassilda*." She pulled out a few yellowed sheets of paper, handed them to Jenny.

They were handwritten scores on lined paper, set out for piano and two voices, and though Jenny hadn't seen the spidery handwriting before she guessed that it was probably Satie's own script. She swallowed, abruptly nervous. "There are people I know at Miskatonic University who would really like to see these," she said.

"Really? You'll have to ask Father—for all I know he's already written to somebody or other about them." She reclaimed the sheets, set them on the music rack atop the Zann pieces, and settled on the bench. "Do you know the words?"

"In English, yes."

"Oh, we can certainly sing them in English, then." She shook her hands, rested her fingertips momentarily on the keys, and then began to play.

Even for a piece by Satie, the music was strange, full of unexpected dissonances that emerged and dissolved a note at a time. The opening bars seemed to conjure up an architecture of dark pyramidal shapes, and against that background the two of them began to sing:

> "Upon the shore, the cloud waves break,
> The twin suns set beneath the lake,
> The shadows lengthen in Carcosa."

The music flowed out from under Charlotte's hands.

> "Strange is the night where black stars rise,
> "And strange moons circle through the skies,
> "But stranger still is lost Carcosa.
> "Songs that the Hyades shall sing,
> "Where flap the tatters of the King,
> "Shall die unheard in dim Carcosa.
> "Song of my soul—"

All at once Charlotte stopped playing, and her face went pale. She slid off the bench, darted across the room and turned out the lights, leaving only the dim glow of morning through the curtains for illumination. One finger pressed frantically to her lips, she all but dragged Jenny across the room to a hiding place behind the door.

A moment later Jenny heard the sound that had caused all this: footfalls on the stair. At first she thought it was Aunt Lisette, but then realized that there were two people descending, one whose steps clumped heavily down the stair, the other exact as a drumbeat. A whisper of voices, male, came through the near-silent air.

Jenny looked at Charlotte, then back toward the door. The footfalls grew louder, then faded, and the sound of the great front door opening and closing rang down the hallway.

Charlotte let out a shuddering breath. "We need to be somewhere else," she whispered, took Jenny's arm and hurried with her out of the room. Afterward, she would not say why.

CHAPTER 7

THE TERRIBLE OLD MAN

T he next morning, when Jenny sat before the statue of
Saint Toad, an image as clear as a photograph took shape
in her mind. She recognized it after a moment: the public
library she'd passed on the way from the bus to the Chaudronnier mansion. Along with the image came a sudden wordless
awareness that she needed to go there that day.

She considered that over breakfast. The trip seemed rather
pointless. Still, the thought of a walk appealed to her, even
though the weather was still windy and wet; also, of course,
she'd offered to do things for Saint Toad, and didn't want to
take back the promise. She made a mental note to pocket her
smartphone and see if she could get a signal on the way, and
finished her eggs.

The Chaudronnier mansion had a side door that opened
onto the carriage port and led through a wrought iron gate to
the street. Charlotte was busy that morning, waiting on her
mother, and so Jenny slipped into her ordinary clothes—jeans,
blouse, cardigan, jacket, the sort of outfit that would doubtless
summon a shriek from Aunt Lisette—and hurried down the
stair to the ground floor in the gray morning. Nobody was up
and around but the servants, and none of them spotted her. She
slipped out the side door, leaving it unlocked, and a moment
later was standing on the sidewalk beside Green Lane.

The day was cold and blustery, with rain spattering down from flat gray clouds to set the streets gleaming in the uncertain light. Jenny tried to remember the route she'd originally taken from the bus, and despite a few wrong turns, managed to find her way back along the winding deserted streets to the Kingsport Public Library.

It was a pleasant old brick building with a much-repaired air to it. Big arched windows let lamplight from within spill out to mingle with the gray indifferent light outside. Jenny stood outside for a moment. Part of her wanted to get back to the mansion on Green Lane before anyone noticed that she was gone, but the message she'd gotten from Saint Toad hovered in her thoughts, and it occurred to her that going to the library usually included the last steps in through the doors. She climbed the stair, wiped her shoes on the mat, and went inside.

It could have been any public library in the country, with beige steel shelves full of books, a couple of tables loaded with well-aged computers, a children's section over to one side with half-sized chairs and tables and a bin full of brightly colored stuffed toys that had obviously seen plenty of use. Two librarians at the desk inside gave her incurious looks. She nodded to them, crossed to a nearby bookshelf—Fiction, Co to Ha, the sign on the shelf told her—and spent a few minutes looking at nothing in particular.

About the time she had decided to leave, the library door swung open again, letting in a brief rush of street noise. Boots sounded in the entry, hushed suddenly on the carpet further in. A woman's voice—one of the librarians, Jenny guessed—said, "Good morning, Mr. Coldcroft."

"Good mornin', Agnes," a deep voice replied, rich with the old New England accent. A moment later the newcomer had crossed to the same shelves where Jenny stood. She busied herself with a book, then suddenly realized the man was watching her and glanced up at him.

He was a sturdily built old man, shorter than most though taller than Jenny, the sort of person she could easily imagine fishing from a dory outside Kingsport harbor in all weathers. He had a heavy pea-coat on, over clothes of a cut that looked at least as old as the dresses she'd taken to wearing at the Chaudronniers. White hair spilling from under a woolen cap and a thick white beard framed a face tanned and wrinkled as old leather. He looked as New England as New England could be, Jenny thought; the one thing out of place was the color of his eyes, which were golden yellow. It was that last detail that finally triggered a stray memory: the figure she'd seen briefly from the bus, glancing back toward her from in front of the barque *Miskatonic*.

"I'm sorry, am I in your way?" she said.

"Not a bit, miss." He regarded her for another moment, then seemed to reach a decision, turned to the bookshelf and pulled down something from the long row of C.S. Forrester sea stories. All at once Jenny knew it was time for her to go, and headed for the door.

It felt important that she get back to the Chaudronnier mansion as quickly as possible, so she hurried on, huddling into her thin jacket and thinking ruefully of the stout wool coat the old man had been wearing. The closer she got to the mansion, the stranger the whole business felt to her, but she had no answer to the questions that it raised in her mind: one more puzzle to add to all the others she'd already encountered.

The corridors of the mansion were empty when she slipped back in through the side door, though she heard Aunt Lisette's voice rising in complaint from the open door of one of the parlors and, after a while, a subdued response from Charlotte. She climbed the stairs as quickly as she could without making noise, got back into her rooms, shut the door and let out a ragged sigh. Her own clothes went back into the closet and the dresser as quickly as possible, and she slipped into a day dress and got herself presentable by Chaudronnier standards.

Only then did she notice her smartphone, sitting where she'd left it on the little round table, with its charger plugged in to a wall socket. She considered it for a long moment. Part of her wanted to go outside and try to get a signal, but something warned against that, and that latter impulse was the stronger. Finally she shook her head, left her rooms and went back downstairs.

Michaelmas nodded a greeting to her as their paths crossed on the first floor. Other than that and Aunt Lisette's voice, which was still rising and falling in tones of exasperation, the mansion might have been deserted. The face of Saint Toad guided her to the library as before, but this time the spell of the books offered no solace. She walked over to the great central table, gave it a long moody look.

After a while, the table lost whatever interest it might have had for her, and she walked over to one of the shelves of poetry and literature, looking for something to still her circling thoughts. The book by Justin Geoffrey she'd seen down in the basement of Orne Library was there, and she pulled it out, opened it at random. A quatrain from a poem caught her eye:

> Until the blade of Uoht shall rise,
> Until the ring of Eibon burns,
> Until the one appointed turns
> The pages of the Ghorl Nigral,

She shut the book in a sudden burst of irritation. Why, she wondered, was she wasting her time with all this superstitious nonsense, the Ceremonies, the Mao games, the Book of Eibon, when she should be getting a head start on her reading for the next semester? For that matter, why was she here at all, wasting her time waiting for some eccentric family festival and making believe there was some kind of presence in the hideous little statue in her sitting room—

She stopped there, staring at nothing in particular, and then said out loud, "Why am I thinking like this?" Faint echoes were the only answer she got, but a cold whisper of memory had already responded. After a moment, she crossed to the locked bookcase, opened it, and pulled out the *Livre d'Ivon*.

The great volume creaked audibly as she set it on the table and opened it. Somewhere in here, she thought. Somewhere in the second book.

The thoughts, by turns panicky and jeering, circled faster and faster through her mind as she paged through the ancient tome, but growing up short and plain and poor in a world that despised all those things had taught her stubbornness, and that stubbornness kept her mind focused enough to find the passage she wanted. *Si un sorcier ou un mauvais esprit envoyait pensées nocives*, the heading ran: if a sorcerer or an evil spirit sends hurtful thoughts …

The notion of trying to use any of the incantations in the *Livre d'Ivon* had scarcely occurred to her before, but she did not hesitate. She pressed the thumb and ring finger of her right hand together, and with the joined tips traced the necessary sigil in the air, then drew in a deep breath and spoke the Words—

"CADOS ESCHERIE ANITH SABLAC SAHUN ABA ABARIDOEL."

—and all at once, as the last Word echoed back from the ceiling, every trace of the harassing thoughts vanished.

She stood there by the table and the open book for what seemed like a very long time, staring at nothing in particular.

Sorcery?

Maybe, she told herself. Maybe not. The stark reality of what had just happened tried to dispute the matter with her, but she did not want to listen, not yet. She closed the *Livre d'Ivon*, took it back to its place, locked the door, and then went to one of the shelves of literature and pulled out a book at random, hoping to find something harmless. Unfortunately the book that she pulled out was the Oscar Wilde translation of *The King in Yellow*.

Despite herself, she started laughing, and thought: I really can't get away from it, can I? The Beardsley illustration on the cover—a crowned figure in scalloped and tattered robes, with an abstract mask covering its face and long white hair swirling in the wind—stared back at her in perfect silence. She took the book to the nearest chair and settled down to read. That was an evasion, and she knew as much; the rising spiral of unknown forces that surrounded her would not go away just because she didn't have the courage to confront it; but she needed a respite, at least for a while.

* * *

The morning slipped away faster than she thought, and she barely had time to get up to her room and change into a nicer dress before it was time to go to Aunt Lisette's rooms on the second floor. By the time she got there, she felt flustered and out of breath, and she took a moment and a few deep breaths before tapping on the door.

A tall pale woman opened the door and considered Jenny. She wore a maid's uniform, and her hair and eyes were the identical shade of gray. "Miss Parrish."

"Yes."

"Please come with me." The maid led her down a little hall with doors on either side, and then into a sitting room that was easily four times the size of Jenny's, and still managed to look crowded. A pair of mismatched bookshelves held paperbacks with garish lettering on the spines; cabinets cluttered with an assortment of bric-a-brac leaned against the walls, and a gathering of low tables muttered to one another beneath assorted burdens. Over to one side, a big television crouched atop a low hutch, babbling quietly to itself as the talk show of the screen lurched through its predictable routines.

Lisette sat on one end of an ornate overstuffed sofa facing the television. The window behind her looked out over a formal garden toward the wrought iron fence along Hall Street. She got up as Jenny came in, waved the younger woman to a chair, slumped back onto the couch, and fumbled with the remote for a moment before the television screen went black. "Thank you, Coral," she said to the maid. "We'll have the first course at twelve-fifteen."

"Of course, ma'am," said the maid, and left the room.

Lisette watched her go, and an uncomfortable silence descended. Finally, without looking at Jenny, she said, "I don't suppose you read romance novels."

"Some, yes," Jenny said. "What are you reading?"

Her aunt's eyes snapped over toward her, then looked away. After a moment, Lisette named something by a popular writer of a generation back.

"I haven't read that one," Jenny said, "but I did read *Brash Breathless Love*."

That got another sudden glance. "What did you think of it?"

"I liked it," Jenny said truthfully enough—there was no point, she decided, in mentioning that she'd been thirteen at the time and no judge of literary quality.

Lisette took that in. "That was the first of her novels I read," she said after a moment. "I think I've read everything of hers in print by now."

"I have a lot of reading to catch up on when I finish college," said Jenny.

That got another sudden glance, but it wasn't guarded, as the earlier ones had been. There was something starved and desperate in it. "I certainly did."

"Someone told me that you went to Miskatonic," Jenny ventured.

"Yes. Yes, I did. That's where Martin and I met, in fact."

That was apparently enough common ground to still the desperation in Lisette's eyes, at least for the moment.

They talked about romance novels and Miskatonic University until the tomato bisque, the creamed veal, and the olives and pickles had come and gone, and a plate of miniature croissants drizzled with chocolate and a tall pot of coffee made their appearance. Then, for all the world as though she had suddenly remembered something, Lisette changed the subject. "And now here you are," she said. "I can't imagine what it would have been like, hearing about all these—" She gestured vaguely. "Traditions, superstitions, in the family."

"I never was told very much about them," Jenny said.

That was apparently not the answer she was expecting. "Poor Sophie must have taught you something."

"No, Mom never said much about the family. I asked, but—" Jenny shrugged. "She was never willing to talk. I don't know why."

"And—please forgive me for even mentioning this, Jenny—your father—"

"She never told me anything about that at all."

Lisette contemplated her coffee for a long moment, and then tried again. "And Martin keeps on talking about this Festival. I wish I knew more about it."

"So do I," Jenny said. "Really." She sipped coffee. "I'd kind of hoped that you could fill me in, in fact."

That got her a wary, troubled look, which Lisette replaced with a forced smile as soon as she realized that Jenny had noticed it. The conversation veered back to Miskatonic University, and the rest of the lunch went by without incident.

That evening at dinner, though, Lisette was as distant and brittle as ever, and did her best to pretend that Jenny didn't exist. It was Willis Connor, to Jenny's surprise, who leaned ever so slightly forward in his chair and said, "Jenny, Lisette tells me that you've been to the public library here in town. I've got a business question I have to deal with—I know, you'd think my boss would leave that alone for the holidays. But the library—it's up on Carter Street, isn't it?"

"Is there a branch there?" Jenny replied. "I didn't know. The one I've been to is down on Circle Street."

"Big gray building?"

"No, red brick," she said. "I think it's a Carnegie library." Then, remembering her one glimpse at the collection: "But I don't think they have much in the way of business or reference books there. You might be better off driving up to Arkham— I'm pretty sure that Orne Library's open weekdays through the break, and they've got a big business section."

He nodded, gave her a long and searching look. "Thank you."

It was only later, when she was getting ready for bed, that she realized that Connor had been trying to catch her out in a lie about the library—and that in turn made it uncomfortably clear that he'd somehow guessed what library she'd actually been in when Lisette went looking for her two days before.

All at once, she recalled the intrusive thoughts that had circled through her mind that morning. If those had still been repeating themselves when she'd gone to Lisette's rooms, or when Connor had asked his question …

When she sat before Saint Toad's shrine a few minutes later, that was still much on her mind, and she set out her worries before him.

You evaded a trap, the not-voice told her. *That was well done— but there will be others.*

* * *

The next morning, Charlotte knocked on the door when Jenny had scarcely finished breakfast, with good news: Aunt Lisette would be shopping in Boston that day and the next with her brother, and Willis Connor had left the house on some errand of his own at first light. "And I was wondering …" Charlotte said, her voice trailing off.

Jenny waited for a moment, then: "Wondering?"

"If—if you'd like to sing the rest of *Le Chant de Cassilda* with me, and maybe some other pieces."

"Of course," Jenny reassured her.

The halls and stairs of the old mansion creaked and murmured around them as they descended to the music room on the first floor. Charlotte insisted on leaving the door open a little—"in case someone comes," she murmured—but got the music out and settled on the piano bench with every sign of enthusiasm. They sang Cassilda's song twice over, then three of Fréneville-Forgeron's poems set to music by Erich Zann, and then Jenny managed to convince Charlotte to play Satie's Prelude to *Le Roi en Jaune*.

There were three movements. The first, quiet and meditative, wove a gentle theme in and out of strange harmonies. The second seized the theme in a taut grip and slowly twisted it into a parody of itself, a vapid, vulgar little melody that could have featured in a commercial, then crushed it beneath a rising tide of dissonance until its final notes rang out like a despairing cry and sank with the rest into brooding silence. Then came the third movement, opening with three terrible chords that, Jenny guessed, proclaimed the presence of the King in Yellow. From there the music rose up in a torrent of harsh discords that must have shaken the rafters of the theater in that one legendary Paris performance. They didn't shake the rafters of the Chaudronnier mansion, for Charlotte wouldn't play them *fortissimo* as the score demanded; even so, the music set Jenny's teeth on edge. Finally, though, the last tremendous chord sounded, and in the final bars all the discords somehow resolved themselves into harmonies and the quiet flowing theme of the first movement returned to put an improbable benediction on the whole.

As the echoes of the last notes faded, the telephone rang in the hall outside.

Charlotte tensed visibly, but kept her seat on the piano bench. The phone stopped on the fourth ring, and a voice Jenny could just recognize as Michaelmas' said something she couldn't hear clearly. Silence followed, and then the low groan of a door opening and closing put punctuation at the end of the call. After a long moment, Charlotte gathered up the sheets of music and put them back in the cabinet, then relented and brought back another Satie piece from *Le Roi en Jaune*, the *Valse Masqué*.

"This is the dance from Act One," Charlotte confided. "I wish I could see it performed someday." She drew in a ragged breath, shook out her hands, and started to play it rather less than half as loud as the score suggested. The music conjured up images from the play in Jenny's mind: Cassilda and the Phantom of Truth dancing in the great hall of the palace of Alar among scores of other dancers, all of them masked, while Camilla looked on with cold jealous eyes and Thale waited with his poisoned dagger.

Finally the waltz finished, its last triumphant notes belying the terrible events that were about to happen, and Charlotte let out a long pleased sigh. At that moment, someone cleared his throat just outside the door.

Charlotte twisted suddenly around. Jenny, turning not quite so quickly, saw her cousin relax and then the reason for it: the person standing outside the door was Michaelmas.

"Miss Jenny," he said, "Mr. Martin desires to see you in the study. I should probably mention that he wishes you to pay a visit with him in town."

Charlotte got up from the bench. "Should I come?"

"I suspect not, Miss Charlotte. The visit will be to Mr. Enoch Coldcroft."

Charlotte drew in a sudden sharp breath. Jenny glanced at her in surprise, to find that the younger woman's face had gone pale. Still, Michaelmas was waiting, and after a moment Jenny went to the door and followed him.

* * *

"Tea for ye, I'll warrant," said the old man with the yellow eyes. "Cream and sugar?"

"Please," Jenny replied, and let him wave her to one of the two high-backed settles that flanked the cast iron Franklin stove in front of the great stone fireplace. Martin had already taken a low chair next to the window, which was made of little diamond-shaped panes and let in ample light but only the vaguest blurred sense of what was outside. Low ceilings crossed with great oaken beams, paneled walls marked with the twisting marks of worms, and big gray flagstones covering the floor completed the picture. It was, Jenny thought, a very comfortable space—unlike most rooms she'd known, it was almost sized for someone as short as she was.

The old man vanished through an open doorway. Jenny watched him go, then turned to Martin, but her uncle was evidently not in a communicative mood and stared at the flames through the little glass window of the Franklin stove.

They'd driven, Michaelmas at the wheel, the dozen blocks from the mansion on Green Lane to the cottage on Water Street, just back of the waterfront in a line of battered, crumbling houses that had to date from before the Revolutionary War. It had taken Michaelmas some trouble to get around the corner into the narrow street, but finally the car rolled to a halt and Michaelmas got out and opened her door and then Martin's. The rain had stopped by the time they arrived though puddles pooled dark in the street, and she and Martin picked their way along the weathered flagstones of the walk to the front door, past stark gray stones carved into blurred shapes Jenny didn't recognize. They hadn't needed to knock; the door opened as they approached, and the old man she'd seen in the Kingsport library bowed and waved them in.

A kettle shrieked a room or two away, and a moment later the old man came back through the door with three mugs in his hands and handed them around. Jenny's held black Chinese tea with a smoky, tarry scent barely restrained by molasses-scented sugar and what, from the look of it, had to be actual cream; the other mugs held stronger stuff, some brew that smelled of rum, spices, and lemon. She and Martin thanked him, and he made a little bow and perched on the other settle, facing her.

"Jenny," said Martin, "this is Enoch Coldcroft, a very old friend of the family. Enoch, this is my niece Jenny Parrish."

"Aye," said Coldcroft, "damme if I didn't know her for a Chaudronnier at a glance. If ye'd called her Marie I shouldn't have blinked."

Jenny remembered the portrait in the brown room, and sipped tea to hide her thoughts. It felt oddly as though the room itself was watching her.

"You wanted to speak to us," Martin said, after a long silence.

"Aye," said Coldcroft. "I've news, to begin with, and a warning. With the Festival so close I daresay it's no surprise to ye or anyone that the other side's nosin' about. There's been books stolen in town—nothin' that can't be done without, but still, ye'll want to be more than careful about that library ye have."

"I've taken some steps," Martin said.

"'Tis well. I'd counsel ye likewise to stay safe indoors until the Festival's past." He turned to Jenny. "Ye even more than th'others. I know why ye went out, girl, and who sent ye, but that's not a thing to do a second time, not 'til we've been to the Festival and come back again. There are dangers about, some ye can see, some ye can't." He shook his head. "There's a right storm blowin' up just now. I don't know if either of ye heard tell of the business at the college up in Arkham the month just past."

Jenny blinked, and after a moment found her voice. "If you mean the fire and—the rest of it—a little, yes. Nobody from the university's talking about it, but there are rumors."

"Ye live up Arkham way?"

"I'm going to Miskatonic," Jenny told him.

"I don't know a thing about any of this," said Martin.

"No? It's quite a business," Coldcroft said. "Ye know the other side had some deal of strength there? There was a pitched battle of a night, and the buildin' they was in got burnt out hollow. I hear tell a certain gentleman in black was in th'thick of it."

Martin stared at the old man. Jenny watched him, and wondered why.

"So th' other side's lost a battle," Coldcroft went on, "and they'll be lookin' to strike a blow in return. Your books 'd make a temptin' target, if they could get to 'em. So would certain folk they'd have cause to want. Or—" His voice went low. "A certain ring."

Martin was silent for a long moment. "I wish we had it," he said at length. "We've spent years trying everything we can think of, Enoch, but the Ring of Eibon is lost."

Jenny glanced at him, trying to remember where she'd heard of a ring of Eibon.

"That's bad," said Coldcroft. "That's very bad. Still, if it can't be found, there's no help for it, and ye'll just have to abide what happens."

"I know," said Martin, and bowed his head.

An uncomfortable silence came and went, and then Coldcroft asked Martin about one of the other old Kingsport families, and they plunged into a conversation that Jenny, knowing none of the people involved, couldn't follow at all. She gathered, though, that the preparations for the Festival were finished, and the missing ring had been discussed with the heads of the Kingsport families and with someone else whom neither Martin nor Coldcroft would call by name.

"Well, then," said Coldcroft finally. "That's as much news as I have, and that's why I sent for ye—that and some tests ye know of, better done here than elsewhere." He glanced at Jenny.

"I really don't think that was necessary," Martin protested.

"Martin," Coldcroft said, "ye know better. Now of all times we dasen't take risks."

Martin nodded after a moment, unwillingly. They said their goodbyes, and then it was back out into the wet street, where Michaelmas waited imperturbably by the car.

When they were in the back seat again and the car started forward, Jenny turned to face her uncle. "Uncle Martin," she said, "what have I gotten myself into?"

Martin glanced at her, looked away again. "Our religion has its enemies," he said. "It's nothing you have to worry about."

"There was somebody inside Belbury Hall when it burned last month," Jenny said. "At least one person. I think that's something to worry about."

He considered her, and finally nodded. "Once the Festival happens," he said, "you'll understand. I hope you'll be willing to be patient until then."

With that equivocal answer, Jenny had to be content.

* * *

"Well, that was—remarkable," Jenny said to her cousin. "I wish I knew more about Mr. Coldcroft." She'd found Charlotte in the music room on returning from the drive, though the sheet music was back in its cabinet and Charlotte had been standing by the window staring out at the brown wet garden when Jenny came in.

Charlotte gave her a wide-eyed look, as though the thought of knowing more about the old man frightened her. "He's lived in Kingsport since I don't know when," she said in a low voice. "Since our people came here, I think. He's got a nickname, too. You know how ship captains are called the Old Man? People here call him the Terrible Old Man." She would say nothing more, and a few minutes later excused herself and fled up the stair to her rooms. Jenny watched her go, and then shook her head and went to the library.

It took most of half an hour, but Jenny finally remembered where she'd seen something about the ring of Eibon, and went looking along the shelves until she found the copy of Justin Geoffrey's *The People of the Monolith and Other Poems*. It took her only a few minutes to find the quatrain she recalled, and then to read the whole poem:

IN CARCOSA

Vast pyramids of night-hued stone
Rise stark above that nameless strand,
Where on the black and hissing sand
The waves of cloud break endlessly,

Where, in a place of mystery
Beneath the black unhallowed stars,
The pale night-scented nenuphars
Shed perfume for the King alone.

He walks there in the darkling hour
When both the suns have passed from view,
And stops to feel the wind blow through
his tattered robes, from lost Yhtill:

His vow is unforgotten. Still
The Pallid Mask conceals his face:
The shadow of a distant place
And time obscures each floating flower.

Until the blade of Uoht shall rise,
Until the ring of Eibon burns,
Until the one appointed turns
The pages of the *Ghorl Nigral*,

That figure, terrible and tall,
With tattered robes and windblown hair,
Shall keep his nightly vigil there
Beneath those white and wintry skies.

She read it twice, stood there looking at nothing in particular for a long moment. The part of her mind her college years had trained leapt at once to pick the poem apart, fitting it into the history of twentieth century popular romantic poetry, noting among other things the references to *The King In Yellow*— Geoffrey knew the French original, no question, since the Wilde translation put lotus flowers instead of nenuphars in the King's garden. Still, something else caught the deeper levels of her mind: the old sense of presence and strangeness opening up around her, revealing a world unknown.

This time, though, the wider world so briefly revealed wore a different aspect—

Danger.

She could feel it in the air around her, as though an unknown beast crouched to spring, and she knew instinctively that she was among the prey it had in sight.

After a cold moment, she put Geoffrey's book away, went to the locked bookcase at the far end of the library, and got out the *Livre d'Ivon*. The spell she'd cast to clear away whatever had descended on her after she'd gone to the library had been much on her mind, but it was far from the only incantation in the book. If she was going to have to contend with unknown forces, she decided then and there, she was not going to go unarmed.

CHAPTER 8

THE SUSSEX MANUSCRIPT

"Sylvia," Jenny asked, "what is the ring of Eibon?"

They were in Jenny's sitting room, with a pot of tea and two bone china cups on the little round table between them. Outside the weather still seemed determined to hold winter at bay. By the time Jenny left the library to find Sylvia and ask the questions that she knew had to be asked, the clouds had begun to break up, and now afternoon sun splashed across the rose garden and the wet Kingsport roofs outside.

The old woman gave her a long considering look, then sipped tea before answering. "Where on earth did you hear about that?"

"No, you don't," said Jenny. "I asked first—I'll answer your question just as soon as you answer mine."

"Fair enough," Sylvia allowed. "It's a piece of jewelry that's been in the family for a very long time—according to the stories, since long before we came to this country—and it has some very strange traditions associated with it."

Jenny waited, then rolled her eyes and gestured for her to go on. Sylvia laughed, then said, "Okay. Marc d'Ursuras brought it here from France, but it's supposed to have been made in Hyperborea—that's Greenland nowadays, but this happened long before the ice sheets covered it. Eibon was the sorcerer who made it. You might be interested to know that he was a friend of Saint Toad. Is that enough of an answer?"

"Eibon," Jenny said, then realized why the name seemed so familiar. "Oh, of course. Is he the Ivon of the *Livre d'Ivon*?"

Sylvia's eyebrows went up. "Now I'm wondering where you heard of that."

"I found it in the library here, of course," Jenny said. "Though I wouldn't be surprised if there were copies at Orne Library."

"More likely than not," the old woman said. "We've actually got another copy of the same book, though you might have a little bit of trouble reading it—it's titled *Llyfr Efon y Dewin*, and it's in sixteenth-century Welsh."

"Well, that certainly leaves me out," Jenny said, laughing. "But—we actually have his original ring?"

Sylvia shook her head. "No, you don't. I answered your question. Now it's your turn to answer mine."

Jenny nodded, conceding the point. "Uncle Martin took me to visit Enoch Coldcroft this morning, I don't know why, and they talked about the ring—I gather it's been lost. But I also read about it in a poem by—" She had to search her memory for the name. "Justin Geoffrey."

"'Vast pyramids of night-hued stone rise stark above that nameless strand,'" Sylvia quoted at once.

Jenny blinked in surprise. "That's the one."

"I know it well. But, yes, we have Eibon's own ring, or we should have it."

"Should have it?"

"As you heard, it's lost."

"What happened?"

Sylvia paused, poured more tea for them both. "Claire mentioned that the two of you talked about family history the other night. Did she say anything about your grandfather Charles Chaudronnier?" Jenny nodded, and her great-aunt went on. "He was a very difficult man, and I don't say that just because of the way he treated me. You'll have a hard time getting Martin to talk about him at all, and of course you know how your mother was. But Charles was a student of the old lore— a very deep student. I'm pretty sure that he didn't limit his studies to theory."

"You're saying," Jenny said, "that he practiced—sorcery."

Sylvia looked away, didn't answer. "He and Martin got into the most terrible fights," she said, "and I'm honestly not sure if Martin would ever have come back here at all if Charles hadn't died suddenly. They weren't on speaking terms after he went to Miskatonic—and that's just it. Charles knew where the Ring of Eibon was kept; that was part of the family lore he got from Father when he came of age, but he didn't pass any of that on to Martin. Then all of a sudden he was dead, and we searched the house from top to bottom and couldn't find the Ring. We found the most astonishing things: secret passages, for example."

Jenny's eyes went wide. "Really?"

"Really. In fact, there's one in your rooms—Claire and I have one just like it in ours. Push on a panel in back of the bedroom closet and you'll find a stair going down to the second floor. We found those, we found false walls with hiding places behind them, we found the oddest bits of old furniture and whatnot, but the Ring, no."

Jenny took that in. "And there were no clues at all?"

Sylvia regarded her for a long moment. "I think it's time to talk to Martin."

* * *

Afternoon light filtered through the stained glass of the skylight as Martin unlocked the bookcase at the library's far end, pulled out a book from the shelf below the one where the *Livre d'Ivon* rested. Jenny looked on, uncertain.

Sylvia had taken her straight down to Martin's office on the first floor, where he spent his days managing the family's assets; the Chaudronniers apparently owned a great deal of real estate in and around Kingsport. Martin was constantly on the phone, fielding inquiries, sending out repairmen, making arrangements with tenants who'd had this or that crisis land on them and needed time to cover the rent, or couldn't afford it at all—there were, Jenny gathered, people who still had places to live because Chaudronnier pride scorned the thought of turning a destitute tenant out onto the street. Martin had been up to his elbows in tax forms when they'd come into the office, but the moment Sylvia mentioned the Ring of Eibon he'd pushed the paperwork aside, motioned for them to follow, and led the way into the library.

"It's one of the rarest items in our collection," Martin said, "copied out by hand by Marc d'Ursuras. The original used to be in the British Library—they insist they don't have it now, but I have my doubts. There was a printed edition out of London in 1598, and Golden Goblin Press did a photostatic reprint of that in 1934; we've got them both, but they're riddled with errors and omissions. This is another matter entirely."

He carried the book to the table, set it down, opened it and leafed through it to the title page, where great flowing letters read: *Baron Frederic I of Sussex his Manuscripte*. Below, in smaller script, was *Marc Ursuras transcripsit 1831*.

Jenny nodded, wondering what this had to do with the Ring of Eibon.

Martin glanced at her, as though he'd heard the thought. "According to one of the few scraps of family tradition I had the chance to learn," he said, "the secret of the Ring of Eibon's hiding place is supposed to be somewhere in this book. I used to wonder if that was just rumor, but almost twenty years ago Sylvia and I found something tucked between the pages of the book on sorcery that Marc d'Ursuras wrote—a little scrap of paper in his handwriting. It said that he'd written the location of the R of E in the clean copy he'd made of the *Sussex*

Manuscript. This is the clean copy. If he was telling the truth, the secret is right here."

Jenny considered the title page. Something about it bothered her, though she wasn't at all sure what it was.

"I'm assuming," Martin said then, "that Sylvia's already told you about your grandfather, and his interest in the old lore."

"A little," said Jenny.

"Did she mention that your mother helped him in his studies?"

Jenny's gaze snapped up from the manuscript to his face. "No."

"That should have been my job," Martin said, "but Father and I—we had a troubled relationship, I suppose you would say. He was a difficult man, and I was full of myself and didn't want to waste my life, as I saw it, on a collection of musty old books. When I went to college, Father wanted me to study the classics—Miskatonic still had a classics program in those days. Instead, I studied business administration." He shrugged. "And so Sophie helped him in his studies, in—whatever it was that he was trying to do." Then, turning away from Jenny: "It's occurred to me more than once that she might have taken the Ring with her when she left."

"I don't remember her ever wearing a ring at all," Jenny said.

"She wouldn't have worn this one," said Sylvia. "No one's worn it since Eibon's time. Let me correct that: no one's worn it and survived."

"It's a thing of immense power," Martin said, turning back toward Jenny and meeting her shocked gaze squarely. "More power than human beings can endure. It can be used in certain limited ways without wearing it, and a great many people have done that down the years, but—" An equivocal gesture. "It's happened at least a dozen times, or so I've read in the old books, that great sorcerers and sorceresses convinced themselves that they were strong enough to wield its power, put it on—" He mimed the gesture. "—and died shrieking."

"Did Eibon wear it?" Jenny asked

"Yes," said Sylvia, "but he was only half human. His father was Saint Toad."

Jenny considered that for a long moment, then asked, "What did the ring look like?"

"It's of red gold," said Martin, "with a purple stone."

"If she had anything like that I didn't see it, and it wasn't in her things after—" She let the sentence drop.

Martin nodded. "It was just a thought."

"But it's a problem that it's lost, isn't it?" Jenny asked then.

"Very much so," said Martin. "The family had custody of it, and one of the duties we have as its keepers is that of bringing it to the Festival. I've talked to the other families, and nobody's sure what will happen if we have to go there emptyhanded, but I doubt it will go easy for us. I've already told—the appropriate people—that I take full responsibility."

Jenny considered that for a while, then at the manuscript. "Would you mind if I looked at this?" she asked. "I know there's not much of a chance that I'll find anything you missed, but—I don't know why, but it feels important."

That was an understatement. Something pulled her toward the manuscript, silent and insistent as whatever it was that had drawn her to the shrine of Saint Toad her first afternoon at the Chaudronnier mansion. Whether or not Martin felt it too, she could not tell, but he gave her a long unreadable look and said, "It should stay in the library for safekeeping. If you want to study it here, though, and see if you can find anything, I can't see any harm in that."

* * *

She spent several hours that afternoon reading the manuscript, but had something else to distract her that evening. Aunt Lisette and Roger had come back from Boston that afternoon, and Charlotte had been called to her mother's rooms promptly thereafter. At dinner, Lisette seemed even more brittle than usual; Martin was wrapped in silent thoughts; such talk as took place at the table came in brief bursts, separated by long silences, but that was ordinary enough. What was different was Charlotte. She sat up close to her father's end of the table as she usually did, across from Jenny, but she would not look at Jenny at all. She ate her dinner in silence, and all but bolted out of the room as soon as the meal was finished. Jenny watched her go, wondered whether her visit to Enoch Coldcroft earlier that day and Charlotte's reaction to that had anything to do with it, and turned her thoughts to other things.

The next morning Henrietta looked more cheerful than usual as she set out breakfast, and explained that her cousin had finished a new dress for her in time for the Festival.

"I didn't know your family kept it too," said Jenny.

"Oh, yes. We've been in Kingsport even longer than the Chaudronniers—we came here almost four hundred years ago."

"From Averoigne?" Jenny guessed.

"No, straight here from the old country—well, what was left of it above water. When I was little, my Nana used to tell Lettie and me stories about the really old times before the seas rose, when it was all terraced gardens of orchids and mangoes, green groves around the temples of the Great Old Ones, and Susran's white towers, with birds from the mainland flying around them." She finished pouring the coffee. "They say that by the time we left, all that was still above water was the little island of Bal-Sagoth, and that went under I don't know how long ago." The last details of the table set, she smiled and went to the door. "Enjoy."

"I will," said Jenny. "Maybe I'll see you at the Festival."

"Oh, probably," Henrietta said with another smile, and left the sitting room.

She finished breakfast, got dressed for the day, and waited for Charlotte—they'd arranged the morning before to go to the library together and talk. Time passed, though, and Charlotte did not show. Jenny waited, feeling increasingly uneasy. To distract herself, she went to the bedroom closet, pushed aside the dresses, and looked for the entrance to the secret passage that Sylvia had mentioned. It took a little searching, but eventually she found a panel that, when pushed, opened onto a narrow dark stairway. She pulled it shut again, shaking her head in wonder.

More time passed. She got out her set of stones for the Mao games and played the first voola of the Second Game, which was supposed to clear away obstacles; even so, nothing happened. Finally she left her room, went to Charlotte's door, and listened. No sound came through the door. After a moment, she gathered up her courage and knocked.

A long silence, then: "Who is it?"

"It's Jenny."

A longer silence slipped past. Finally the lock turned with a surprisingly deep and heavy click, and the door opened a foot or so. "Charlotte, I—" Then she saw the younger woman's face, pale and tense, frozen into a mask of itself. "What's wrong?"

Charlotte turned away sharply and went back into the room, leaving the door open. After a moment Jenny followed her, and closed the door behind her. It was a good deal more massive than the other interior doors in the house, with solid oak planking on the inside face.

Once inside, she looked around, as she had never before been in Charlotte's rooms. The sparse and carefully chosen furniture and the handful of paintings on the walls, eighteenth-century landscapes by French masters, spoke of depths and nuances to her cousin that she hadn't expected. Bookshelves full of volumes by Jane Austen and Georgette Heyer, and a rack of DVDs of old black-and-white romantic movies, added to the impression.

"I don't want to talk about it," Charlotte said indistinctly, crossing to the windows on the far side of the room.

"Is it something I did?" Jenny asked.

Charlotte answered her by bursting into tears. Jenny, perplexed, got her to sit down on a nearby settee and found a box of tissues. It took some coaxing, but finally Charlotte burst out, "Mother—Mother told me that—when the two of you had lunch—that you—you—you kept on talking about how stupid I was—"

Jenny's mouth fell open. "She said *what*? Charlotte, that's a lie! I didn't say anything like that, and I wouldn't!"

Wet red-rimmed eyes peered up at her.

"All we talked about," Jenny went on, "was what Miskatonic University was like when she was there, and—oh, I forget the title of the book she was reading; it was by the woman who wrote *Brash Breathless Love*."

Charlotte blotted her eyes, looked at her again. "Have—have you read that?"

"Yes."

"What did you think."

"Well," Jenny temporized, "I was thirteen at the time."

Charlotte choked. It took a moment for Jenny to realize that the sound was a first faint attempt at laughter.

"I can't believe she said that," Jenny said then. "That's just so horrible. And—why?"

Charlotte looked up at her again, and all at once her eyes went wide. She looked away, then, and stared at the floor for a long moment. Jenny had already learned that Charlotte's insights had to be coaxed to the surface, and waited for her cousin to speak.

"Jenny," she said finally in an unsteady voice, "do—do you remember *The King in Yellow*?" Jenny nodded, and Charlotte went on. "In the first act—the way Naotalba set Camilla and Cassilda at each other's throats, so they wouldn't talk to each other?"

"Oh, yes," Jenny said. Then: "You think she was playing Naotalba."

"Not just her," said Charlotte.

Jenny waited.

"That brother of hers has been filling her ears with I don't know what nonsense for years," Charlotte burst out. "I know he's been talking about you. I've seen the way he looks at you. And that friend of his, Willis Connor—he's worse still. He doesn't say anything at all, not when I'm in earshot, but I don't trust him." She started crying again. "It was when he started coming here with Roger to visit that—that everything went—" Whatever else she might have meant to say got lost in the sobs.

Jenny waited. When Charlotte had stopped crying and was blotting her eyes again, she said, "This time, though, Camilla and Cassilda are going to have a good long talk, and maybe the King in Yellow will show up and drag Willis Connor away."

She'd meant it as a joke, but Charlotte looked up. In a very low whisper, she said, "He'll be there at the Festival, you know—the King." Mouthing the words: "Hastur himself." Then, laughing: "I hope he does come home with us. Father will know how to pray to him, Sylvia can dance for him the way the madwoman did—do you know she used to dance ballet, and still does her exercises every morning?—and he can drag Roger and Willis Connor off to the depths of Demhe and we won't have to put up with them any more." The laughter guttered. Sadly: "And maybe he can put some sense back into Mother. She used to be such a sweet person."

"Claire told me the same thing," Jenny said.

That got her a sidelong glance. A long moment passed. Finally: "I always used to wish I had a sister," Charlotte said in a small scared voice.

"So did I," Jenny admitted. "Next best thing?"

"Close enough," Charlotte said, with a sudden delighted smile. Then, abruptly serious: "And I'll never, ever believe a single word Mother tells me about you again. I promise."

* * *

It was past noon when Jenny finally left Charlotte's sitting room and went down to the library. The lie Lisette had told still left her speechless with anger. The cool deliberation with which her aunt had targeted one of Charlotte's deepest insecurities—or had the idea been Roger's, or Willis Connor's?—left her wishing fervently that she could slap whoever was responsible hard enough to send teeth flying.

Still, she had no shortage of other things to think about. On the assumption that the point of the lie was to keep the two of them from talking, she and Charlotte had talked about everything they could think of that might have to do with the Festival, or the family, or Jenny's presence in the Chaudronnier household. She'd described her visit to the Terrible Old Man in as much detail as she could manage, and Charlotte had listened, even though Enoch Coldcroft all too clearly terrified her. In return, Charlotte told her every scrap of information she knew about Roger Applegate and Willis Connor, going all the way back to her childhood.

It was not a comforting account. Once Charlotte reached her teens, Roger's behavior bothered her increasingly— "I don't like the way he looks at me," she'd explained, reddening. When she came home from the boarding school in New York State where she'd finished her education, she'd talked to Sylvia, who'd talked to Michaelmas, who'd replaced the door of her rooms with the massive oaken door that Jenny had noticed and the ordinary lock with a heavy deadbolt that couldn't be forced open. There had apparently been scandals in Danvers, where Roger lived. Lisette would not hear any criticism of him, but Charlotte had noticed that her mother went out of her way not to leave Roger alone with her even for a moment.

Willis Connor was another matter. He showed no least scrap of interest in Charlotte or any other woman, or for that matter in men; every word he said was measured, every change of expression deliberate; he deflected questions about his background and profession with practiced ease, and kept his thoughts and his agenda wholly out of sight. From him, Charlotte guessed, came the influence that had twisted itself around Lisette's mind and heart, but that was a guess, based on scraps of conversation between them that Charlotte had overheard from time to time. Coral, Lisette's maid, had some kind of understanding with Connor—she wasn't from Kingsport, unlike the rest of the servants, and Charlotte distrusted her.

With the coming of the holiday season and the approach of the Festival, though, something new and uncomfortable seemed to be happening. Roger and Willis had arrived three days before Jenny, Charlotte explained, and from that moment on, she'd noticed them watching her—not the way Roger usually did, but with a colder look in their eyes. Day after day, she'd spotted one or the other of them sitting in one of the parlors downstairs with the door open and a good view of the hall, ostensibly reading a newspaper or typing on a laptop but glancing up whenever anyone passed by. At night, unfamiliar sounds whispered down the halls of the old mansion. They were looking for something, Charlotte guessed, and whispered—to Jenny's great surprise—"I think they're looking for Eibon's ring."

Only when Jenny stepped into the library was she able to shake her mind free of the conversation with Charlotte and focus on the task at hand. With so little time to spare before the Festival, she could feel necessity pressing hard around her, and whatever drew her to the *Sussex Manuscript* pressed harder still. College classes and seminars had taught her some of the ways that authors liked to weave hidden messages into their books—acrostics, anagrams, simple ciphers—but finding any of those required close attention to the text. With that in mind, she sat down at the big central table in the library with the old volume open before her, and gave it the kind of attention she was used to giving a book when her grade point average depended on it.

Since she'd already read the manuscript once and had some sense of the architecture of the text, she plunged straight into a word-by-word reading, looking for patterns that might conceal the secret. Like the *Livre d'Ivon*, it was a free mix of philosophy, mythology, and incantation. It had much to say about the Great Old Ones, though some of that was so incomprehensible that Jenny guessed the author hadn't actually understood whatever source he was using, and some of the spells which were also in the *Livre d'Ivon* were pretty obviously garbled. By the time she'd finished, the Tiffany skylight overhead was reddening with sunset, and she spent the remaining time that day looking for the obvious possibilities—acronyms made up of the first or last letters of each line, misspellings that might conceal an anagram, and so on—without finding anything.

A little later, just before she had to go upstairs to dress for dinner, she thought she'd figured out what it was about the title page that bothered her. After dinner, she made an opportunity to talk to Sylvia privately. "On the first page of the *Sussex Manuscript*," she told her great-aunt, "it says Marc Ursuras, not Marc d'Ursuras. Do you happen to know why?"

"Why, yes," said Sylvia. "You know that the *de* is a marker of nobility, right?" Jenny nodded. "Marc dropped that when he came to this country. Some French emigrés did that if they came from noble families, or they dropped the *le* if they came from the lower classes—we used to be 'le Chaudronnier,' you know."

"I didn't," Jenny said, and managed to conceal her disappointment. She made an early night of it, got up while it was still dark, and was back in the library the next morning by the time the first hints of dawn trickled through the skylight.

By ten o'clock she was out of ideas, but just then she thought of something that might make the whole question moot. She got the *Livre d'Ivon* out of the locked bookcase. Maybe, she thought, just maybe, if a spell can chase off thoughts, it can find something that's been lost.

She spent most of half an hour paging through the old tome, looking for something that might do the trick. Here and there she found something that was almost right. At the beginning of the second book, for example, was the Sigil of Cykranosh, which she'd memorized earlier while looking for useful spells: you pointed your left thumb at someone or something you wanted to command, formulated the sigil in your mind, concentrated on it, and said a single word, and whoever or whatever you commanded would obey that word until the spell wore off some hours later. She tried to think of some one word that would make the Ring of Eibon reveal itself, and then realized that she had no idea where to point her thumb. She kept reading.

A little further on was an incantation to summon a being called the Warder of Knowledge, but she'd already read warnings about the dangers of summoning beings unless you knew how to send them back where they came from, and turned the page. Twenty pages later, though, she found a spell that was exactly what she needed. *S'il faut à voir de loin une certaine personne ou chose*, the heading ran: *If it is necessary to see from afar a certain person or thing …*

The spell required a crystal, and for a moment she was at a loss, until she remembered the oddly shaped crystal in the drawer next to the box of marble counters for the Mao Games. She went to the bookcase, got it out, set it on the table, and read the spell carefully. It would, the book said, show three images in the crystal, and they had to be asked for one at a time. She sat down facing the crystal, traced the proper sigil over it, recited the Words, and then said aloud, to test the spell, "My room at 324 North Halsey Street in Arkham."

She looked into the heart of the crystal, and suddenly there the room was, as though she was looking down through a hole in the ceiling. She could see her copy of *Le Roi en Jaune* lying on the desk where she'd left it, next to the unicorn statue, and the rumpled mess of the bedding she'd forgotten to straighten out before she'd left for Kingsport.

That was promising. She'd had several ideas in mind for the second thing to ask, but one of the options forced its way to the front of her mind, and she decided to attempt it: "Owen Merrill. I want to see where he is right now."

The image of the room vanished, and after a moment she seemed to be looking down into another room, one she didn't recognize at all. It looked like a motel room, but the furniture was old and well-used even by cheap-motel standards. Two people sat on the bed, with a big leatherbound book open in front of them, and they both seemed to be leaning forward, studying it. One was certainly Owen—she knew the sandy hair and broad shoulders at a glance—but she didn't recognize the other: a young woman with brown curly hair and skin that was something between light brown and olive. There was something decidedly odd about the way her legs were tucked up under her skirt.

Jenny watched for a moment, and then blinked and shook her head, wondering where Owen was, who the young woman was, and what might have brought the two of them to a motel room somewhere—the obvious reason didn't apply, since the Owen Merrill she knew wasn't likely to throw away his university career for a love affair, and the book the two of them had been reading looked disquietingly like one of the old tomes in the locked bookcase there in the library. She shook her head again, tried to clear her mind. Now for the one that counts, she told herself. "The location of the Ring of Eibon," she said aloud.

Nothing appeared at all.

She waited, and nothing happened. Staring at the crystal, she sensed—what? A barrier, maybe, something that turned sorcery aside. She let out a long annoyed sigh, stared at the crystal for a while longer, and then traced the sigil in reverse and took the crystal back to its place in the drawer underneath the locked bookcase.

As she came back to the table, she heard murmured voices outside the door to the library. She stopped and then, thinking she recognized one of them, went to the door. As she moved away from the center of the library, the voices fell silent. She went back to the table, and listened: somehow, standing there, she could hear them clearly.

"... right around here," said a voice that was unmistakably Willis Connor's, in a low murmur she still had no trouble following. "I've watched them turn down this corridor half a dozen times and vanish without a trace."

"Some kind of spell?" Roger asked him.

"Something like that. The thing is, if it's like every other example I've heard of, they'll be able to hear us from inside the library."

"That could be a problem."

"Not at all," said Connor's voice. "It just has to be used in the right way." Something in the tone of his voice made Jenny's skin crawl. "Come on. Let's see what we can find ..."

The voice faded into silence. Jenny listened for several minutes, but she could hear nothing more. She gave the door a long uneasy look, then turned toward the table.

The *Sussex Manuscript* lay open to the title page. She glanced at it, and all at once realized what it was that had been bothering her about it. She stared at the title for a long moment, then went to the shelf of reference books and started looking up the details.

* * *

The mansion seemed even more silent than usual as Jenny settled into a chair in her sitting room, waved her great-aunt to another. Sheets of paper lay on the dark wood of the table, covered with Jenny's precise writing. Pale winter sunlight angled down from the window across the sheet on top and the words written on it: *Baron Frederic I of Sussex his Manuscripte.*

"As soon as I looked at the title," Jenny said, "I knew there was something wrong with it, but I wasn't sure what. I had to look some things up—thank Saint Toad the library has an *Encyclopedia Brittanica* from the nineteen-twenties, and an old copy of *Burke's Peerage*. With those, it took me about fifteen minutes to be sure that Baron Frederic I of Sussex is an impossible name. There never was such a person and there never could have been."

Sylvia's eyebrows went up. "Please go on," she said. "This is fascinating."

Jenny held up one finger. "First, Sussex is a county, not a barony. There have been earls of Sussex and dukes of Sussex, but there's never been a baron of Sussex; that would be like calling someone the mayor of Massachusetts." Another finger went up. "Second, peers in England don't use Roman numbers after their names, ever. Only kings and queens do that." Another finger. "Third, no English peer below the rank of earl puts 'of' after their title. So even if Sussex were a barony, which it's not, and it had a baron named Frederic, which it didn't, you'd say Frederic, first Baron Sussex. You'd never say Baron Frederic I of Sussex."

"And Marc d'Ursuras had to have known that," Sylvia said. "The Countess brought him to England when she fled the Revolution, and he didn't see France again until after Waterloo. While he was in England, he ran with a very exclusive set—the family still has letters he exchanged with Beau Brummell, for example." She shook her head. "How very puzzling."

"That's what I thought," said Jenny. "And it occurred to me that there might be some kind of hidden message in it. So I tried a few things, and—well, it's an anagram." She pulled the second sheet of paper out of the stack. "If you take this—" Her finger traced the title, *Baron Frederic I of Sussex his Manuscripte.* "—and rearrange the letters, you get this." She handed the sheet of paper to Sylvia. It read: *marc ursuras hides eibon's secret on p. xii f.*

Sylvia's mouth dropped open. "Oh, my," she said. "So what was on page twelve?"

Jenny pulled out another sheet. "That nearly stumped me, because I couldn't find anything there about Eibon at all. Then I noticed that there's a symbol at the bottom of every page—but they're not the same from one page to the next. I'd still have been stumped, except for a volume I happened to notice once when I was in the library, a French translation of Abbot Trithemius' book on codes and ciphers."

"The *Steganographia*," Sylvia said.

"That's the one. It was printed in the early eighteenth century, so I guessed it was one of the books Marc d'Ursuras brought with him from France, and started looking through it. It took a while, but the symbols are from one of Trithemius' ciphers. The first eleven pages have nonsense symbols. The message begins on page twelve, and goes on from there. Once it finishes, the nonsense symbols start up again, and go on to the end of the book."

"And the message?" Sylvia asked.

Jenny handed the sheet of paper to her. On it was written: *crypte dessous caveau pierre détaché centre de mur oriental étends en haut*

"'Crypt below vault,'" Sylvia said aloud. "'Loose stone middle of east wall reach up.' That's clear enough, except that the family doesn't have a vault."

"I read *caveau* as 'cellar,'" Jenny said.

"There's certainly a cellar," said Sylvia after a moment, "and a space below it. There's a trapdoor in the cellar floor. Martin told me that he opened it when he was searching for the Ring of Eibon—other than that, I don't think anybody's been down there since before I was born."

Jenny considered her. "Is there any way to ..." She let the sentence drop.

"It would have to be done late at night, so nobody finds out," Sylvia said.

"By 'nobody' you mean Lisette," said Jenny.

"Not just her," Sylvia said. "I've heard some rumors—and I think you heard about the books that were stolen from the Ambervilles." She nodded after a moment. "If you're up for it, the two of us could go look tonight."

The thought of venturing down into an unknown crypt in the middle of the night wasn't exactly comforting, but Jenny nodded anyway. "The Festival's so close," she said. "We'd probably better do that."

CHAPTER 9

THE RING OF EIBON

After her evening prayers, Jenny pulled on jeans, a blouse, and a cardigan, and nestled down on the settee. She managed to get a little sleep, but every noise the old house made around her jarred her to wakefulness. When Sylvia's stealthy knock finally came, she was grateful for it.

She opened the door just enough to glance out. Light from the lamp beside the settee showed Sylvia, dressed in a dark baggy sweatshirt and slacks; she pressed a finger to her lips for silence, motioned for Jenny to follow. Jenny slipped out into the hall, closed the door as silently as she could, and followed her great-aunt down the unlit hall.

Dim light from windows lit the main stair as they picked their way down. To Jenny's ears, every faint rustle and creak rang as loud as a trumpet. Even so, they got to the main floor without any sign that they'd been heard, and Sylvia gestured to the left and led Jenny back around the foot of the stair to an unobtrusive door. She opened it at a snail's pace to keep it from creaking. Within was another stair, far plainer than the one above, with a dim light filtering up from below.

Sylvia pulled off her shoes, motioned to Jenny to do the same thing. Once they were in stocking feet, she led the way down the stair. Halfway down was a landing with a door to the left, and light filtered around the door. As Jenny passed, she could

139

hear quiet voices beyond the door, the clatter of cookware, and then a long unhuman moan she recognized, after a moment, as the sound of an oven door being opened. Then they were past the landing, and the sounds faded into silence.

At the bottom of the stair was another door. Once it was safely shut behind them, Sylvia whispered, "Shoes back on again. We're in the cellar, and there's damp—and other things."

Jenny got her shoes on as quickly as she could. Sylvia pulled a little flashlight from her pocket and turned it on. By its pale gleam, Jenny could just make out the cellar around her, the square pillars and great rounded arches that supported the ceiling, the gray flagstones that paved the floor. Something scuttled in the shadows, and Jenny looked away from the noise, hoping not to see what made it.

"Over here," Sylvia whispered, and waved her over toward one side of the cellar. Jenny followed her to the far side of one of the pillars. There, one side of a wooden trapdoor peeked out from under an old metal steamer trunk, festooned with cobwebs, that looked as though it had last been used for a voyage on a Victorian-era steamship.

As Jenny went to move the trunk out of the way, soft footsteps sounded on the stairs, descending toward the cellar.

Sylvia motioned for her to hide behind a stack of crates in one corner, hurried to a hiding place of her own. The tiny flashlight clicked off. Utter darkness surrounded Jenny. The footsteps drew closer, stopped just outside the door. For a moment Jenny thought that they would turn and climb the stair again, but then the hinges let out a high thin shriek. A faint glow splashed across the cellar, and then a bright beam from a powerful flashlight played this way and that.

As the light slid past, missing her, Jenny pressed herself into her hiding place. After a few moments, a familiar voice spoke: "I shall probably have to call the police, you know."

Jenny found her courage and her voice. "Please don't do that, Michaelmas," she said.

"Miss Jenny." The light snapped in her direction.

She stepped out into view. "Yes."

"Are you alone?"

"No, she isn't," said Sylvia.

The light swung over toward the old woman. "Miss Sylvia," said the butler. "Under the circumstances, I'll have to ask for an explanation."

"Of course," said Sylvia. "Jenny may have figured out where the Ring of Eibon is hidden, and we're seeing if she's right. As for the hour—we didn't want to give certain other people any idea where we were searching for it."

"That was wise," said Michaelmas. He went to the door, closed it, and turned a switch; a single pallid light bulb in the center of the cellar cast long shadows outwards. "Mr. Applegate and Mr. Connor have been searching the house and the grounds. They have Madame's key ring. I believe she lent it to them."

Sylvia stared at him. "That's—very troubling."

"Indeed," said Michaelmas. "That being the case, perhaps I may offer my assistance."

"Thank you," said Jenny. "If I'm right, though, we're almost there. The ring is in a hiding place in the crypt below here."

"Ah. I had wondered more than once if that might be the place Mr. Ursuras chose." The butler stepped over to the trapdoor, took hold of the handle on the end of the trunk blocking it, and swung it effortlessly out of the way. He stooped, then, and just as easily pulled up the trapdoor, revealing emptiness below. His flashlight shone down, illuminating a stone wall with footholds cut into it.

"I'm not at all sure I can climb that," Sylvia said after a moment. "Michaelmas, can you go down there with Jenny?"

"I am forbidden to enter the crypt," Michaelmas replied.

Jenny gave him a startled look, but Sylvia simply nodded. "In that case," she said, "Jenny, do you think you can bear going down alone?"

"I'll manage," she said. "Can I borrow your flashlight?"

Sylvia handed it over. Jenny gripped it between her teeth, crouched beside the opening, and lowered herself in. Michaelmas stepped over and shone his flashlight down from above, and Jenny got her feet securely lodged in one of the footholds and began the descent.

* * *

It took some scrambling, but a minute or so later she was safely down. She looked around, and the breath caught in her throat. She'd expected more of the plain stone construction of the cellar above, not a mosaic floor that returned the flashlight's beam in an intricate play of green, blue, and purple stone. In the center of the floor, surrounded by fantastic arabesques, was a central disk, maybe two feet across, that gleamed like onyx. The walls of the crypt were made of great blocks of plain gray stone, but someone had daubed strange hieroglyphics on the walls in something that didn't look like paint. The symbols seemed familiar. A long moment passed before she recognized them as part of a ritual from the third book of the *Livre d'Ivon*.

She shook her head, reminded herself of the reason why she was in the crypt. A question she'd forgotten to ask earlier came suddenly to mind. "Which way is east?" she called up to the trapdoor above.

In response the pool of light from Michaelmas' flashlight slid away from the wall she'd descended, toward the far wall. "That way, Miss Jenny," said the butler.

She crossed the vault to the far wall, started testing the stones toward the middle. The third one she tried gave slightly as she pushed. Probing with her fingers, she found depressions on the sides where she could grip it, and pulled. The stone came loose. Behind it was darkness.

She shone the flashlight into the gap, and saw nothing but a hollow in the stone. A pang of disappointment passed through her, but suddenly she remembered the last words of the message she'd deciphered: *étends en haut*. She slid her hand into the opening, brushing the upper surface with her fingers, and found a void toward the back. Twisting her arm up and around, she managed to force her hand up through it to a little shelf, and her fingers closed on something cubical and cold.

She pulled it out, examined it in the light from Sylvia's flashlight. It was a box of some dark untarnished metal, maybe three inches on a side, with a seam dividing it in half and a round button of metal next to the seam. "I've got something," she called up. "A little metal box."

"The ring is inside," Michaelmas said at once. "Don't put it on your finger for any reason, Miss Jenny. It has killed many people who attempted to wear it."

"I know," she said. "But thank you."

"You're most welcome."

Fortunately her cardigan had pockets. She tucked the box into one of them and began to climb out of the crypt. The way up was considerably more difficult than the way down, but once she was within reach of the trapdoor Sylvia and Michaelmas both knelt and caught hold of her hands, and with their help she clambered up into the cellar.

Michaelmas closed the trapdoor once she was through it, and pulled the steamer trunk back into its place. Jenny took the flashlight out from between her teeth, dried it on her sweater, and handed it with an apologetic look to Sylvia, who laughed and pocketed it. "Now, the ring," the old woman said.

Jenny pulled the box out of her cardigan pocket, held it up so both the others could see it, and pressed the button with her thumb. With a soft click, the seam widened. She pulled on the upper half of the box, and it swung slowly open on a concealed hinge.

The gold, impossibly red, blazed in the lamplight. A somber purple spark smoldered in the heart of the gem. Jenny's breath caught. She glanced at the others; Sylvia stared at the ring with wide eyes, while Michaelmas gazed upon it without expression.

"The Ring of Eibon," the butler said.

"I've never seen gold so red," Sylvia said. "Is it an alloy, I wonder?"

"No," Michaelmas said. "The gold's a product of alchemies that were lost before Poseidonis drowned, or so I was taught, and the making of the stone was a secret that only Eibon ever mastered. There's none like it in the world, nor will there ever be another."

Sylvia nodded. "The question in my mind," the old woman said, "is what to do with it until the Festival."

"If I may offer a suggestion. Miss Sylvia," said Michaelmas.

"Of course."

"It can be worn about the neck on a chain without the least danger," said the butler. "It's made to be difficult to detect when it's close to a living body."

"That's true," said Jenny. When the others turned toward her, startled, she went on: "I read that in the *Book of Eibon*."

They looked at each other, then back at her. "How much of the book have you read?" Sylvia asked her.

"All of it," Jenny admitted. "A couple of times. It was—interesting."

The old woman and the butler looked at each other again, and then Sylvia nodded and smiled. "Well," she said, "once I can find a chain, I think you should wear it."

Jenny nodded uncertainly. "That makes sense. Yes, if you think that's best."

Michaelmas went to the door. "Give me five minutes to make sure the way is clear," he said, and slipped out through the door. His soft footsteps faded to silence on the stair.

Jenny watched him go, then turned to her great-aunt. "That's funny," she said, "that he still calls you Miss Sylvia."

"He's called me that ever since I was a little girl," the old woman said.

Jenny blinked, and gave her an astonished look. Sylvia smiled and changed the subject. "You have no idea how much this is going to mean to Martin," she said. "To all of us, really. To be able to bring the Ring of Eibon to the Festival—what an amazing thing that will be."

* * *

A quarter of an hour later, Jenny slipped through the door into Sylvia's sitting room. Claire was sitting on the couch, wide awake and watching. Behind Jenny, Sylvia came in, turned to murmur a few words to the butler, and then closed, locked, and bolted the door. She turned back toward the others with a ragged sigh of relief.

"And?" Claire asked.

"We found it," said Sylvia.

Claire blinked in surprise. "That's wonderful. May I—"

"Of course," Sylvia said at once. To Jenny: "If you don't mind, of course."

Jenny had already extracted the metal box from the pocket of her cardigan. She pushed the button and opened the box, revealing the red-gold ring and the purple stone.

Claire blinked again, but not in surprise. "That's odd," she said. "My eyes won't focus on whatever's in there."

All at once Jenny remembered what Michaelmas had said, set the box down on the drum table, and drew her hand back. Claire drew in a sudden sharp breath.

"You see it," Sylvia said.

"Yes," Claire said, staring at it. "I've never seen a stone like that."

"It's older than the human race," Sylvia said.

"I can well believe it," said Claire.

"Let me see about a chain," Sylvia said to Jenny then, and went into the bedroom. Jenny slumped down on a nearby chair.

"Tired?" Claire asked.

Jenny managed a smile. "I hope I don't have to get used to searching basements in the middle of the night."

Claire laughed, shook her head. "It usually isn't one of Syl's habits either."

All at once Sylvia came back into the sitting room. She had a silver chain in her hand, but her face was tense. "There are people in the garden in back," she said. "Two of them, with flashlights. They were carrying something, I think"

"Connor and Applegate?"

"That's my guess." She turned. "Jenny, if you're willing, I'd like you to bed down on the couch here for the rest of the night, and Claire and I will keep watch by turns." She frowned. "Put it down to an old woman's worries, but I don't want to take unnecessary chances."

"I've slept on plenty of couches before," said Jenny. "I'm fine with it."

"Thank you." Sylvia extracted the Ring of Eibon from its box, threaded the chain through it. "Here. Let's get this around your neck, so nobody will be able to see it."

Jenny let her great-aunt fasten the chain, then tucked the ring under her clothing. "There we go," Sylvia said. "Now let me see about some blankets."

* * *

She slept, and woke once in near-darkness. Over on the far side of the room, Claire was sitting in a pool of lamplight with a book open in front of her She wasn't looking at the book, though. She was watching the door with narrowed eyes.

Jenny blinked and shifted so she could see the door. Claire caught the movement, glanced toward Jenny and raised a finger to her lips. Jenny nodded, said nothing. After a moment she noticed a soft sound coming from the hall outside: a faint droning noise too steady to be anything but a machine. It grew slightly louder as the moments passed, as though whatever was making it was coming down the hall toward the door.

As the source of the noise approached, something strange happened to the air inside the room. A faint glow shimmered through the near-darkness, but it didn't seem to be any color Jenny could name, and the walls somehow looked less solid than they'd been a moment before. The glow played back and forth, and all at once Jenny was certain that whatever made it was searching for the Ring of Eibon.

She put her hand to her chest, felt the hard shape of the ring under her blouse. She didn't remember any spells from the *Livre d'Ivon* that could hide a magical ring from whatever was shining into the room, but she recalled some of what the same book said of the ring's powers, and thought at it: Hide. Don't let yourself be found. Then, hastily: not by anyone but me.

The ring didn't respond. It didn't have to. As her hand rested on it, she felt something for which neither of the languages she knew had a name: an immense architecture of forces balanced and counterbalanced against one another, turning in complex arcs through some continuum that was neither space nor time. One great facet of that architecture had already pivoted outward in response to the glow, and Jenny sensed that the ring was concealing itself.

It was not concealing her, though. She sensed that with equal clarity. If the glow was searching for her, she would have to fend for herself.

Whisper of sound from the bedroom door made her glance that way. Sylvia stood there in a bathrobe, staring out at the glow. In her hand was a gleaming shape that Jenny recognized after a moment as a pistol. Claire glanced back at Sylvia, gestured at the door to the hall; Sylvia nodded; the two of them waited in perfect silence while the glow moved from side to side.

Then, as gradually as it had come, the faint drone faded out, and the glow guttered and was gone. Claire and Sylvia remained motionless and intent, waiting. Nothing happened. Finally Sylvia let out a long ragged sigh of relief. She pocketed the gun, turned to Jenny, and placed her hands against the side of her face, saying more clearly than words could: go to sleep.

Jenny nodded after a moment, and pulled the blankets back up around her. The last thing she saw before sheer exhaustion swallowed her was Claire's face, as the old woman glanced her way and then turned her attention back to her book.

* * *

When she woke again, the view through the open curtains showed pale morning sun glinting from snow on the roofs of Kingsport and the brown brick of the abandoned hospital off in the distance. Jenny blinked and rubbed her eyes, and all at once smelled browned butter, egg, and spices. She pushed back the covers and sat up, still blinking.

Next to the window, Claire bent over the chafing dish, which was clearly the source of the odors. Sylvia, who stood nearby, noticed Jenny's movement. "I've told you more than once," she said to Claire, "that the smell of your French toast would wake the dead."

They laughed, and so did Jenny. "What time is it?" she asked.

"Just past eleven."

"Wow."

"Well, it was an exciting night—and it's probably just as well you slept so late." In a low voice: "I went downstairs earlier. After we came back up here, somebody went into the cellar and searched it. I don't know if they moved a certain steamer trunk, but I suspect so."

Jenny took that in, nodded, said nothing.

She got up a moment later, used the bathroom, then came out and stood for a moment looking at the shrine with its two statues. "Is it okay if—" she asked her great-aunt.

"Of course." Sylvia gestured at the clutter. "Help yourself to a chair."

Jenny found one, placed it before the shrine, sat and repeated the words: "*Iâ, Iâ, G'noth-ykagga-ha, Iâ, Iâ, Tsathoggua.*"

The contact with the Great Old One came suddenly, and with it the not-voice: *Once you leave this room you will be in danger*, it said, *and there is only so much I can do to help you. If you can, if they come for you, flee to the deep places.* A sudden image of the cellar appeared in her mind's eye. *If you are able to reach the deep places, I may be able to protect you there.*

Jenny blanched, but managed to nod after a moment.

You have Eibon's ring, the not-voice went on. *If all goes well and you bring it to the Festival, you will be asked to present it to one who waits for you. You must say these words to him.* With an effort Jenny could feel, the unhuman mind on the far side of the little statue forced through words: *"Sire, Tsathoggua bids me present you this token." Repeat them to me.*

Jenny whispered the words.

Good, said the not-voice. *Remember them, and say them just so. Much depends on it.*

Then the sense of connection faded, and Jenny drew in a long uneven breath and tried to nerve herself up for the day ahead.

French toast with maple syrup did much to improve the morning, though. So did the news that she would not have to leave the safety of Claire's and Sylvia's room until well into the afternoon. "Martin and I worked out the details yesterday," Sylvia explained. "We'll meet in the brown parlor at three—just the four of us who are going to the Festival, for a light meal and final arrangements. After that, you'll have the chance to wash up and dress; wear a day dress and comfortable shoes, because we'll be walking to the Festival. I have some preparations to make; once those are done, Michaelmas and I will come to your room and bring you down to the library. Then we'll get Charlotte—I don't imagine anyone will bother either of you, but better to be on the safe side."

"And I," said Claire, "will cook up a splendid dinner and eat it all myself." With a sudden grin: "When you get back, depending on how late it is, I can probably fix something then, too."

* * *

Just before three o'clock, Sylvia left the sitting room, Jenny at her heels. An unfamiliar hush seemed to crouch in the halls. As she followed Sylvia down the stair, Jenny realized what it was: the quiet sounds that announced the servants at work, the faint hum of the vacuum cleaner and the subterranean rumbling from the laundry room, were silent. If Lisette was watching television, she had the sound off. The stillness set Jenny's nerves on edge. So, absurdly, did the thought that Lisette might see her dressed the way she was, in jeans and a cardigan still marked with dust from the cellar, creased and rumpled by a night's sleep on Sylvia's couch.

Still, the two of them reached the first floor without incident, and Michaelmas stood outside the door of the brown parlor, imperturbable as always. He bowed to them both and brought them in. "Sir? Miss Sylvia and Miss Jenny."

Martin was standing by the window, looking out at the garden. He turned around, waved them to seats as Michaelmas left the room. "As soon as Charlotte arrives we can start," he said.

As though his words had summoned her, the door opened again, admitting Charlotte and Michaelmas. "Sir, Miss Charlotte."

"Thank you, Michaelmas. Have the other servants been sent away for the night?"

"Other than Madame's maid," said the butler, "yes."

"I trust you won't have any trouble seeing to Lisette and her guests."

"I anticipate no difficulty, sir."

"Good. We'll have lunch right away."

"Of course, sir." Michaelmas bowed and left.

Martin considered the three women for a long moment, and then said, "Well. A few more hours, and—the Festival. Charlotte, Jenny, I apologize for keeping the two of you in the dark about what's going to happen, but you'll understand the reasons soon enough, and this will be something you'll remember for the rest of your lives."

"What do we need to do?" Jenny asked him.

"All any of us have to do now is be waiting in the library when the sun goes down. That's where we'll await the summons, where every Chaudronnier who's attended the Festival has awaited the same summons since this house was built. And then—we'll go."

His face showed tremendous strain. Jenny wondered what it meant, and then thought of the Ring of Eibon and what Martin had told her about the consequences of its loss. She was about to tell him that the ring has been found when the door opened and Michaelmas came in with a tray on his shoulder. He went to the sideboard and busied himself there for a moment, setting out platters, plates and silver, then bowed to Martin and left as silently as he'd come.

As the door closed, Martin started talking again. "Listen carefully, both of you," he said to Charlotte and Jenny. "Some of the things you're going to see will be very strange, and some may be—rather frightening. It's one thing to pray to the Great Old Ones and read about their creatures and servitors, and quite another thing to meet them. Please believe me that no harm is going to come to you or anybody—"

Muffled voices sounded outside the door. Martin turned, frowning. Sylvia got up from her seat and stood behind Jenny.

After a moment, one of the voices suddenly got louder and more shrill, and Jenny recognized it: Lisette's. Charlotte blanched visibly and backed away to the far end of the room. Martin, his frown deepening, went to the door and opened it. "Lisette, I—"

"You will *not* lock me out of a room in my own house," she shouted at him.

"Lisette," he began again, but all at once she shoved past him and darted into the room. She glanced around, spotted Jenny, and came toward her. "Jenny, you poor child," she said. "I tried to find you earlier in your room—to warn you."

"Lisette," Martin said once again, in an agitated tone.

"Will you be quiet!" she snapped at him. "It's not enough for you that you have to practice this bizarre cult of yours. It's not enough for you to draw my poor daughter into it, and turn her against her own mother. No, you have to lure this poor child here, and you and I both know why." She turned back to Jenny. "Don't you realize what this is all about, Jenny? The only reason they brought you here was so they could sacrifice you at this festival of theirs."

"Lisette," Martin said after a moment of stunned silence, "that is quite enough!"

Lisette ignored him. Jenny, staring up from her chair at the flat hard mask of her aunt's face, suddenly glimpsed what lay behind it. "Aunt Lisette," she said, "you don't have to listen to them, you know."

The mask cracked. Through the gap, for an instant, Jenny glimpsed the same starved desperation she'd seen so briefly when the two of them talked over lunch. It was only for an instant, and when that ended, the gap closed hard and Lisette's face went stark white. Her mouth worked, but no words came out. All at once she darted out of the room, slamming the door behind her.

A long silence filled the room in her absence. Finally Martin turned. "Jenny," he said, "I hope you don't believe—"

"Of course not," she said.

"Thank you," he said. Then, after another moment: "Well. Despite—what just happened—I'm going to encourage everyone to have lunch. None of us should eat again until after we get back from the Festival, and it's likely to be a long night." He motioned Charlotte and Jenny toward the sideboard.

Lunch was scalloped oysters, watercress sandwiches, a platter of winter pear slices surrounding a ripe brie cheese, and coffee. For a long time no one talked. Finally, when the platters were looking decidedly empty, Martin turned to Jenny and Charlotte and said, "I hope the two of you recall the chant I taught you."

Jenny glanced at Charlotte and raised an eyebrow. Charlotte managed a shaken smile. They each drew in a breath, and in perfect harmony, a fifth apart, chanted:

"*Iâ, Hastur, khai'wan shrai-ghnagh'gwa,*
"*Iâ, Hastur, khai'wan khlw'mna.*"

Martin's eyebrows went up. Sylvia, delighted, put a hand to her mouth. "That," said Martin, "will do very well indeed." A little of the tension left his face, but only a little. Once again, Jenny drew in a breath to tell him about the Ring of Eibon, but he forestalled her. "Well, we all have preparations to make. I'll go directly to the library now. I'd like you to meet me there—" He glanced at the grandfather clock in the corner. "Will an hour be enough for you, Sylvia?"

"That should be fine," the old woman said.

"Good. I'll see you all then."

* * *

Sylvia and Michaelmas escorted Jenny and Charlotte up the stairs, stopped outside Charlotte's rooms. "Don't open the door, no matter what, until we come to get you," Sylvia told her. "I'll knock, or Michaelmas will—you know how. I don't think there'll be any kind of trouble, but—"

Charlotte nodded, unlocked her door and slipped inside. The deadbolt shot home with an impressive thud.

The three of them climbed the stair to the third floor, walked down the silent hall to the door to Jenny's rooms. "The same goes for you," Sylvia said. "Lock your door, and don't unlock it until I knock like this." She glanced around to make sure no one but Michaelmas was watching, tapped an odd rhythm on the back of Jenny's hand. "It'll be about an hour. Remember— day dress, and shoes you can walk in."

"I remember," Jenny assured her. "See you in an hour." She went into her sitting room, closed and locked the door behind her, glanced up at the clock and then busied herself getting ready for the Festival. She'd decided to wear a sober, comfortable dress of dark green wool with elbow-length sleeves and a cowl neck, and that went onto her bed while she washed up and made a first, mostly unsuccessful attempt to get her hair to behave itself. A second attempt after she'd dressed finally did the job, and she put on her one pair of pearl earrings and an enameled brooch with a rose on it— another thrift store find, that, but it looked as though it might once have graced a dress not too different from the one she was wearing.

She considered her reflection in the mirror, turned from side to side, and smiled, thinking about how startled her house- mates in Arkham would be to see her at that moment. Then, out of nowhere, another thought whispered itself to her in the silence of the room: all dressed up for sacrifice. She scowled and forced it out of her mind.

A little makeup, a few drops of perfume, a second glance at the mirror, and she was ready. She settled the Ring of Eibon against her chest, made sure the chain was invisible, and then turned to look at the clock, to find that she still had nearly twenty minutes left.

She considered getting the Amadeus Carson romance from her bookshelf and trying to read some of it, but her nerves were sufficiently on edge that she knew she wouldn't be able to concentrate on it. Instead, she sat on the settee next to Saint Toad's shrine. The statue sat on its silk cushion with a brood- ing, watchful air that troubled her, and after a moment she looked away.

Just then a faint sound came through the door. Only the hush that gripped the mansion let Jenny identify it as the noise of hinges turning as a door opened and closed. Silence followed, and then the whisper of footsteps approaching her door. For a moment she thought it must be Sylvia and Michaelmas, finished early with their preparations, but the rhythm was wrong.

She got to her feet, suddenly uneasy. The footfalls slowed to a halt just outside. Something that might have been a whispered word stirred the still air. Then, all at once, a muffled, heavy blow slammed against the door.

CHAPTER 10

THE NIGHT OF THE FESTIVAL

After an instant of raw panic, Jenny ran for her bedroom. As she locked the bedroom door behind her, she heard a second blow and the sound of cracking wood as the door to the hall began to give way. The bedroom door wouldn't keep anyone out for long, she knew.

All at once she remembered the secret passage. She darted across the room to the closet, pushed dresses out of the way as the bedroom doorknob rattled behind her. It took only a moment to find the panel; she shoved it with all her strength, and it flew open. Jenny pulled the closet door closed behind her, then plunged into the space beyond and pushed the panel shut.

She could see nothing, but found steps leading to her right and went down them as quickly as she could. Muffled noises behind her warned that the bedroom door had been forced open. All at once her downward flight ended at a wall. Frantic, she felt to one side, then the other, and found a doorknob. Opening it, she stepped into a bare closet that held a scattering of old cleaning supplies and not much else. She slipped out the closet door.

She was on the second floor of the mansion, on the main corridor, and the stair was nearby. Someone was shouting something in a high-pitched voice further down the hall, though she couldn't make out who it was or what was being said. As she

156

started for the stair, a door on the floor above slammed open and footfalls drummed on the hall. She took off running.

As she neared the top of the stair, Roger Applegate lunged out of the shadows toward her. He shouted up past her: "Connor! She's down here. I'll get her."

Jenny tried to dart past him, but he moved too quickly. As his hands closed on her, sheer panic made her kick and claw at him with all the strength she had. One of her knees drove upward, connected somewhere below his ribs; he gasped and lurched forward; she scratched and twisted and flailed, and all at once broke free, tumbling past him to the floor. An instant later she had scrambled to her feet and was running down the stairs as fast as she could.

The deep places, Saint Toad had said. *If you are able to reach the deep places, I may be able to protect you there.* Jenny knew with cold certainty that Roger and Connor could outrun her if she tried to flee the length of the first floor hall to the library, and that left only the Great Old One's advice. She reached the bottom of the stairs before Roger, stumbling and cursing, had gotten halfway down them, and sprinted for the door she and Sylvia had used the previous night. It was unlocked; she darted through it, locked it behind her, and then all but threw herself down the long narrow stair.

The doorknob above rattled before she was more than a few steps down, and then Roger shouted something she couldn't make out. Other noises she couldn't identify came after that, and then a sudden loud crack that sounded far too much like a gunshot for her peace of mind. A few moments later, a blow landed against the door. Wood splintered, but not enough of it. She flung herself down the last of the stairway, got to the foot as a second blow hit and the door gave way.

She threw open the door to the basement and ducked into the darkness beyond it. She'd intended to lock it, too, but found the lock visibly broken, hanging half off the door, and hurried on. In the faint light that came through the open door, she could just make out the place where she'd hidden from Michaelmas' flashlight the previous night. Shadows gathered thick around the walls. Shaking with terror, she flung herself into the space behind a pair of stacked crates, crouched motionless as footfalls reached the foot of the stairs, praying hard: Saint Toad, please. Help me if you can.

The footfalls slowed. A moment later, the basement light clicked on.

"You've wasted my time and yours," Willis Connor said. "Fortunately I have the time to spare. You, on the other hand, don't."

His footsteps whispered on the flagstones of the floor, coming closer to her hiding place. She twisted, pressing herself further back into the gap behind the crates, and only then, through the haze of panic that pressed against her thoughts, noticed something strange.

One of the shadows she'd seen hadn't changed or moved when the light went on. It filled the space between the stone wall and an old trunk, black and liquid as a pool of ink, and no trace of light came through it. From it came a swampish smell. She stared at it, and saw ripples pass through it, as though it tensed.

Just then Connor came around the far end of the crates and saw her.

"Don't bother with your spells," he said. "They won't work on me." His eyes, cold and narrowed, remained fixed on her. "Did you really think we couldn't figure out why your foul masters sent you—that I wouldn't know you were here for Eibon's ring, or recognize you on sight for the half-human monstrosity you are? I don't want to think about why your mother betrayed her species and gave herself to the toad god, but I can certainly take care of the result." He reached inside his jacket and pulled out a pistol.

At that instant the shadow lunged out from behind the crate with blinding speed. Connor saw it a moment too late, and before he could spring back it had swallowed the gun and the hand that held it. He tried to pull his hand free, but the black thing held it fast. His other hand reached for something inside his jacket pocket as he shouted, "*Ya na kadishtu*—"

The rest of the blackness flung itself away from the wall and swallowed his head and face. His voice turned into a wet choking sound, then to silence, and the rest of the incantation went unsaid. The black mass drew inward, engulfing more of him, and where the gun, the hand, and the head had been, nothing at all was left.

A moment later the shape that had been Willis Connor crumpled to the basement floor and fell forward, and the shadow flowed over it. For a brief instant, the silhouette of a headless and handless corpse lay there, absolute black against the gray stones. The shadow sank down upon him, then, and when it flowed back to its place behind the old trunk, no trace of Connor remained.

* * *

Jenny crouched there behind the crates for a long moment, trembling and hoping she wouldn't vomit. Her blood pounded in her ears. Finally, as her panic lessened, she straightened up and came out from her hiding place, edging as far as she could from the place where Connor's corpse had so briefly rested, and started for the door.

A sudden flurry of noise, and then all at once Roger Applegate came stumbling into the basement, his face dripping blood from the scratches Jenny's fingernails had left. "Connor!" he shouted. "I had to shoot the damn butler. You've got to call the others—" Then he saw Jenny. He lurched to a stop, staring at her with round frightened eyes, and scrabbled for something in his pocket. As he did so, the black shapeless thing surged out from behind the trunk and flowed across the floor toward him.

For one frozen instant Jenny stared at him and the flowing darkness. The man disgusted her, and the thought that he might have killed Michaelmas was almost more than she could bear. She need only do nothing and the black thing would swallow him as it had swallowed Willis Connor, but she knew at once, instinctively, where that decision would lead. Instead, she did the only thing she could think of: she pointed her left thumb at him, formulated the Sigil of Cykranosh in her mind, and shouted, "Stop!"

He stopped.

Motionless as a wax dummy, he stood there with a panicked expression fixed on his face and one hand frozen in mid-fumble in his pocket. Jenny's mouth fell open. The shapeless black thing slowed and stopped as well, extruded part of itself into the form of a muzzle, and turned that toward her, as though asking a question.

She tried to speak, failed, swallowed and tried again. "It's okay," she told the black thing. "He can't do anything to me now." The thing dipped its muzzle in acknowledgment, and slid back across the flagstones toward the edge of the cellar.

A rush of soft footfalls came down the stair. Michaelmas appeared at the door. Something was wrong with his face, though Jenny couldn't make out what it was at first. He had a gun in his hand, an old revolver with a long barrel. "Mr. Applegate," he called out, "if you move a muscle I shall shoot you dead."

"He can't move," Jenny said.

Her voice seemed to startle him. "Are you unharmed, Miss Jenny?" he asked.

"Yes. Yes, I think so."

Michaelmas came closer, and stepped around Applegate, considering him. "You've bespelled him, I believe," he said in a tone of surprise, turning toward Jenny. Then: "Is something wrong, Miss Jenny?"

"Your—your face has come loose, Michaelmas," she managed to say. It was hanging at an angle from the right temple, and she could see intricate shapes of yellow metal, gears and wheels and rods, behind it.

"Oh dear." He reached up with his free hand, pulled the face back into its proper position. "And Mr. Connor?" Before she could answer, he looked past her, toward the place where the black thing waited. "Ah," he said. "Tsathoggua looks after his own."

"Is that his?" Jenny asked.

"His spawn and servant. It's dwelt here in the cellar since Mr. Ursuras' time." He thrust the gun into the waistband of his trousers, tried to adjust his face with both hands. After a moment, he turned to her. "Could I ask for your assistance, Miss Jenny?"

"Of course."

He pulled a length of wire from a pocket. "If you could, please fasten this side up, perhaps to my ear. I can do a proper repair in my rooms once you're safely in the library, but something more temporary will suffice for now."

He bent forward so that she could reach his face. Something—a bullet, she guessed—had punched through the edge of it and dug a shallow trench across the cheek, stripping off what looked like flesh-colored porcelain to reveal yellow metal beneath, and breaking off the fastening that held it in place. She found an eyelet on the metal inside his face, below his left eye, and got the wire attached there, then looped it around his ear twice and twisted the end around to hold it in place. "That ought to do," she said.

"Thank you most kindly. You're needed in the library now. If you please—"

"Sure."

They went to the door; Michaelmas turned off the light and closed the door behind them.

Sylvia was at the top of the stair, her pistol in her hand. When they came into sight, she let out a little cry, and the moment Jenny came within reach the old woman threw her arms around her and held her, shaking. As she drew back,

Sylvia said something to the butler, but Jenny couldn't quite make sense of it. She was shaking, too, as panic slowly let go its hold on her nerves; Willis Connor's last moments replayed themselves over and over again in her mind's eye—and so did his last words.

Sylvia and Michaelmas seemed to understand. They each took one of her arms, and steered her as quickly as possible to the library door.

* * *

Jenny was still shaking when she stepped into the library. Uncle Martin surged to his feet. "Jenny! Are you hurt?"

"No," she said. "No, just winded, and—and scared."

Sylvia helped her into a chair, patted her arm, and then got to work brushing the dust from the cellar off her dress with a handkerchief. Jenny slumped back in the chair, felt the pounding of her heart gradually slow to a more normal pace.

"Sir, Mr. Connor is no longer with us," Michaelmas said then. "He broke down Miss Jenny's door, which I shall have repaired at once. Miss Jenny had the good sense to flee to the cellar, and Mr. Connor followed, with consequences I need not describe to you."

"Did he fire the shot I heard?" Martin asked.

"No, sir. That was Mr. Applegate, and fortunately he fired it at me. He is currently in the basement, where he will be unable to move for some hours." In response to Uncle Martin's raised eyebrow: "Miss Jenny has apparently put her time in the library to good use."

"I used the Sigil of Cykranosh," Jenny said.

Martin and Sylvia both stared at her. "That," said Sylvia, "is really quite remarkable."

"I'm not sure why I didn't try to use it on Connor," Jenny said then. "I didn't think of it. I was—" Her voice broke. "Really scared," she managed after a moment.

"It probably wouldn't have worked on him," said Sylvia.

Martin gave her a startled look. "How so?"

"I'm starting to think," Sylvia said then, "that he might have been an initiate of the Radiance." Jenny wondered what that meant, and why it made Martin draw in a sudden sharp breath and then clench his eyes shut.

"With your permission, sir," Michaelmas said then, "I will make sure Miss Charlotte is safe, and bring her." Martin nodded distractedly, and the butler left.

Martin watched him go, and then shook his head. "Jenny, I'm horrified that anything like this would happen to a guest in this house. Please accept my apology."

Jenny nodded after a moment, hearing generations of long-dead feudal magnates whispering their antique creed in his voice. "Of course."

"Thank you." Then, after a moment: "I didn't think that anything of the sort would happen at all, and I'm even more baffled that you would have been the target."

"There's a reason," Jenny admitted. "I don't know how they knew, but—" She stood up, pulled the silver chain from around her neck, and raised her hand so that the Ring of Eibon gleamed in the air between them.

If she had slapped Uncle Martin across the face the effect would not have been half as dramatic. His mouth fell open and his eyes went wide, and only a sudden grip on the back of a nearby chair kept him from staggering. "How—" he began, and stopped. A moment later: "Did—did Sophie take it after all?"

"No," Sylvia said. "Once you told her that the secret was supposed to be in the *Sussex Manuscript*, she sat right down with it and solved the riddle we've been beating our heads against for all these years. We found the ring last night."

Martin steadied himself by a visible effort of will. "Where was it?"

"In the crypt below the cellar," Sylvia said.

"I went there," said Martin, his voice unsteady. "Years ago, with the *Livre d'Ivon*. I called on the powers—the ones Father used to invoke—in the place where they tore him apart." Sylvia cried out, horrified, but he ignored her. "I called on them and commanded them, and they could tell me nothing. Nothing!"

"It's protected against sorcery," Jenny said. "I tried to use a spell to see it in a crystal, and didn't get anything either."

Once again Martin and Sylvia both stared at her. "You used a scrying spell," Sylvia said, wondering. "Where did you learn that?"

"In the *Livre d'Ivon*," said Jenny, looking from one to the other, uncertain.

"That's not easy work," Sylvia said.

Jenny gave her a puzzled look, remembering how readily the little pictures had leapt into the crystal. "Oh," she said. Then, to Martin: "There's a stone in the east wall that you can pull out, and a little space up behind it. I wonder if Marc d'Ursuras might have put it there when he built the house."

"That's very likely true," Martin said, beginning to recover his composure.

Jenny lifted the ring again. "Will you take it, Uncle Martin?"

He considered her, then the red gold of the ring, drew in a long uneven breath, and then nodded once. "Of course."

She unfastened the silver chain, slid the ring off it, and handed it to Martin, who put it in an inside pocket of his jacket. The chain, refastened, went to Sylvia, who shook her head slowly in astonishment and then put the chain in her purse.

* * *

Just then, the door to the library opened, and Charlotte came in, with Michaelmas behind her. Her face was pale and rigid, and she walked straight over to Martin as though she didn't see anyone or anything else in the room. "Father," she said, her voice shaking, "this Festival had better be important. Really, really important. If it isn't, I will never speak to you again."

"It matters more than you can imagine," Martin said. "You'll understand soon enough."

She faced him for another moment, and then crumpled into a chair and started to cry.

"Sir," said Michaelmas, "Madam was standing outside her door, screaming words I will not willingly repeat. From the condition of her voice I think she had been doing so for some time. She called for Mr. Applegate and Mr. Connor when I arrived, and then ran to her rooms."

Martin clenched his eyes shut and bowed his head. Sylvia had already gone to Charlotte's side, pressed a handkerchief into her hand, and was murmuring something into her ear.

"She said the most horrible things," Charlotte burst out, still crying. "About the family, about the Great Old Ones, about—about me. And she wouldn't stop. She just wouldn't stop."

Of course, Jenny thought. Of course. "She wanted to get you to open the door," she said aloud. "It's a good thing you didn't. Roger and Willis Connor tried to kill me a little while ago."

Charlotte's head snapped up suddenly, and her eyes went wide. "You're all right?"

"Pretty much. I had—help. I don't know what they would have done to you if you'd come out, but—"

That was not quite true. Remembering the words she'd heard from inside the library, she could see all too clearly what their plan must have been. They'd known the whereabouts of the library door, and guessed that sounds from outside could reach those inside. Charlotte's screams would have been audible inside the library as they did whatever was necessary to bring Martin and Sylvia out of the library, and into the line of fire of Connor's gun. After that—

Her thoughts came to a sudden stop. What Willis Connor might have done if he'd had the Ring of Eibon to give him power did not bear thinking about.

Charlotte was nodding slowly. After a moment, she wiped her eyes with the handkerchief, blinked several times, and then drew in and let out a long ragged breath. "I wish I knew why all of this happened."

Jenny looked at Martin, who nodded, and reached inside his jacket. "I can't be certain," he said, "but I think they were after this." He brought his hand out. The red gold and the brooding purple gem caught the light of the lamps.

"We found it," said Jenny.

"The Ring of Eibon?" Charlotte whispered. "Then—we can do what we're supposed to do in the Festival. "

"Yes," Martin said, as though the thought had only just occurred to him. "Yes, we can." He turned back to Jenny. "I'll keep the Ring for the moment," he said, "but during the Festival, it needs to be taken to—someone—who will bless it. I'd like you to do that, Jenny. You've earned the right."

"I'll do my best," Jenny said, remembering what Saint Toad had said that morning.

"It's simple enough," Sylvia said. "You'll hold the Ring in both your hands, carry it across the floor to the one who will bless it, and then bring it back to where we'll be sitting. Two other people will do the same thing with other items first."

"That sounds pretty easy," Jenny allowed.

"Sir," said Michaelmas, "given the time, it might be well to prepare for the summons."

"True," Martin said. "Thank you, Michaelmas."

"Of course, sir." Michaelmas went discreetly to the door and stepped outside it; the click of a lock turning followed a moment later.

Martin went to the table in the center of the library, returning with a stack of folded black garments. He handed them to Jenny, Sylvia, and Charlotte, and kept one for himself. Jenny unfolded hers; it proved to be a black hooded cloak.

"Put it on," said Martin, "and sit down."

Jenny shook her cloak out, settled it over her shoulders, fastened the clasp and pulled the hood up over her head.

"Now this," Martin said. He went to the table again, brought back two short glasses full of something pale, translucent, and faintly green, and handed one glass to Charlotte and the other to Jenny. Returning, he brought back two more, for himself and Sylvia, and stood waiting. Jenny sniffed the glass; the liquid in it smelled of grain and herbs, the almost-mint scent of penny-royal strongest among the latter.

"Down it goes," Martin said. "This is the *kykeon*, the drink of the old Mysteries."

Jenny nodded, raised the glass to her lips, tasted it—it was bitter, but not unpleasantly so—and drank. A numb tingling feeling spread through her mouth. Martin took the glass, gathered up the others, put them on the table, and then returned to his chair and settled on it, arranging the cloak around him.

A curious brightness filled the air, and all at once Jenny noticed that there was a door in the wall of the library in front of her, between two bookcases, where no door had been a moment before. She stared at it, then nodded slowly. It somehow made sense to her that they would go to the Festival by no ordinary route.

Time passed. The clock in the corner ticked out its solemn rhythm. The odd bright quality spread through the air, while the skylight darkened visibly. Then, finally, a heavy knock sounded against the door between the bookcases: once, twice, thrice.

"That is the summons," Uncle Martin said. His voice sounded as though it came from some vast distance. "Come with me."

Jenny stood up. She had the oddest feeling that she was leaving something behind on the chair, but for some reason the thought of turning to look didn't occur to her. With the others, she followed Uncle Martin to the door. He pulled it open, and one after another, they stepped through it into the night.

* * *

Outside a cold wind was rising, and scraps of dark cloud went scudding overhead across the panoply of the stars, veiling and unveiling a gibbous moon. A thin shroud of snow covered streets and roofs, glowed when the moonlight shone on it. Jenny went with the others down the steps onto Green Lane, followed Martin's lead as he turned left and headed toward the corner. Charlotte, looking pale and frightened, huddled in her cloak and stayed close to her father, while Sylvia went ahead. Jenny looked around, wondering if the others Roger had mentioned might put in an appearance, but the streets remained silent.

A few others in dark hooded cloaks were already heading up Caldecott Street, and as the Chaudronniers reached the corner, two more cloaked figures came out from one of the houses, though somehow Jenny didn't notice the door open to let them out. No one spoke, and no sounds of traffic broke the silence. Only the keening of the wind sounded low and clear as the old families of Kingsport left their homes and gathered for their ancient rite.

The street wound uphill between old houses. Seven blocks on, it crested a rise, and the northwestern quarter of Kingsport lay spread out below. Where all the unsold condominiums on the outskirts of town should have been, a scattering of distant farmhouses climbed the slope, and there seemed to be no traffic at all on the streets nor any lights in the windows. Impulsively, Jenny touched Sylvia's arm and pointed. What with the dim light and the shadows from the cowl, she couldn't see Sylvia's expression at all. The old woman nodded, as though the fields and scattered houses had been there all along, and gestured to the right, toward the last steep block of Summit Street leading up to the top of the hill.

The brown mass of the long-closed Congregational Hospital should have been straight ahead of them, Jenny thought she recalled, but that was not what stood pale against the stars. A soaring white steeple edged with moonlight rose there instead, and the windows of the church beneath it were golden with the glow of candles. A faint murmur that was more than the wind came from the open doors, though Jenny could not make out what it was. Beyond it, the cliffs north of Kingsport rose up one after another against the glittering sky, and a point of golden light burnt on the furthest and highest crag of all. Jenny wondered what that meant.

Summit Street was half full of cloaked figures, climbing up the street from the old houses below and spilling from the streets to either side. Jenny and the others joined them. One of the hooded shapes glanced Jenny's way, and she thought she saw Henrietta's face smiling at her from inside the hood. The short figure next to her looked very like Fern. Jenny smiled back. A moment later, though, she lost sight of them both as more cloaked figures joined the procession.

With the others, Jenny climbed the hill to the lich gate of the old church and crossed the churchyard, where leaning tomb-stones rose stark out of thin windblown snow. Strange pale lights flickered atop the stones; Jenny wondered what they were. As she crossed the churchyard, two other things caught her attention. The first was that none of the people filing into the church ahead of her left footprints on the snow. The second was that her shoes left no trace either.

Beyond the churchyard the ground fell away steeply. The dim lights of Kingsport sparkled in the night, and the masts and rigging of a dozen tall ships stood black against the moonlit water of the harbor, but Jenny barely noticed any of these. She made sure she was still with the other Chaudron-niers, kept close to them as the crowd of cloaked figures flowed up to the church door and filed inside one by one.

An old woman in a black hooded cloak like the others stood there with a leatherbound book in one hand and a pen in the other. At first glance, Jenny wondered what was wrong with her face; a second revealed that she was wearing a mask the color of bone, an abstract shape with a pointed chin, a straight line for the nose, and dark eyeholes through which Jenny could see nothing. When it was the Chaudronniers' turn to enter, Martin approached the masked woman, nodded a greeting, and indicated Charlotte, Jenny, and Sylvia with a gesture. The old woman made an entry in the book and motioned them through.

Inside, the church was dimly lit. Jenny, who had never been inside a New England meeting house before, looked around with some curiosity at the white box pews that ran up both sides of the aisle, and the pulpit standing where all the churches she'd seen before had an altar instead. In front of the pulpit, though, the carpet had been taken up and a trapdoor exposed; this stood open, revealing a steep stair. The cloaked figures went down the stair in single file.

The stair descended into a vault beneath the church, where stone tombs in a style centuries old lay in silent ranks. One of the tombs was open, and Jenny was startled to see the file of cloaked figures climbing into it and vanishing from sight. When she got close enough to see into the tomb, though, she discovered there was another stair inside it, leading steeply down into darkness. Martin went into the tomb and descended out of sight. Charlotte followed him, visibly trembling. Then it was Jenny's turn; she climbed over the side of the tomb, made sure of her footing, and started down the stair.

The dim light from above soon faded into blackness, but Jenny found that somehow she could see the way clearly. At first the wall next to her was made of great square stones set with crumbling mortar. Further down, as the stair bent into a descending spiral and plunged into the heart of the hill, the masonry gave way to smooth unbroken rock. The air felt cold and damp, and only the rustling sounds made by the figures before and behind her and the dripping of water from the dank stone walls kept it from perfect silence. Questions Jenny could not answer pressed around her. She kept going.

Finally, after half an hour or more, a dim shimmering glow the color of sunlight through spring leaves began to filter up from below, and a high faint piping gradually resolved into the sound of a flute. The stair widened and straightened, and then opened out onto a vast cavern full of the ornate shapes of the underworld, stalagmites, stalactites, still pools of black water, pale shapes like stone mushrooms, and terraces edged with intricate traceries of water-formed rock. Through the midst of it ran an underground river, surging and roiling over the water-carved stone of its bed. In the broad space on the near side of the river, scores of cloaked and cowled figures gathered in silence.

Jenny scarcely noticed any of these at first, though. All her attention went to the source of the light, a column of pale green fire that rose upwards from a chasm in the middle of the cavern floor to play against the ceiling high above. Bright as it was, it cast no shadows, and no heat flowed from it. Jenny stood awestruck for a long moment, staring at the pillar of flame, and then hurried after the other Chaudronniers.

She joined a swelling crowd around the column of green fire. An old man wearing another of the abstract white masks stood next to the flame and led the ceremony; the gleam of yellow eyes through the mask's eyeholes told Jenny who it had to be. She listened to chants in a language she thought she recognized from passages in the *Livre d'Ivon*, watched as offerings were made to the fire and the river, curtseyed with the other women as the men bowed low. The flautist, a dim hunched figure over to one side of the cavern, played on. After a time, the Terrible Old Man gestured with one hand, and the music changed to a different tune full of unexpected trills.

In response, out of the shadows on the far side of the cavern, an ungainly creature came flopping into the half-light. It had great wings like a bat's, folded at its sides, and webbed hind legs on which it hopped. Its head looked vaguely birdlike, a little like a crow's, a little like a vulture's, though it had a mane of coarse hair spilling back over its shoulders. Thick short fur covered its body, which had odd flaps and protrusions in various unlikely places. Another of the creatures followed the first, and another.

One of the women who had made offerings to the river walked over to the first of the creatures, clambered up onto its back, and lay flat on it, grasping the mane. All at once the great wings unfurled, rose and swept down, and the creature leapt into the air. Clumsy on the ground, it was the opposite in flight, and in an instant it had soared out of sight into the shadows.

More of the creatures came hopping out of the darkness. One by one, the cloaked figures climbed onto the creatures and flew away. Jenny made sure she was close to Uncle Martin and the other Chaudronniers, waited with them until their turn came.

Then Martin was helping Charlotte onto one of the creatures. Jenny saw her face briefly, pale but composed, though her hands shook as she knotted her fingers into the mane. The great wings swept up and then down, and the creature carried Charlotte off into the darkness. It was Jenny's turn next. Her knees wobbled as she crossed the stone floor to where Martin stood next to her winged beast. Still, she put one foot into her uncle's cupped hands, let him boost her up onto its back, and then crawled forward between the wings until she could take hold of the mane.

The creature made a chuffing noise deep in its throat. It turned its head so that one great yellow eye could see her, and then muscles shifted beneath her and two of the protuberances on its back pressed inward, gripping her sides. The wings unfolded and rose up. Jenny drew a deep shuddering breath, and all at once the wings swept down and flung her and the creature together up into the darkness above.

CHAPTER 11

THE TATTERS OF THE KING

For a moment Jenny could see nothing, and then the darkness dissolved around her and she and the creature she rode were in the open air under bright stars. As the great wings swept down, she looked past the beast's shoulder, expecting to see the lights of Kingsport rushing past below them. What she saw instead made her gasp: a vast plain sweeping out in all directions to the circle of the distant horizon, and clusters of jewel-colored lights floating just above the plain, moving slowly at an angle to her, as though drifting on the wind. The stars above her were not the winter constellations she knew.

For a time the creature flew steadily onward above the plain, the lights drifted past below them, and the wind rushed cold past Jenny. She clung to the beast's mane and felt the muscles work beneath its hide. Then, without warning, the scene dissolved, and the unknown stars gave way to a pale green sky streaked with veins of light. Below, an ocean the color of jade reached away to the emerald rampart of a distant shore half hidden in mist. Ahead, Jenny could see a long ragged line of the flying creatures beating the air with great strokes of their wings. They seemed to be flying toward the shore, but long before the first of them got there the green sky and the jade sea dissolved around her and another landscape took its place.

Now the sky was deep purple, fading to violet at the horizon. Directly ahead, a huge and silent tower rose up from a sullen crag of stone on the highest peak of a range of dark mountains. She wondered if it might be their destination, but the beast she rode climbed through the air with labored wingbeats and cleared the tower by a hundred feet or more. Glancing down, Jenny saw something crouched in the shadows on the tower's topmost battlement, a shapeless presence that gazed up at her with cold unblinking eyes. She shuddered involuntarily. A moment later it had vanished from sight in the darkness behind her. After another moment, the violet sky dissolved into the red hue of rubies and dying coals, and the mountain range was replaced by a vast flat delta striped with curving channels carrying water to a dark sea.

It's as though we're flying from world to world, Jenny thought. Then she remembered the passage from the *Livre d'Ivon* about the true shape of the world, and wondered if Kingsport, the plain, the ocean, the mountains, and the delta might all belong to the vaster Earth that Eibon had described, bending anthward and ulthward toward poles she had never before imagined. Dazzled and delighted, she clung to the creature's mane, let it carry her onward.

After a time—they were flying over a brown desert beneath a tawny sky just then, passing high above a city of domes and slender towers fashioned from stone the color of cinnabar—she noticed something that puzzled her. With each change in the landscape, even though the winged creatures didn't climb at all, the ground below seemed further away. The winged beast she rode began to descend, angling its wings downward, but each further change took the surface further away still. Finally the creature was plunging almost straight downwards, chasing the fleeing ground as world after world rushed past, and Jenny clung to the mane and shook with something halfway between exhilaration and terror.

Then the great wings swept up and down again, beating the air, slowing the descent, and a final strange landscape unfolded around her. The sky was a blank expanse of featureless white glare, dotted with black stars that sparkled like polished jet. Below her, the land crouched low beneath the jagged shapes of ink-black trees. Ahead, she could make out great dim angular masses that rose up above the line of the horizon.

The creature flew onwards, and the masses drew closer. They were black pyramids, Jenny realized, dozens of them clustered together, some smaller, some larger, and one vaster than any. The flying beast she rode descended until it was less than a hundred feet above the harsh lines of the treetops. The beasts ahead had already done the same; Jenny risked a glance back over her shoulder and saw a long line of the creatures behind her, descending out of the cold white glare of the sky in her wake.

As she looked forward again, the forest gave way abruptly to a shore of black sand, and then to something that looked like thick white cloud but surged and ebbed like water, reaching out into the middle distance. Beyond the far shore of the cloud lake, the black pyramids rose up stark against the sky. Before them, Jenny could see tiny shapes of people and winged beasts on the black ground just past the shoreline, and the flying creatures in front of her descended one by one to join them.

The cloud lake rushed past below, rolling in great silent waves. The creature she rode angled its wings as it neared the shore, and then slowed in a great rush of wingbeats as the shore came close. A final flurry, and the shock of landing shook the muscular back beneath Jenny. She looked past the creature's wing to make sure the ground was where it should be, and unclenched her grip on the mane. The beast made another chuffing noise in its throat, and the two protuberances that held her sides loosened their grip.

She scrambled down off the creature's back. Her knees nearly buckled beneath her as she reached the ground.

Once she'd steadied herself and made sure her legs would support her, she started across the beach toward the nearest group of cloaked figures on the shore.

* * *

One of the figures turned toward her and hurried across the black sand. It was Charlotte, her eyes shining. "We can talk here," she said in a whisper. "Mrs. Amberville told me. Do you know where we are?"

"No," Jenny admitted.

"Carcosa," whispered Charlotte. "The City of the Pyramids. I can hardly believe it." Then, looking past Jenny's shoulder: "Oh, here comes Sylvia!"

Jenny turned. Another of the flying beasts was landing in a flurry of wingbeats a little further down the shore. Once it had folded its wings, the two of them hurried over to help the old woman down from the creature's back. "Thank you," Sylvia whispered to them.

A few moments later, still further down the beach, another of the creatures landed, and Martin swung down from it and came to join them. "We'll want to get in line," he said in a low voice once he'd greeted them. "The procession will start as soon as everyone's here."

They hurried toward the city as yet another of the winged beasts came down to land. Away from the cloud lake and its pale silent waves, the beach rose up into a low black dune dotted with shore grass the color of the sand, bending and nodding in the cold steady wind. Past the dunes lay a flat black pavement that reached unbroken to the city. Beyond that, the nearest of the pyramids rose into the black-dotted glare of the sky.

They took their places in a long uneven line of cloaked and cowled figures, standing on the pavement. Once they were in place, Sylvia bent close to Jenny and Charlotte, pointed off to the left, into the cold wind, toward where the lake curved around the furthest of the black pyramids. "Look that way," she whispered. "What do you see?"

Jenny looked. At first glance she could see nothing there but the blank white of the sky, but none of the black stars shone there, and after a few moments she was sure that there was movement in the distance, like mist rising from a lake or curtains stirring on a windy day. Nor was it quite the same color as the sky; the longer she stared, the more visible the difference became. It was—

Yellow. She was sure of it: faint but definite, like the gleam of antique gold.

"What is it?" Charlotte whispered.

"That way lies Yhtill," said Sylvia, "the ulthern pole of the great world, where the powers who were before the Great Old Ones danced at the making of things. It's hidden away now, from us and from everyone in the great world, and the veils that hide it—" She gestured. "—are the tatters of the King." She leaned closer, intent. "We were promised, a long time ago, that they will not hide Yhtill forever."

Jenny took that in. One by one, more of the flying beasts landed, folded their wings, let their passengers down to the somber sand, and hopped away down the beach. One by one, cloaked and cowled figures climbed over the low black dunes and joined the line. Jenny considered the line, and then leaned close to Sylvia and asked, "Is everyone here from Kingsport? I didn't think there were this many with us when we went to the church."

"No," Sylvia whispered back. "No, not at all. There are people here from wherever the folk of the drowned country settled." She gestured further up the line. "Our French cousins are up there—we'll be sitting with them once we reach the Hall of the King."

The wind blew cold, drove sand across the pavement, fluttered in the folds of Jenny's cloak. Time passed. Finally, the last of the flying beasts landed in a flurry of wingbeats, the last of the cloaked figures found its way into place, a shudder of movement ran down the line as everyone turned to face the same way, and a high thin note from a flute far up the line joined with the muttering of the wind. Uncle Martin turned to Charlotte and Jenny, and said in a low voice, "The chant will begin soon." They both nodded. He turned back, and they waited.

Finally the line began to move. Somewhere behind the Chaudronniers, another flautist began to play, first a single long note, then a slow solemn melody. Jenny drew in a breath, and she and Charlotte both started chanting at the same moment:

"Iâ, Hastur, khai'wan shrai-ghnagh'gwa,
"Iâ, Hastur, khai'wan khlw'mna."

Others took up the chant, and once everyone had the melody, the flautist began playing variations high above the voices. The procession stopped, started, stopped again, and then began to move steadily across the black pavement into dim Carcosa.

* * *

A broad path paved with smooth black stone led between ranks of pyramids into the dark heart of Carcosa. At intervals along the route, altars stood in pairs on either side of the path, garnished with wreaths of jagged black leaves that Jenny guessed came from the forest over which she'd flown. Black stone bowls sat at the foot of each altar, half full of smoldering coals. As the procession passed between each pair of altars, small groups of cowled figures left the line to either side, poured libations of dark wine on the altars, and cast incense on the coals, intoning words that blended with the slow somber chant of those still in the procession. Their duty fulfilled, they rejoined the procession and resumed the chant.

From somewhere up ahead, the deep shimmering voice of a great gong rang out, beating a slow rhythm over which the chanting voices flowed and the music of the flutes leaped and gyred. Incense smoke streamed across the pavement in the steady wind. The procession went on, passing between one pair of altars after another. Ahead loomed the greatest pyramid of all, rising stark and somber against the unearthly sky. Jenny had guessed all along that this would be their destination, and she was not mistaken.

Ahead, a deeper darkness broke the smooth side of the pyramid where it met the pavement. As Jenny came closer she recognised it as a corbelled arch hundreds of feet high. The gong stood to one side of it, huge and dark, supported by a great dark frame, and those who beat it stood to either side with great dark mallets in their hands. On the gong, yellow on black, was the first shape of bright color Jenny had seen anywhere in Carcosa or the lesser world on which it stood. It looked a little like a Chinese character and a little like a word in Arabic, but Jenny remembered what she'd read in the *Livre d'Ivon*, and knew it for the Yellow Sign.

Ahead, the cowled figures leading the procession vanished into the shadow of the vast arch. Jenny tried to let the chanting voices and the harsh astringent scent of the incense shut out troubled thoughts, and failed. Once she'd passed the outermost pair of altars, a cold whisper of dread had begun to circle somewhere in the deep places of herself. Aunt Lisette's frantic words murmured themselves in her mind, and though she thrust them away they kept returning.

The arch came closer, and closer still. Jenny glanced at Charlotte, who walked beside her with a dazed but calm expression on her face, and tried again to concentrate on the chant. Those ahead of her fell silent when they passed into the shadow of the arch. Jenny wondered what that meant, tried not to think about what might be waiting inside the pyramid.

Then she and Charlotte came under the shadow of the arch. Two elders wearing white masks, one to each side of the procession, placed index fingers where lips would be to signal silence, and gestured for them to draw back their cowls. As they did so, two more masked elders stepped from the shadows, dipped curiously carven sticks into little bowls they carried, and traced a symbol with scented oil on her forehead and Charlotte's. Though she couldn't see it or follow the quick movement, Jenny felt sure that the symbol was the Yellow Sign.

At a signal from the elders, she and Charlotte both pulled their cowls forward again and went on. Beyond the arch, a stair rose up into distance, lit at intervals by torches that burnt with a pallid yellow flame. They began to climb, slowly, keeping pace with the shrouded figures in front of them.

Without the chant to distract her, Jenny's thoughts circled back again and again to Aunt Lisette's accusation. If the Festival was to end in blood, she could not help realizing, if a human life had to be offered to Hastur once each century, a stray member of one of the Kingsport families with no money or influential friends would be a logical choice for the victim. If it had happened in Kingsport, there might be clues for the police to find, but this way there would be no trace of her anywhere on the lesser Earth. When her housemates in Arkham reported her as missing, and the police finally came around to the Chaudronnier mansion, Uncle Martin could simply tell them that she'd left to catch the bus and that was the last he knew of the matter.

Then, a sudden icy realization: Or they could leave her suitcase beside the Miskatonic and throw her jacket into it, and talk about how depressed she'd been, and the Arkham police would treat it as one more student suicide, just like Owen's.

She was trembling as they neared the top of the stair. No, she told herself, no. It's not true. Aunt Lisette just repeated what Roger told her, and Roger got it from—

All at once she remembered Willis Connor's face when he'd had her cornered in the basement. From the man who tried to kill me, she reminded herself. If anyone would have staged my suicide, it would have been him. A moment later, she wondered: was that what happened to Owen?

She reached the top of the stair, followed the others down a short passage, and passed through a high dark door. All at once those and all other stray thoughts scattered. She had reached the Hall of the King.

Above her, the vaulted ceiling was lost in shadow. To either side of a long central aisle, rows of stone benches like pews in an ancient cathedral extended out to sheer black walls on either side, where more torches burned pale and dark banners hung still in the motionless air. The benches were divided into sections by low, ornately carved walls of black stone, oddly like the box pews in the meeting house in Kingsport, and beside the entrance to each section was a sculpted shield bearing a coat of arms. Ahead, the benches and the aisle gave way to open space; beyond that was a dais, and on the dais, towering above the cowled figures, rose a mighty statue of a yellow-robed king upon an onyx throne.

It was a splendid statue, Jenny thought, astonishingly life-like, though its proportions were far from human and it was easily six times the size of any living man. The crown on its head was of the same impossibly red gold as the Ring of Eibon, massy about the base and rising to jagged twisting spires above. Long white hair carved in fluid lines cascaded down past the harsh angles of the shoulders. The face lay hidden behind an expressionless abstract mask the color of bone, broad at the top and tapering to a point below, with a long straight line for the nose and eyeholes that revealed only darkness within. Heavy robes that looked like stiff yellow brocade worked with gold, tattered and scalloped at their lower edges, hinted so perfectly at the unhuman form within that Jenny wondered if the folds were actually made of cloth. The hands that rested on the

night-hued arms of the throne were perhaps the most triumphant detail of the statue: six-fingered, angular as a spider's
legs, pallid and abstract as the great mask above, they hinted
at terrible power even in repose.

Behind the statue, against the far wall, a long black banner
descended from unguessable heights. On it, high above the
statue's head, blazed the Yellow Sign.

Uncle Martin turned to the other Chaudronniers, motioned
to one side. Jenny caught sight of the cauldron and three serpents emblazoned on the dividing wall a moment later. She
filed in with the others, sat on a bench between Sylvia and
Charlotte. A dozen people were sitting there already, and Uncle
Martin nodded greetings to them: the family's French relatives,
Jenny guessed, and turned to look at the statue again.

The position of one of the great six-fingered hands had
changed.

She stared with wide eyes. A moment later she noticed a
slight inclination of the great pale mask, a slight movement of
the mighty head. It was not a statue, she realized then. She had
come into the living presence of Hastur, the King in Yellow.

* * *

The last of the cloaked and cowled figures filed in and took
their places on the stone benches. Silence settled into place in
the Hall of the King for a time, and then a high shrill chime
sounded. It echoed off the stone walls and then, moments
later, came back as a distant whisper from the unseen ceiling
far above. After the echoes faded to silence, the chime sounded
again, and after another long pause full of echoes, again.
Nine times in all it rang, and when the last shuddering echo
faded into silence, nine cowled figures rose from their seats
and went out into the open space before the King.

Since she'd first read the letter from Sylvia, Jenny had wondered what might take place at the Festival. Her only previous

encounters with ceremony were high school and university graduations and a few church services she'd attended to please a high school friend, and none of them had been particularly inspiring. She'd guessed from the first that the Festival would have nothing in common with those experiences, and the more she'd learned about her Chaudronnier relatives and their heritage, the more certain she was of that. What had never occurred to her, even after reading the *Livre d'Ivon* and working a little of its magic, was that the ceremonies of the Festival might be intended to make something happen.

The moment the ceremony began, though, she sensed purpose moving through it. The movements of the nine cowled figures on the black floor, as they paced out from an unmarked center to space themselves evenly around a wide circle and stand there in silence, were too intent and too focused to be empty formalities. More figures followed them, moved out into the space they defined. One carried an ornate golden cup, into which she dipped her fingers at intervals and flicked them outwards from the circle, spraying droplets of water; another followed with a censer hanging from a chain, which he swept around in great arcs, sending smoke billowing. Both chanted syllables in a language Jenny did not know.

As they retired from the circle, more followed, nine of them, carrying wands tipped with elaborate symbols. They moved to the spaces between the first nine, traced patterns in the air around the outside of the circle, and then turned inwards and came together at the center. There they brought the tips of the wands together, and something that was not quite light shimmered through the smoky air. Once the shimmering was well established, they turned and walked outward to the edge of the circle again, and the not-quite-light spread with them, swept out past the nine motionless figures at the rim of the circle, filled the hall. Jenny felt it as it reached her, a subtle pressure that flowed past her but left the air changed where it had been.

The bearers of the wands filed back to their places in one section of benches, and more cowled figures replaced them. Jenny watched it all and tried to make sense of it. Even as she made the attempt, she knew that whole worlds of knowledge she would need to understand the Festival were hidden from her. One thing was clear to her, though: a link of some kind was being renewed, a portal kept open that might otherwise have closed forever.

Finally, after many more things had been done, the nine figures who had kept their stations at the edge of the circle from the beginning of the ceremony returned to the center and then filed back to their places. Jenny wondered for a moment if the Festival was over, but memory told her otherwise.

All at once, then, utter silence filled the Hall. A moment later, she realized its source. The King, who had remained all but motionless until that moment, had raised one hand. As Jenny watched, the six long fingers gestured a silent invitation.

In response, several of the cloaked figures seated on a section of the benches close to the Chaudronniers' stood up and went to the edge of the open space. One carried a thin object that glittered in the dim light—a long dagger or short sword in an ornate scabbard, Jenny realized after a moment—and held it out to another, who bowed, and then unfastened his cloak. The others drew the cloak and cowl from him, revealing a tall middle-aged man with a dark pointed beard, in formal dress of European cut. He took the weapon upon the palms of both hands, and walked across the floor to the dais, carrying it before him.

Sylvia leaned close to Jenny then, and whispered, "You'll be the third to go before the King. Be ready." Jenny didn't trust herself to answer, and simply nodded.

When she looked back across the Hall, the man with the long dagger was kneeling on one knee, head bowed, saying something in what Jenny guessed was Spanish. Holding the weapon level to the floor, he lifted it high. The King leaned forward in his throne, reached down, took it in his great pale hands and drew the blade. The shimmering that was not quite light flared and sparkled around the weapon, and then the King sheathed it and returned it to its bearer. The man rose, bowed deeply, backed off the dais, and returned to his place.

The King gestured again. Another group of people rose and went to the edge of the open space, and repeated the same process. This time the object to be presented was a book bound in an ancient style, with hasps and hinges of pale metal over oddly patterned leather that looked, Jenny thought, as though it had scales upon it. The book's bearer was a tall woman with deep brown skin, dressed in brightly colored clothing Jenny dimly recognized as West African. She crossed the floor to the dais, knelt gracefully and presented the book, speaking in a flowing many-voweled language. Once again the long white hands of the King took the offering, and something not quite visible flared and shimmered around it. Then the King returned the book to its keeper, and the woman left the dais and returned to her place among her relatives.

The King gestured a third time. "Now," Sylvia whispered. Jenny stood up, and so did the other Chaudronniers from Kingsport. As they filed out of their section of the benches and came to the edge of the open space, a startled murmur went through the crowd of cowled figures. Of course, Jenny realized after a moment. They didn't know that we found the ring.

Uncle Martin brought out the Ring of Eibon from his pocket, held it out. Jenny curtseyed and unfastened her cloak, let Charlotte and Sylvia drew it off her. Then the ring was in her cupped hands, and she started across the open space toward the King in Yellow.

In all her life she had never felt as completely alone as she did in those minutes, as she crossed the black stone floor to the dais and the throne. It's okay, she told herself. He'll take it, and bless it, if that's what he did with the others, and give it back to me, and everything will be okay. She tried not to look at the towering unhuman figure before her, tried not to notice the silence, the watching eyes behind her, or the bitter chill that gathered in the air as she advanced.

Then she was on the dais before the King in Yellow. She knelt on one knee, bowed her head, held up the Ring of Eibon in her right palm, and said in the clearest voice she could manage, "Sire, Tsathoggua bids me present you this token."

Sudden cold, intense as the heart of winter, brushed her palm as the King took it. A moment later, before she could lower the hand, she felt the same terrible cold close around her wrist and forearm. Another moment, and fire flared suddenly against the cold: searing, blinding. Involuntarily, she looked up.

Her arm was held immobile in the King's icy grasp, and the Ring of Eibon blazed like a hot coal on the forefinger of her right hand.

Terror surged through her, and with it returned the memory of Aunt Lisette's words. The thought burst into her mind: Is this how they'll sacrifice me?

Then, past the ring and the incandescent pain that flowed from it, she saw the King. His head bent down, as though to consider her, and all at once she saw through the eyeholes of the Pallid Mask and glimpsed the great dark eyes within. In them, she read not death but destiny.

The King released her arm, then, and she crumpled to the dais, still looking up at him with wide stunned eyes. He nodded, to one side, to the other, and two elders with white masks came, bowed, and helped her to her feet. They half-carried her back to where the Chaudronniers were waiting. She saw, in brief splintered glimpses, Martin reaching for her and helping her back into cloak and cowl, Charlotte's face streaked with tears, Sylvia nodding slowly and making sure that the hand with the Ring of Eibon upon it was supported by a fold of Jenny's cloak. The hand glowed faintly from within, and streaks of light were spreading up the inside of her forearm, visible through her skin.

Afterwards, she recalled little of the rest of the ceremony. The nine figures with wands, the bearer of the cup and the bearer of the incense, the nine who stood silent at the outer limits of the circle, all these returned to the open space and did various things: that she was sure of. As the procession formed to depart from the Hall of the King, elders in white masks conferred with Martin and Sylvia, she knew that, but all that stayed in memory after that were dim glimpses of the City of the Pyramids as Martin carried her to the shore where the cloud waves break. Then her hands clutched the mane of one of the winged beasts, the protuberances on its back closed around her sides, the mighty muscles strained and surged, and she rose up toward the black stars: that much she remembered.

Then came another memory, no more than a momentary fragment. She was in the library of the Chaudronnier mansion, sitting in the chair she'd been in when the summons came. Martin, Sylvia, and Charlotte were in their chairs, silent, wrapped in their hooded cloaks, eyes closed. She tried to stand up, but her legs buckled beneath her, and she crumpled to the carpeted floor.

After that, there was nothing but darkness.

CHAPTER 12

THE HERITAGE OF CARCOSA

The darkness lifted once, in a dim place full of shadows and echoes that woke whispers of memory she couldn't trace. A cool damp cloth moved across her forehead, soothing her. It smelled of herbs she didn't know, resinous and astringent. She was naked, she realized vaguely, lying on the thick soft fur of some great animal's hide, with a coarse blanket thrown over her that felt as though it must be made of woven hair. She couldn't feel her right arm from the elbow down, and the rest of her body ached as though she'd been beaten, but some sort of crisis had passed, she sensed that.

Two voices stirred the trembling air, one dimly familiar to her, one not.

"It would be distinctly unwelcome to me," the familiar voice said in a meditative tone, "if any harm were to come to her."

"Oh, she'll be fine," said the unfamiliar voice. It was deep and resonant, with a trace of an accent Jenny didn't recognize. "The King chose wisely."

"Perhaps," the familiar voice replied. "I don't appreciate his logic."

The other laughed softly, said nothing.

The cloth crossed her forehead again, and she sighed, enjoying the coolness and the scent. The thought occurred to her that

188

she should thank whoever was tending her. With what seemed like an immense effort, she forced her eyes open.

The one who was tending her wasn't human. Its eyes were twice as large as hers, and its muzzle jutted outward. Its skin was the color of yellow umber, and so was the short fur that covered much of its body and the thick mane on its head. The great eyes regarded her with kindness, though, and the thin doglike lips curved in what looked like a smile. It turned, and said something in a language that sounded like the yaps and howls of a hound.

"She's awake," said the unfamiliar voice, amused. "And listening to us. No, the King chose wisely indeed."

Jenny managed to turn her head, or more precisely let it slump over in the direction of the voice. Only the dimmest of lights filtered through that place of shadows and shuddering air, but she could just make out two figures near her, half-silhouetted against the stone wall behind them. One she knew at once: rather like a toad, something like a bat, a little like a sloth, a huge half-shapeless presence that regarded her with eyes that glowed from within like smoldering coals. The other she didn't recognize at all. He looked more or less human, a tall lean figure that seemed to be wearing a long black coat and a broad-brimmed black hat.

The one she didn't recognize approached, knelt smoothly beside her, considered her for a moment. "Sleep, little one," he said. "You have much to learn, and much to do." Then he extended a long finger that glittered with rings, and touched her on the forehead with it. The touch sent her instantly back into the darkness.

* * *

She woke again to the sensation of a cool moist cloth moving across her forehead. This time, though, the cloth smelled of lavender, and even through closed eyelids she could tell that the space around her was full of light.

She blinked, opened her eyes, tried to focus. A dim shape near her turned. "I think she's awake," said Claire's voice.

Jenny blinked again, and her mind and her senses slowly came clear. She was in her nightgown, tucked into bed in her suite in the Chaudronnier mansion. Pale sunlight of a winter morning splashed through the window, and also through the doorway from the sitting room; the door itself seemed to have been replaced, for it showed no sign of the night's violence. Claire was perched on a ladderback chair next to the bed. Beside her was a folding tray with a basin of lavender water on it, filling the air with the scent.

Just then Sylvia came in through the door. "I think you're right," she said to Claire. "Bless Saint Toad for that." Then, to Jenny: "How do you feel, dear?"

Jenny tried to say something, but her throat was too dry. She swallowed, and managed a broken whisper: "Okay."

Claire wrung out a washcloth in the lavender water, held it up with a questioning look. "Please," Jenny said. "That smells so lovely."

The washcloth brushed her forehead again. The coolness and the scent were so pleasant that her eyes drifted shut, and she sank back into the darkness.

She woke again to find the last gray light of evening filtering through the window. Sylvia was sitting in the chair next to the bed, reading a book by the light of the bedside lamp. She looked up before Jenny could speak, put the book aside. "Awake?" she asked.

"I think so," said Jenny, in something like her normal voice. "How long have I been asleep?"

"It's Thursday evening—" She pulled a watch out of her cardigan pocket, glanced at it. "—just past six o'clock, so about fourteen hours since we got back from the Festival."

Jenny lay in silence for a long moment as the memories of the night settled back into place. "I was so frightened," she said at last, "when he put the ring on my hand. I hope I didn't embarrass the family or anything."

A firm shake of Sylvia's head denied it. "You did nothing of the kind. We had people from the old families here in town come visiting all afternoon, asking after you; Mr. Coldcroft called, and we also got a phone call from Jean-Laurent d'Ursuras in Vyones. They were worried about you, of course, but I think every one of them mentioned how graceful you looked and how well you handled it all."

"I'm glad," Jenny said, feeling overwhelmed. "It's like remembering a dream." Another memory came back into focus. "Do you think there'll be any trouble about Willis Connor?"

Sylvia shook her head. "As far as anyone knows, he left here during the night, and no one's seen him since. There are those who will make sure it doesn't go further than that: friends of ours—and also enemies of ours, allies of Connor's and the cause he serves."

"You called him—" Jenny struggled to recall the phrase. "An initiate of the Radiance." When Sylvia nodded: "What does that mean?"

The old woman paused for a long moment. "The Radiance is an organization—an order, I suppose would be the better term. It's had many other names—it's been around for thousands of years, just as we have. But its members are the enemies of our religion and of the Great Old Ones, and its initiates and adepts—those who've committed themselves body and soul to the Radiance—they have strange powers of their own."

Jenny nodded. Still another memory had come clear, bringing perplexities she had no idea how to answer. "Can I ask a question that's probably going to sound really stupid?"

Sylvia raised an eyebrow. "Go ahead."

"Did we actually go anywhere last night?"

"Why do you ask that?"

"Because—" She struggled for a moment to find words. "After I got on the winged beast to fly home, I—woke up, I think, and I was in the library downstairs. You and Charlotte and Uncle Martin were there, too, in your cloaks, with your eyes closed. I tried to get up, but I fell—at least I think that's what happened."

"That'll explain a few things," Sylvia said, nodding. "When the rest of us got back from the Festival, we found you lying curled on the carpet in front of your chair." She leaned forward. "Jenny, you should know already that not everything real is material, and there are real places—as real as a rock—that human beings can only reach by stepping outside of the realm of matter as we know it. Carcosa is one of those places. Long ago human beings could go there, and other places in the great world, in their material bodies, and we've been promised that someday we'll be able to do that again. For now, though, to keep the Festival, we leave our material bodies here and travel to Carcosa in the other bodies, the subtle bodies, that every human has. That's what happened last night."

"But how can it be real, if—" She stopped, unable to go on.

"Have you looked at your right arm yet?"

"No," Jenny admitted, and pulled it free of the covers. The Ring of Eibon gleamed on the first finger of her right hand. The spark of somber light in the great purple stone had grown and spread, glowing like a coal. She reached for the Ring with her left hand, touched it, and found that it did not shift at all. She could move her hand freely, but the Ring was as immobile as though it had fused to her finger bone.

"Pull up the sleeve," Sylvia said.

Jenny did so, and her breath caught in her throat. The skin of her forearm and wrist looked as though it had been bleached. The pallid marks weren't evenly spread over the skin, though. As she turned her arm, she could see the pattern they formed. The King's cold hand had marked her with its grasp.

"It was real," Sylvia said, "all of it. And for the first time since long before the ice covered Hyperborea, someone wears the Ring of Eibon. That's amazing, and it's even more amazing that the one who wears it is my very own grandniece."

Jenny blushed, and then flung herself toward the old woman and threw her arms around her. Sylvia hugged her, patting her shoulders, and then helped her back into a stable position in bed. "Speaking of material bodies," she said then, "it occurs to me that you haven't had a single bite to eat in rather more than twenty-four hours. Do you think you can handle a bit of food?"

Jenny considered that. "Please," she said at length. "Toast, and a couple of poached eggs. And—coffee with cream and sugar, if that's not too much trouble."

"No trouble at all." Sylvia smiled, got up from the chair.

* * *

Jenny was most of the way through the toast and poached eggs when a tentative knock sounded on the door of the suite. Sylvia, who had been keeping her company and answering her questions, got up and went out into the sitting room. She came back a moment later. "It's Charlotte," she said. "Would—"

"Please," Jenny said. "I'd like to see her."

Sylvia went back out, and after a moment Charlotte came into the bedroom. She looked pale and drawn, but brightened when she saw Jenny sitting up in bed. "How are you feeling?"

"Okay, I think. Has something happened? You look dreadful."

She slumped into the chair next to the bed as the sitting room door shut with a soft click. "It's been a stressful day. Mother's left."

Jenny's mouth fell open. "I'm so sorry," she said. Then: "What happened?"

"It was almost funny," said Charlotte, with a weary little laugh. "Do you remember what happened after we all got back from the Festival?"

"Not a thing."

"We got you up off the floor and about half awake, so you could stand with a little help, and I volunteered to get you up here so you could sleep off—what happened—and we left the library, all four of us. You were stumbling and swaying, I had your arm over my shoulder, and you mumbled something really silly I don't remember at all now, and I started laughing, and who should come out of the lilac parlor then but Mother. She stopped in the middle of the hallway with an expression on her face I can't begin to describe, and then said—" She started laughing, then managed a fair imitation of Lisette's most awful voice: "'Charlotte, you're drunk.'"

Jenny burst out laughing, and Charlotte joined her, shaking with laughter that sounded uncomfortably close to tears. After a moment, she shook her head. "And I just couldn't help myself. I looked at her and said, 'Mother, don't be absurd.'"

Jenny blinked in surprise. "How did she take that?"

"Not well at all. Before she could say anything, though, Father said, 'I'll accept an apology for your words earlier.' Of course he meant the horrible thing she said about how you were—were going to be sacrificed—and Mother turned absolutely white and spun on her heel and went up to her rooms and locked herself in. So I got you up the stairs and helped you get into bed and everything, and I figured that was that.

"But it wasn't. We got back about four in the morning, and about seven I woke up hearing Mother out in the hallway literally shrieking at Father. Of course I hid in my room for the rest of the morning, but Alison came in with breakfast at nine, and that's when I learned what happened when we were at Carcosa."

She leaned forward. "Jenny, Mother called the police when she couldn't find any of us, and she told them that you'd been taken away to be sacrificed to some pagan idol or I don't know what nonsense. So an officer came by in the small hours, and Michaelmas told him that the four of us were at a Christmas party and would be back around dawn. Then when morning came around, Father told Mother that she had to call the police herself and tell them that she'd been overwrought and you were fine, and that's when she started shrieking at him and saying the most hateful things about the family, and finally locked herself in her rooms again.

"Then the police came—it was about nine o'clock, and I was downstairs in the brown parlor trying to talk to poor Father, and he was just standing there looking out the window and saying nothing, the way he does when he's upset. But Michaelmas showed them in, of course. They wanted to make sure you were okay, because of what Mother said, so I brought them up here and showed them that you were alive and told them that you'd come down with the flu when we were out. Then it turned out they wanted to know where Willis Connor was, and of course nobody knew. Michaelmas let them into the rooms where he was staying, and right out there on his desk were some things that had been stolen in town in the last two weeks or so—some old books, and I don't know what else. So they searched his things, and found three different sets of identification in three different names."

Jenny took that in. "That must have stirred things up," she said.

"You have no idea," said Charlotte. "Someone told Mother, and she came out and started screaming at Father again, and they were down in the lilac parlor while the police brought in a couple of detectives and everything was upside down, and all at once who do you think came up from the basement?"

Jenny put her hand to her mouth, suddenly realizing who it had to be. "Uncle Roger," Charlotte said, confirming it. "Who couldn't explain what he was doing in our basement, or where he'd been since last night, or why his face was all scratched bloody. Two of the detectives took him off to the dining room to question him, and Mother lit into Father again, and he finally lost his temper and told her right there in front of everyone that she owed him one apology for accusing him of planning to murder you, and a second for calling in the police and embarrassing the family, and a third for letting her brother bring a thief under his roof, and she was going to give him those apologies then and there before she said another word to him.

"And she didn't say another word to him. I was listening from the foot of the stair, and she never spoke to him after that. As soon as the police finished with Uncle Roger, she came out into the hall and said, 'Roger, you'll please take me away from this wretched place.' And she said to Michaelmas, 'Have Coral pack my things,' just like that. So they went out the door and drove away, back to her family in Danvers, I imagine. And—" She swallowed visibly. "I was standing there at the foot of the stair, and she saw me and turned away. She wouldn't look at me or speak to me. She just left." Her eyes clenched shut, and she bowed her head.

Jenny put a hand on her shoulder, and after a moment Charlotte put one of her hands on top of Jenny's. "Thank you," she whispered.

A long moment passed. Jenny remembered the starved desperate look she'd seen in Lisette's eyes, and wondered if things could have ended any other way. Willis Connor had spent ten years worming his way into her thoughts, that much seemed plain, exploiting her weaknesses so that he could use her as a weapon against the Chaudronniers and the Festival. Could she have turned on him, there at the last? Jenny didn't know, and the question haunted her.

Finally Charlotte raised her head again, blinking; her eyes were wet. "So that's what happened while you were asleep."

"I'm almost sorry I missed it," Jenny admitted.

A faint uncertain smile showed on her cousin's face. "It really was quite a spectacle."

Jenny considered her. "What will you do now that—" She stopped, drawing back from the necessary words.

Charlotte forestalled her. "Now that the voola's complete? I don't know. I really don't—except that some things are going to change."

Something stirred in the younger woman's face as she said the words, a thing Jenny had never seen there before: an expression that reminded her just for a moment of the soldiers, pirates, and sorcerers who looked down from the portraits below. That things would indeed change in the Chaudronnier mansion, Jenny saw no reason at all to doubt.

* * *

She slept again after Charlotte left, and when she next woke it was morning and she was alone. After a long while, she decided to risk getting up. She tottered into the sitting room on legs that felt uncomfortably like rubber, regarded the shrine of Saint Toad for a few moments, and then lit the candles, renewed the scent of the potpourri, sat on the chair and let herself sink into the sleepy hush that surrounded the Great Old One.

Stilling her mind was no easier than it had been before, but once she managed it, geometries of meaning that previous mornings and evenings had left unrevealed moved through the silence. The Ring of Eibon drank in the candlelight, radiated it back in a smoldering purple glow. She lifted her gaze, sensed the familiar presence of Tsathoggua.

You didn't tell me, she said in the wordless language she'd learned.

You never asked, the Great Old One responded.

She considered that for a moment. *But is it true that I'm—*

Yes. Then, in answer to a question she hadn't yet dared to frame, even to herself: *She came to me willingly. It was only later, after your grandfather unleashed forces he could not control and perished, that she turned away and sought the fate you know of—and my protection cannot save those who flee from it.*

Jenny nodded slowly, and then, suddenly nervous, asked: *Will—will I, like, sprout tentacles, or anything like that?*

Only if you wish to, the answer came.

She laughed. Just then she wanted nothing so much as to fling herself against his great toadlike bulk and press her face against his furry hide in affection and gratitude. Lacking that option, she sat in his presence for a long while and simply welcomed his company.

The ceremony done, she rang the bell to ask for breakfast. Henrietta came in response, as she'd hoped. "You're okay?" the maid asked.

"I think so," Jenny said. "A little wobbly, maybe."

"Oh, good. I was so worried when—well, when you went up to the King, and the rest of it happened. But you know who's been fretting herself sick, though? Fern. She was just about in tears when Mr. Martin carried you away, and she's been asking about you ever since."

"You tell her that I'm fine," said Jenny, "and pass on my thanks." Then: "I hope the Festival wasn't too difficult for her."

"No, she did okay. Me and Alison stayed with her the whole time, and so did her brother Kenny—the one who works in the fishing fleet; he's really protective of her, you know."

They settled the details of breakfast, and Henrietta went away promising to reassure Fern. Jenny bathed, dressed, and then sat at the round table by the window and ate while flurries of snow drifted down outside. The Ring of Eibon glowed somber on her finger, reminding her of questions she still had to learn how to ask. Long after she'd finished her breakfast, she sat there, watching the snow fall, thinking about what had happened and what she needed to do, now that her world had turned inside out.

A sudden awareness whispered through her mind, and she called out: "Please come in." Only after she'd spoken did she realize that no one had knocked on the door.

The door opened anyway, to reveal Michaelmas. Whatever repairs he had made to his face had left no mark of the bullet behind. "Miss Jenny," he said, "I trust you're well?"

"More or less—thank you for asking."

"You're most welcome. Mr. Martin wishes to know how soon you think you might be able to come down to the brown parlor."

"Now, I think," Jenny said. "I may need some help on the stairs, but that's all."

"I would be happy to oblige."

She stood up, and found her legs considerably more willing to bear her weight than they had been before breakfast. "Then let's go."

They walked together down the hall to the great stair. "May I ask you a personal question, Michaelmas?"

"Of course, Miss Jenny."

"How long have you been with the family?"

"A matter of definition. I was created by Luc le Chaudronnier in 1362, on the feast day of St. Michael and All Angels, thus my given name. He bequeathed me to his daughter Sybille, who married Geoffroi d'Ursuras, and I remained with the d'Ursuras family until Marc d'Ursuras brought me here, after whom I returned to the Chaudronniers."

"Luc le Chaudronnier," Jenny said. "Who had the Ring of Eibon in his keeping."

"Exactly. He used it in my creation." In answer to Jenny's questioning look: "Brass heads capable of speech were very much in fashion among sorcerers in those days, but an entire man of the same substance, able to move and think as well as speak—that was, as I recall, quite a different matter. It was through certain rituals that made use of the ring that Master Luc obtained the necessary lore. I don't believe anything of the kind had been done since Vergil of Seville's time, and of course he had the ring as well."

Jenny nodded. They had reached the top of the stair, and she took hold of Michaelmas' proffered arm for support on the way down. Beneath the sleeve, she could feel smooth hard metal, and something within it—a shimmer that reminded her of the ritual at Carcosa, the presence of ancient sorceries.

She had meant to ask another question, but a whisper of sound echoing up the stairwell sent the thought spinning off into nothingness. It was music, she was sure of that from the first, and as they went down the stair she recognized it: the terrible third movement of the Prelude to *Le Roi en Jaune*, played as thunderously as Erik Satie himself must have played it on that night when the play had its one and only Paris performance. The great crashing dissonances came sweeping up the stairs like cloud waves onto the black sands of Carcosa.

"Charlotte?" Jenny asked.

"She has been playing since six o'clock this morning," Michaelmas said. "I think she must have played nearly every piece of music in the collection."

"I'm glad to hear that."

"You're not alone in that, Miss Jenny."

The movement rose to its final crescendo as they came down the stair to the first floor, paused, and then tumbled down in the last, almost miraculous bars, where all the dissonances resolved into harmonies and the gentle theme of the first movement emerged again to bring the Prelude to its conclusion.

As the last notes faded to silence, Michaelmas brought her to the brown parlor and opened the door. "Sir? Miss Jenny."

"Thank you, Michaelmas," said Martin.

He was sitting in one of the velvet-covered chairs. His face was lined and haggard, as though he hadn't slept in days, but something in his eyes and his posture spoke of a burden long carried that had finally been set down.

"Jenny," he said. "I'm glad to see you on your feet."

"I'm glad to be on my feet," she replied. "I heard about—what happened. I'm so sorry."

He nodded, gestured her to a seat. A moment later, as she was settling into place on one of the divans, the door opened again and Charlotte came in. Her eyes were red, as though she'd been crying, but she greeted them both cheerfully and let Martin wave her to another seat.

Minutes passed. Martin looked fixedly at the floor. Finally the door opened a third time, and Sylvia and Claire both came in, with Michaelmas behind them. Martin motioned toward the divan; the old women sat down, while the butler stepped back slightly, saying, "I believe you wished me to remain, sir."

"Please," Martin said. He drew in an unsteady breath, and then said to all of them: "We have some decisions to make as a family."

"Should I be here?" Claire asked him directly.

He met her gaze briefly, looked at the floor again. "Yes. Under the circumstances, I see no further point in acting as though you're not a family member by marriage."

Claire blinked. "Thank you, Martin," she said, obviously moved. "That means a great deal to me."

Uncle Martin nodded. "I'm sorry it took this long." Then, raising his head again: "The first things we need to discuss, I think, have to do with you, Jenny. I don't know if you've had any chance yet to think about your future, now that you've returned to the family."

It took her a moment to realize what he was implying. "A little," she said. "I'll be going back to Miskatonic University when the holidays are over. I've made some commitments there that I don't want to break, and I want to finish my degree."

He nodded, as though he'd expected it. "In any case, I hope that from now on you'll consider this house as your home. Any time you wish, announced or unannounced, the door will be open for you and we'll be delighted to have you here."

"Thank you," she said, fighting a lump in her throat.

"It's the least the family can do. Now I believe you'll have had to take out loans to pay for your education."

Jenny nodded glumly.

"I'd be much obliged if you could send me the details, so we can clear those, and any further bills should simply be forwarded to me."

"I can't let you do that!" Jenny objected.

"There speaks the Chaudronnier pride," Sylvia said with a little laugh. "Jenny, if things had gone the way they should have gone, there never would have been a question of loans. The family would have paid for your education as a matter of course, the way it paid for mine. Please let us make that right—it might make it just that little bit easier for someone else to get the financial aid they need."

After a moment, Jenny ducked her head and nodded. "Thank you," she said indistinctly.

"Charlotte," Martin went on, "has also raised the possibility that you might be able to spare the time to come with us to France this summer. Quite a few of our French cousins have been asking after you since the Festival. Jean-Laurent d'Ursuras in particular gave me quite a grilling on the phone about why we hadn't brought you to visit him yet—I had a fair amount of explaining to do. I hope you'll be willing to gratify his curiosity."

"I'll have to talk to Dr. Akeley and make sure," Jenny said, "but I should have the summer free, and I'd love to go." Then, a sudden memory surfacing: "Doesn't the Université de Vyones have some kind of relationship with Miskatonic?"

"I don't know," Martin said, his eyebrows going up.

"I believe it does," said Claire. "There was something about that in the *Arkham Advertiser* a few months ago—do you remember the article about Greenland, Syl? But it's not just the polar research program, if I recall correctly."

"If that's the case," Martin said then, "and you decide to spend a semester or two there, I know our French cousins would be delighted to have you stay with them—in fact, you may have some trouble finding time for your studies."

"They'll behave," Sylvia told him. "I'll sic Emmeline Grenier on them if they don't."

That got a general laugh. "There's one other matter," Martin said then, "which I hesitate to mention, but—"

"The Ring of Eibon," said Jenny.

"Yes. That it's on your hand, and you're still—with us—implies certain things. I hope you won't mind if I ask if you've given any thought to that."

"I spent most of this morning thinking about it," Jenny said. "Thinking, and—talking to Saint Toad." She glanced down at the ring, and was silent for a time, watching the somber light burn in the heart of the great purple stone. "I think," she said slowly, "that I'm supposed to study sorcery—to become a sorceress. I think that's what this—" She gestured with the ring. "—is all about. The thing is, I don't know what that involves."

"If I may interject, sir," Michaelmas said.

"Of course," said Uncle Martin.

"Miss Jenny, a certain book from the library may be helpful in that regard. Perhaps I could bring it here."

"Please," Jenny said. Martin nodded to the butler, who bowed and left the room.

When he was gone, Martin considered her. "If that's what you feel you have to do, Jenny," he said, "I won't stand in your way—but I admit I'm gravely concerned. Sorcery is terribly dangerous for any human." His voice dropped. "As my father learned."

Jenny nodded, and drew in an unsteady breath. "There's something you don't know about me," she said then, "something I only learned yesterday. I'm not—entirely human." Stumbling over the words, she told them what Willis Connor had said and Saint Toad had confirmed.

The room was silent for a long moment. "I see," said Martin finally. "Of course that does happen from time to time."

Sylvia snorted. "Well, yes," she said. "By all accounts Marc d'Ursuras' real father was the King in Yellow, not the Comte de la Frenaie. As far as I know, all the old families here have some such connection to the Great Old Ones, and usually more than one."

Martin considered that. "It's said the children of Tsathoggua have—certain gifts in the direction of sorcery. Well." A first slow trace of a smile touched his haggard face. "It's been a very long time since we've had a proper sorcerer or sorceress in the family."

"Past time, if you ask me," said Sylvia. "Do you recall the stories about what will happen when another hand wears Eibon's ring?"

"Yes, but we'll have to see," Martin cautioned.

"'Until the ring of Eibon burns,'" Sylvia quoted. Martin gave her a worried look, and then stared at the floor and said nothing.

"What do the stories say?" Jenny asked her great-aunt in the silence that followed.

It was Martin who answered, though. "According to our traditions," he said, "there are three treasures that embody the heritage our family shares with the others of our faith, the heritage of Carcosa, that came to Poseidonis long before it drowned. The Ring of Eibon, the Blade of Uoht, and the *Ghorl Nigral*, the Book of Night: those are the three. When they awaken—when another hand wears Eibon's ring, when Uoht's blade rises and falls in wrath, and when the *Ghorl Nigral* gives up its final secret—the stars will come round right at last, the long age that began when the holy places were defiled will end, and the world will become—different."

Lines from the poem Sylvia had quoted whispered through Jenny's mind. "And the King waits for that," she said.

"I've seen him at his vigil." Martin did not look up, and his voice was little more than a whisper. "In the wind we felt—the wind from Yhtill."

The door to the parlor opened, and Michaelmas came back in; he had an old leatherbound book in one hand, which he gave to Jenny. "Miss Jenny," he said, "you will find the relevant passage on page forty-two—the first paragraph after the new chapter begins."

She opened the book. "What does it say?" Charlotte asked.

It took Jenny a few moments to find the page and the passage, but once she located it she read aloud:

Of the additional studies required of students of the art of sorcery

While sorcery stands apart from all other arts, it cannot be mastered in its fullness by the unlearned, and indeed more than one who sought entrance into its mysteries perished wretchedly through an inadequate grasp of more ordinary knowledge. Let those who desire to study that which is set forth in this book first be thoroughly versed in such elementary learning as grammar, logic, and rhetoric; in languages as well ancient as modern; and likewise in the four mathematic sciences. Having mastered these studies, let them proceed next to seek full proficiency in philosophy, and most specially in metaphysic, for from this latter, sorcery takes its beginning and root.

"That's Marc d'Ursuras's book," Sylvia said.

"Exactly, Miss Sylvia," Michaelmas replied.

"I'm not sure how much it helps, though," Martin noted after a moment. "Where on earth would you go about learning old-fashioned metaphysical philosophy in this day and age?"

Jenny had been staring at the passage. Around her, the old feeling of a presence and a strangeness, of the prosaic world opening up into something wholly new, built with the intensity of a gathering storm. It had always faded before, but this time—

This time it opened as wide as the sky and did not depart.

She looked up with a quiet smile on her thin plain face. "Oddly enough," she said, "I know exactly where I can do that."

CHAPTER 13

THE FRIENDS OF SAINT TOAD

The bus came into sight around the corner, 13 TO ARKHAM VIA KINGSPORT on the sign above the front windshield. Jenny picked up both her suitcases and waited while it groaned to a halt in front of her. The doors hissed open; she climbed aboard, paid her fare, settled onto a seat two rows behind the driver as the engine muttered to itself below the floor and the bus rolled away along High Street. The marina came into sight, and beyond it the masts and spars and rigging of the *Miskatonic* stood stark against the winter sky. When the bus passed the sturdy old whaler, though, the Terrible Old Man was nowhere to be seen. Jenny imagined him sitting in his little cottage, warming his hands at the Franklin stove and sipping hot buttered rum, and wondered when she'd see him again.

Martin had tried to talk her into letting Michaelmas drive her back to Arkham, but she'd turned down the offer, not without regret. Part of her wanted to cling desperately to what she'd found in Kingsport; the mansion had begun to feel like a home to her, and Sylvia, Charlotte, Claire, Martin, Henrietta, Michaelmas—each in a different way, they gave her something with which she could fill in the blank spaces of that once-baffling word "family." Still, she'd sensed clearly enough that if she was going to return to the life she'd been living a few short weeks earlier, it was best to leave Kingsport the way she'd come there, on her own.

The old houses of Kingsport slipped past, and she had to fight the urge to pull the bell and walk straight back to the mansion on Green Street. To distract herself, she pulled her neglected smartphone out of the pocket of her warm new coat, waited until it got a feeble but adequate signal, then punched in the password and opened her email. As she'd feared, it was crammed to the bursting point; she had sixteen screens of unanswered messages, and though more than half of it was spam and most of the rest could be deleted unread, there were still too many that needed her attention.

Tish Martin had sent her an email that morning. She opened that one first, read that Tish had gotten back from New Jersey to the house on Halsey Street the night before, and closed it, leaving the long chatty account of Tish's holidays for later. Further down were announcements from the Miskatonic University administration. Two of her spring semester classes had been moved to different buildings—none of the announcements mentioned the fire in Belbury Hall, but Jenny could read between the lines easily enough.

Further still was a terse note from Miriam Akeley. *Jenny,* it read, *please come see me as soon as you can. I've received some very bad news. M.* Jenny wondered what that was about, hit the reply button, typed a response, and sent it: *Dr. Akeley, I can come tomorrow if you're free. Let me know. Jenny.*

Below that were fifty-seven advertisements for loans, jobs, and penis enlargement pills, which she sent to the spam folder, and then a frantic email from Tish that put a cold chill down her spine for a moment. There had been a fire at the house on Halsey Street, it claimed, and she needed to come back to Arkham right away to claim everything of hers that hadn't been destroyed. She stared at the smartphone screen for a moment, aghast, and then all at once remembered the first email she'd opened and scrolled back up to it.

Yes, she'd remembered right—Tish had mentioned that everything was fine at the house they shared. Jenny puzzled over that for a moment, then checked the date on the earlier email and scowled. It had been sent the same day she'd had lunch with Lisette, and she had no difficulty guessing who had arranged to fake an email from Tish or why he'd wanted to convince her to leave the Chaudronnier mansion just then.

None of the other messages required immediate attention, so she closed her email, shut the smartphone down, put it back into her pocket. The bus was already well past the outer edges of Kingsport by then, climbing through a landscape of long-abandoned farms toward the gray hills back of the coast. Jenny turned in her seat and watched the great crags north of Kingsport as they disappeared from view one after another, until finally the last, highest crag slipped behind the folds of the nearer landscape. Thereafter the bus made its way through a countryside as empty as the kingdom of Alar, where the countless ages before humanity's birth seemed just as close as the countless ages to come when humanity would have long since passed away.

Hills thick with bare leafless willows rolled past, a few crumbling barns appeared and disappeared, and then the Fair Isles Mall came into sight like some long-abandoned ruin of the elder world. Beyond it, dim in the gray winter air, were the roofs of Arkham, with the great abstract masses of the University off beyond them. Looking out the window, Jenny suddenly felt as though a distance that couldn't be measured in miles had opened up behind her, separating her from Kingsport and everything that had happened there.

That sense of distance increased as Old Kingsport Road wound to its end and turned into Peabody Avenue, and the bus passed through Arkham's half-abandoned downtown on its way to the bridge over the cold gray Miskatonic River. The river itself reminded her of Owen's disappearance and then, all at once, of the glimpse she'd had of him in the crystal. She wondered what that meant and then, with a sick sinking feeling, if she'd really seen him, or simply glimpsed a reflection of her own wishful thinking.

The bus turned right on Derby Street, and there was the statue of Cthulhu out in front of the Lovecraft Museum, decked out in a woolen hat and a scarf against the cold, and brandishing a plastic snow shovel in its outstretched claw. She stared, and all at once reached for her second suitcase, the one Sylvia had given her. It took the solidity of the handle to reassure her that the suitcase was real.

On the hand that clutched the suitcase handle, catching the pale winter light, the great purple stone of the Ring of Eibon smoldered. She managed an uncertain smile, and braced herself as the bus turned again and grumbled to a stop.

* * *

She came around the corner onto Halsey Street just as Tish appeared at the other end of the block, carrying two bags of groceries. They both called out greetings to the other, met where the walk to the front door left the sidewalk.

"Well, don't you look fine?" Tish said with a broad smile. "That's one pretty coat you got for Christmas. Real camel hair?"

Jenny nodded. "You look like you had a good time too."

"Oh yeah," said Tish. "You got my email? That's not half of it."

They got inside, hung their coats on pegs in the entry, went on into the living room. "Let me get this stuff put away," Tish said, "and then I want to hear all about your people in Kingsport." She headed for the kitchen, and Jenny hauled the two suitcases up to her bedroom on the second floor. Her copy of *Le Roi en Jaune* was exactly where she'd seen it in the crystal, and her bedding was a rumpled mess; she pulled it out straight, considered unpacking, decided against it and went back down the stairs.

"Okay," said Tish, emerging from the kitchen. "The whole story, girl. Every bit of it."

That, Jenny thought, was exactly what she couldn't do. She settled on the couch, drew in a breath, and began to tell Tish about Kingsport, the Chaudronnier mansion, her family. Every other sentence left out something that mattered; Saint Toad, the Ring of Eibon, the Festival, the King in Yellow, all had to be omitted, and for good measure she didn't mention Lisette's departure and finessed the relationship between Sylvia and Claire. Even as she told the tale, it felt like rags and tatters around an emptiness that was almost palpable, and when she finished she wondered how Tish would respond to so obviously fragmentary a story.

Tish didn't seem to notice at all, though. By the time Jenny had finished, she was staring with a look of delight. "Girl, that's wonderful!" she said. "So are they going to help with your college?" When Jenny nodded: "Oh, that's so good to hear. I honestly don't know how I'd have managed without all the help I got from Mom and Dad, and Uncle Mike, and my cousins down in Providence—really, the whole family's had my back every step of the way."

A stray gesture of Tish's just then made Jenny notice something she would have seen long since if she'd been less distracted: a ring she didn't remember Tish wearing before, a slender gold band with a diamond on it, glittering on the third finger of her housemate's left hand. Her eyebrows went up. Tish noticed, followed her gaze to the ring, and then broke into a broad smile.

"You didn't mention that in your email," Jenny said. Then, guessing: "Will?"

"You got it. He popped the question over lunch when I met him on the way down. We're going to wait until I'm done with my residency, but—oh, I'm so happy!"

Jenny said the appropriate things, and before long Tish was talking about her holidays, a long tumbling story full of so many names and relationships that Jenny very quickly lost track of who was who. Tish was just finishing the story when the front door slammed, and a moment later Barry Holzer came in, trying without too much success to manage three suitcases, a backpack, and a duffel all at once—it was a household joke that Barry didn't need luggage when he traveled, he needed a mule train. He greeted them both enthusiastically, got everything up the stair somehow, and then came back down and flopped onto his favorite chair.

Then Jenny and Tish both had to tell their stories over again, and Barry made appreciative noises over Tish's ring and then gave a disjointed but amiable account of the two weeks he'd spent skiing with friends of his up in Vermont. By the time that was finished it was pushing time for dinner, and the three of them pooled resources from their respective cupboards and managed a big batch of spaghetti sauce over the tag-ends of four different bags of pasta. All in all, it was a pleasant evening.

The one curious thing about it was that neither of Jenny's housemates mentioned, or seemed to notice, the great golden ring with the smoldering purple stone on her finger.

Later, when she was nearly ready for bed, she went to her room and unpacked. Her clothes and other belongings from the suitcase she'd brought to Kingsport went quickly into familiar places, but she took her time with the other suitcase, the one Sylvia had given her. She took out the contents one by one. Here was a chafing dish, with the stand taken apart for ease of carrying, and a little blue handbound book from a gift shop in downtown Kingsport in which Claire had written out her favorite recipes; here was another handbound book from the same gift shop, this one with a green cover, into which she'd copied with exquisite care two dozen spells from the *Livre d'Ivon*; here, in a little leather album, were eleven pictures of her mother, and as many mementoes of Sophie's school days, from Sylvia's collection; here was Jenny's set of stones for the Mao Games; here were silver candlesticks, a pair of them, and a pair of bowls that matched them; here were beeswax candles, bundles of them, a cellophane bag full of potpourri, a faceted glass bottle full of oil the color of red amber, and a little black silk cushion.

She busied herself for a few moments making a place for these latter atop her bookcase, with candles in the candlesticks, potpourri in the bowls, and the cushion centered between them. That done, she lifted the little black statue of Saint Toad out of the suitcase and set it in its place. She got the suitcases put away in her closet, and then changed into her nightgown, got ready for bed, pulled the chair over from her desk and set it in front of the statue. A moment later, the candles lit and the potpourri freshened with the scent, she sat and said her prayer.

"*Iâ, Iâ, G'noth-ykagga-ha.*" The words flowed easily now. "*Iâ, Iâ, Tsathoggua.*" She cleared her mind, and to her vast relief felt at once the presence of Saint Toad.

She hadn't meant to ask him the question that was foremost in her mind, but he answered it anyway. *Did you expect anything else?* the not-voice said. *You dwell partly in their world and partly in a world they do not know.*

I'm still amazed that they didn't even see the ring, she replied.

It is better that way, said Saint Toad. *You will meet some few who see it, and by that you will know that they, too, dwell in both worlds.*

She considered that for a time, and then allowed an uncertain smile and let the rest of her worries dissolve, for the moment, in the stillness that surrounded the Great Old One.

* * *

A quick exchange of emails in the morning confirmed her appointment with Miriam Akeley for two o'clock that afternoon. Not long before she left for the Miskatonic campus, though, Tish waved her over and said in a low voice, "Something really weird happened. You remember we hauled Owen's things down to the basement? They're gone."

Jenny blinked, and then thought of the landlord as the obvious explanation. "I wonder if Mr. Cohausen got rid of them."

"Nope," said Tish. "I called him first thing this morning, right after I took some stuff down there and noticed they weren't there. He says he didn't come into the house over break—the weather was so warm he didn't have to worry about the pipes, so he just drove by a couple of times to make sure the place was okay." Her voice dropped even lower. "And here's the really weird thing. The trash bags we put everything in—they're still down there. They're just empty."

Jenny stared at her for a long moment. Suddenly she remembered the image she'd seen in the crystal in the Chaudronnier library: Owen and the brown-haired young woman sitting on the bed, leaning forward to study a great leatherbound tome. Absurd as the idea seemed, she couldn't help wondering if he'd somehow figured out a way to send someone—or something—to get his possessions and bring them to wherever he was.

"You're right," she said aloud. "That's really weird."

Tish shrugged: who knows? "Yeah. Well, I thought you'd want to know." She shook her head, turned, and headed back toward the dining room while Jenny went out into the entry and put on her coat.

She left the house and walked to Wilmarth Hall across a mostly empty campus, wondering most of the way there whether she'd ever find out what had happened to Owen. The roar of diesel engines broke into her thoughts at last, bellowing across the campus beneath a gray and lowering sky; the demolition crews were hauling away the last of the rubble from the site of Belbury Hall. Jenny stopped to look for a few minutes, then hurried across the quad toward the wrinkled orifice that served Wilmarth Hall as a main entrance. For a change, the balky main doors were working, and they hissed and clanked open as she approached. Her foosteps chased echoes up the long stair in the middle of the building; she reached the seventh floor and counted seven doors along the rambling hallway, before she remembered that she could just look for the wooden sign above the door to Dr. Akeley's office.

Her knock on the door got an immediate if muffled answer: "Please come in."

Inside, the clutter of the oddly shaped room seemed all but unchanged, and Miriam Akeley was once again trying to manage too many books on too narrow of a desk. This time there were only two books, but one of them made up for it by sheer size—it was a massive folio bound in black leather close to two feet tall, early eighteenth century by the typeface and the age-spotted paper. The other, smaller and bound in yellow, evaded the professor's grasp and slid toward the edge of the desk just as Jenny came in; she hurried over and caught it just before it managed to fling itself onto the floor.

"Thank you," Akeley said. "If you can hold that for a moment—yes, like that." She reached around the other to her keyboard and typed in two sentences.

"More alchemists?" Jenny asked.

Akeley gave her a glance she couldn't read at all. "No, just something Lovecraft used as a source." She got the great folio closed, then took the paperback from Jenny, shut it, and put it face down atop the folio. By then, though, Jenny had already seen the headings at the top of the folio's pages—*ye IV Booke* on the left hand page and *of Hsan* on the right—and glimpsed the title of the paperback, *Die Sieben Geheimbücher von Hsan*; her German was next to nonexistent but it didn't take too much effort for her to leap the language barrier this once. She managed to keep the surprise off her face, sat on the chair the professor indicated.

"I may as well come straight to the point," Akeley said. "I got back yesterday to find an email from the regents in my inbox—everybody on the faculty got the same one. We were expecting to get funding from the state to cover the costs of the Belbury Hall fire, but—well, you know how hard the last round of state budget cuts hit higher ed. The short form is that there's no state money, and so everything discretionary has had to be gutted. Half a dozen adjunct faculty are being laid off, every department's having its budget slashed, and—" Her face took on a bleak expression. "I don't have funding for an assistantship for you for the spring semester. I probably won't have the funds available next year either. I'm really sorry."

"I understand," Jenny said. "But that's actually not going to be a problem for me." Stumbling over the words: "It's—kind of complicated. I have family down in Kingsport that I hardly knew about, but I went to visit them over the holidays and— well, they're going to pay for my college."

Akeley gave her a blank look for a moment, and then let out an uneven breath and sagged in visible relief. "That's very good to hear," she said. "I'd been afraid that you'd be left twisting in the wind." Then: "Your Kingsport family—anybody I might have heard of?"

"The Chaudronniers," Jenny said.

The professor's eyebrows went up; evidently she knew the name. "That's got to be quite a change for you."

If only you knew, Jenny thought. "No kidding," she said. "I'm having to take a second look at pretty much everything I had in mind."

"Are you still planning on your doctorate?"

"Yes, though I probably won't be looking for an academic position after I graduate. There's still room for independent scholars in the history of ideas, isn't there?"

Akeley nodded after a moment. "There are still a few of them, yes. That's probably a good plan, these days, as long as you don't want to teach."

"Honestly," said Jenny, "I wasn't looking forward to that."

"Well, there you are." The professor sat back in her chair, considered Jenny. "Have you put any more thought into what you want to do?"

"Actually, yes," Jenny said, "but you're probably going to laugh. Did you ever find the syllabus for the old program in medieval metaphysics?"

"Funny you should ask about that," Akeley said. "I found it just before I left for break. The original was in pretty bad shape, but it scanned well." She reached for the mousepad, double-clicked once and then again, and the printer over on one end of her desk let out a little growl, hummed to itself, and started disgorging sheets of paper one at a time. "It's pretty detailed—reading lists, lecture topics, and so on. Are you thinking of something along those lines?"

"I think so. I'm not sure yet."

When the printer finished spitting out pages, Akeley reached for the stack, handed it to Jenny. "There you go," she said. "You've got plenty of time to narrow things down, of course."

Jenny nodded. "Of course." After a brief pause, she went on. "But the budget cuts and everything—they're not even going to let you replace Owen and—" She stopped, realizing she didn't remember the other assistant's name.

"Shelby Adams," Akeley said. "No. We had to fight like hell to keep the regents from making us let go of the assistants we've got, and too many of the ones that'll graduate this spring won't be replaced."

"That's got to be difficult for you."

"It'll be rough," the professor admitted, "but I'll manage."

"Well—" Jenny began, stopped, and then said, "Would it be okay if I helped with your research anyway?"

That got her a startled look. "Without pay?"

"Well, I really don't have to worry about money at this point," said Jenny. "And I'd always heard that half the point of an assistantship is to get hands-on training in teaching or research." Then, deciding to take a risk: "Besides, I think we may have some research interests in common."

"Oh?"

"Well, for example, I know about the *Seven Cryptical Books of Hsan.*"

The silence that followed was deep enough that Jenny could hear the distant gurgling and wheezing of Wilmarth Hall's heating system. "And you also have sharp eyes," Akeley said.

Jenny smiled, said nothing.

After another long moment, the professor nodded slowly. "Fair enough," she said. "And I admit the research I'm doing these days could benefit from some help."

All at once she turned, found a notepad, wrote something on it, tore off the top sheet and handed it to Jenny. "Thank you," she said. "That's very generous of you, and you're right, of course, that this kind of work is also an important part of the learning process. What I'd like to ask you to do first, if you don't mind, is take another note to Abelard Whipple down in the restricted stacks—today, or when you next have a chance."

"I can do that this afternoon," Jenny said.

"That'll be fine. I just need to arrange for access to some things from the collection, and I've got more appointments today."

There was more to it than that, Jenny guessed, but let it pass. They said the usual polite things, and then Jenny left the office.

Once the door was closed, she glanced down at the note in her hand. As she'd guessed, it was written in a language she couldn't read. She put it into her coat pocket, and then turned to face the door, drew in a deep breath, and traced a complex geometrical pattern in the air with the first three fingers of her right hand, all the while picturing Miriam Akeley as clearly as possible in her mind's eye. "As Haon-Dor passed unnoticed among his enemies," she murmured, "so pass thou unnoticed among thine."

The spell from the *Livre d'Ivon* set a faint shimmer of sorcery moving through the air. It was not, all things considered, a particularly potent incantation, but it was the best she could do as the rawest of novice sorceresses. Jenny had already cast it on herself, for her own protection, and if Dr. Akeley was studying the ancient lore—and despite the professor's claims, Jenny found herself doubting that the only point of interest to her was their relation to Lovecraft's stories—she would need something to keep her safe from the Radiance.

The shimmering faded as the spell took effect. Jenny nodded once, satisfied, and set out for Orne Library.

* * *

The lock turned, and the heavy metal door of the restricted stacks opened a few inches, just enough to allow one of Dr. Whipple's bright blue eyes to peer out. "Jenny, wasn't it?" he said. "Jenny—"

"Parrish."

"Of course, of course. Please come in." He opened the door wide, closed it behind her. The bare concrete walls and harsh fluorescent lighting of the restricted collections room greeted her. "What can I do for you?"

"Dr. Akeley sent me with a message for you." She pulled it out of her coat pocket, held it out. The old librarian started to reach for it, then stopped, gazing wide-eyed at her right hand.

"That's quite an unusual ring," he said.

Jenny blinked in surprise, and then said, for want of anything better, "It's been in my family for a very long time."

His gaze moved from the ring to her face. "Ah," he said. "Chaudronnier, d'Ursuras, or d'Amberville, I would guess." He gave the names their French pronunciations, flawlessly.

"Chaudronnier," said Jenny. "My mother was Charles Chaudronnier's daughter."

"I knew Charles," said Whipple. "A pleasure to meet you properly, Miss Parrish—and to see that a certain curious story I heard from an old friend a few days ago, which I considered utterly improbable, is in fact quite true." He put his hand to his chin, regarded her for a long moment, and then said, "Well. Let's see what Miriam has to say."

Jenny handed him the note, and he read it and chuckled, shaking his head. "I take it that she didn't see your ring?"

"You're the only person who's seen it since I came back to Arkham yesterday."

The blue eyes, disconcertingly bright, considered her, and something taut and focused showed beneath the old man's air of vague distraction. "I would be very cautious about that assumption," he said. "The only person who mentioned seeing it—that I don't doubt at all."

Jenny nodded uneasily.

"Very sensible of Miriam, though. Did you know she's studying the old lore?"

"I saw two copies of the *Seven Cryptical Books of Hsan* in her office this afternoon," Jenny said, "and she mentioned something about Lovecraft's sources earlier."

"It's usually Lovecraft," Whipple said. "Lovecraft, Smith, Howard, or one of the others who took the lore and put it in their stories. Quite the irony, all things considered—the wisdom of the ages, turned into raw material for pulp fiction." He sighed. "But she wanted to know if I thought it was safe to have you assist her in her research, and that shows a praiseworthy caution. I trust you realize that the old lore and its students have their enemies."

"The Radiance," Jenny said.

Once again, taut focus glinted beneath the surface. "You would be wise never to use that title outside this room," the old man said. "They rely on secrecy, and if they have any cause to think that's at risk—well, I don't think I need say more."

"No," Jenny said. "I was nearly murdered by one of their initiates a few weeks ago."

He took that in, nodded once. "They have initiates here," he said, "and one adept. There's much they don't see, and much they're prevented from seeing, but you'll want to be careful regardless." He chuckled again and shook his head. "But Miriam—there she was, quite possibly reading what Hsan the Greater had to say about the great talismans of sorcery, with no idea that one of the greatest of them was in the room with her when she wrote that note." Then, abruptly serious. "And she shouldn't learn that from you. I'll simply let her know that you can be trusted—those who have the power to bestow that ring don't make mistakes. She'll need your help, now that Owen's had to leave us."

Jenny looked up again, realizing what the old man's turn of phrase implied. She drew in a breath, made herself speak. "Is Owen okay?"

The question seemed to surprise Whipple. He nodded. "Indeed he is."

"Have you seen him, since—"

"No." A slow smile bent one side of his face. "No, but a very old friend of mine has."

Something about his tone of voice reminded her abruptly of a cascade of recent memories: a shrine in Kingsport, a hall in Carcosa, a half-seen cavern full of trembling air in a place for which she had no name. "Dr. Whipple," she said, "if you don't mind my asking, are you a friend of Saint Toad?"

His eyebrows went up, and after a moment, his smile broadened. "Why, yes," he said. "Yes, among others. Your folk are of the people of drowned Poseidonis, as I recall, and I know something of their ways. Some of us have, shall we say, slightly different relationships with the Great Old Ones—but yes, I know the Eldest, and I don't need to ask who hears your prayers."

Jenny's thin face creased in a sudden smile. "Thank you," she said. "That makes it a little less lonely, knowing that you know."

"Oh, there are others," said the librarian. "Here in Arkham, and elsewhere. But the Ring of Eibon on your finger—that means that strange days are upon us, and an ending of many things we've all known. The Great Old Ones didn't give you that as a decoration, you know. You'll have much to learn, and much to do."

"I know," said Jenny. "I'll do my best."

ACKNOWLEDGMENTS

Like the first novel in this series, *The Weird of Hali: Innsmouth*, this fantasia on a theme by H.P. Lovecraft depends even more than most fiction on the labors of earlier writers. Lovecraft's own writings were of course a primary quarry for the building materials I assembled into *The Weird of Hali: Kingsport*, providing the setting, important elements of the plot, and a great deal of incidental detail. His friend and fellow *Weird Tales* author Clark Ashton Smith contributed nearly as much, including two lost continents, an imaginary French province, and an assortment of other plot elements, scenery, and stage properties. The French poem quoted on page 97, "Un Paysage Paîen," is by Smith—most people find it hard enough to write poems in one language; Smith did it brilliantly in three. Those readers who are puzzled by my attribution of the poem to the invented nineteenth century French poet Honoré-Leclerc Fréneville-Forgeron may find it instructive, or at least entertaining, to translate that name out of French.

Also important as sources for this tale were two stories Lovecraft himself considered among the best weird tales in the English language, Arthur Machen's "The White People" and Robert W. Chambers' *The King in Yellow*. Smaller but still important contributions came from stories by Robert E. Howard, Henry Kuttner, and Fred Pelton, as well as from a writer not usually remembered for her contributions to the weird tales genre, the English occultist Dion Fortune.

My broader intellectual debts are the same as those already listed in the acknowledgments to *The Weird of Hali: Innsmouth*; to that list I would add Owen Barfield and C.S. Lewis, who irritated and inspired each other through a long friendship and then managed the same trick posthumously for me. I also owe, once again, debts to Sara Greer and Dana Driscoll, who read and critiqued the manuscript. I hope it is unnecessary to remind the reader that none of the above are responsible in any way for the use I have made of their work.

Printed in the USA
CPSIA information can be obtained
at www.ICGtesting.com
JSHW032302021023
49516JS00007B/44

9 781912 573899